DRAGON BLOOD SERIES

BALANCED
ON THE
BALADE'S EDGE

BOOK ONE

LINDSAY BUROKER

Balanced on the Blade's Edge

by Lindsay Buroker

Copyright Lindsay Buroker 2014

Cover and Formatting: Deranged Doctor Design

No part of this book may be reproduced, scanned, or distributed in any printed or electronic form without permission. Please do not participate in or encourage piracy of copyrighted materials in violation of the author's rights. Thank you for respecting the hard work of this author.

This is a work of fiction. Names, characters, places, and incidents either are the product of the author's imagination or are used fictitiously, and any resemblance to locales, events, business establishments, or actual persons—living or dead—is entirely coincidental.

Foreword

As a writer, sometimes you have a thousand things (or at least five) that you should be working on, but you get an idea for something new and just have to run with it. I wrote this story quickly, because I knew I had other series to get back to, but it also came out quickly of its own volition. I enjoyed these characters and this new world, and I hope you will too. Before you jump in, I would like to thank Cindy Wilkinson, Pam Tkachuk, and Sarah Engelke for reading an early version and for offering feedback. I would also like to thank my editor, Shelley Holloway, for working this one in on short notice. Thank you, too, good reader, for picking up a new novel and giving it a try. I hope you enjoy the adventure.

Part I

Chapter 1

COLONEL RIDGE ZIRKANDER HAD WALKED the hall to General Ort's office so many times he suspected his boots were responsible for the threadbare state of the drab gray carpet runner. The two privates standing guard on either side of the door were too well trained to exchange knowing smirks, but that didn't mean gossip of this meeting wouldn't be all over the citadel by noon. It wouldn't be the first time. Fortunately, uniforms only held awards and not demerits.

"Morning, gents." Ridge stopped before the door. He eyed the privates' rifles—they had the new lever-action repeating models—but neither man looked like he had been given orders to keep visitors out. Too bad. "How's the general's mood today?"

"Tense, sir."

"That applies to most days, doesn't it?" He didn't expect an answer—privates weren't encouraged to chat about officers after all, at least not where said officers might overhear—but the younger one grinned and responded.

"A week ago last Thursday, it elevated to agitated, sir."

"Glad I was in the air that day then." Ridge thumped the fellow on the shoulder and reached for the doorknob.

The private's grin widened. "We heard about the battle cruiser, sir. That was marvelous. I wish I could have seen it."

"Taking down the supply ship was more of a victory for us, but I suppose that didn't come with the added excitement of being shot at by cannons."

"I'd love to hear about it, sir." The private's eyes gleamed with hope.

"Might be at Rutty's later," Ridge said, "if the general doesn't send me down to the kitchen to chop vegetables with the recruits."

He walked in without knocking. Mounds of paperwork were heaped on General Ort's desk, but the man was gazing out the window overlooking the harbor, his weathered hands clasped behind his back. Merchant, fishing, and military vessels sailed to and from the docks, but, as always, Ridge's eye was drawn to the dragon fliers lined up on the butte on the southern end. Their sleek bronze hulls, propellers, and guns gleamed under the morning sun, beckoning him to return. His squadron was out there, overseeing maintenance and repairs, and waiting for him to bring them news. He hoped this ego-trouncing session would also include the delivery of new orders.

When the general didn't turn around right away, Ridge flopped into a plush leather chair in front of the desk, flinging his leg over the armrest.

"Morning, General. I got your message. What can I do for you this fine day?" Ridge nodded toward the blue sky above the harbor, a sky clear of enemy airships as well as clouds.

Ort turned, his customary scowl deepening as he waved at Ridge's dangling boot. "No, no, have a seat. I insist."

"Thank you, General. These chairs do lend themselves to lounging in comfort." Ridge patted the soft leather. "If anyone ever succeeds in foisting an office on me, I hope it'll be furnished just as finely."

"Seven gods, Ridge. Every time you see me, I wonder anew how you got so many bars on your collar."

"It's a mystery to me as well, sir."

Ort pushed a hand through his short gray hair, sat down, and pulled out a folder. Ridge's folder, though he had to have it memorized by now, all of its three inches of thickness. "You're forty years old, Colonel. Are you ever going to grow up?"

"I've been told it's more likely I'll be shot down first."

Ort folded his hands across the folder without opening it. "Tell me what happened."

"In regard to what, sir?" Ridge asked. He knew perfectly well, but he had long ago learned not to volunteer information that might incriminate him.

"You don't *know*?" Ort's ever-present scowl deepened until the corners of his mouth were in danger of falling off his chin.

"Well, my squad's been on the ground four days. Could be a lot of things."

"According to my report, you broke Diplomat Serenson's nose, bruised his ribs, and threatened to rip off his penis. Any of that sound familiar?"

"Oh," Ridge said, nodding. "Yes, it does. Although, I believe it was his flesh pole I threatened to rip off. There were ladies present, and some find anatomically correct terms too blunt for polite company."

The general's jaw ground back and forth several times before he managed a response. "Explain."

"That slimy turf kisser had cornered Lieutenant Ahn and was groping her and trying to usher her outside. She was about to slam a fist into his face herself, but I stepped in, figuring she might not appreciate your plush leather chairs the way I do." Actually, his ace lieutenant, who had nearly as many kills on the side of her flier as he did this year, had been wearing the most conflicted expression, like she might have actually let Serenson drag her outside and paw her up, since he was such an important delegate. To the hells with that—nobody's uniform required *that* kind of sacrifice.

"Breyatah's Breath, Ridge, couldn't you have defended your officer without starting an international incident?"

Possibly, but he wouldn't have found it nearly as satisfying. Besides... "International incident? We're already at war with the Cofah, and this was just a reminder of why we broke away from their rule in the first place. They think they can have anything they want. Well, they can't. Not my country, and *not* one of my people."

Ort sighed and leaned back in his chair. "It's good to know

you care beneath all your irrepressible impudence, but the king was at my throat like an attack dog this morning. This is serious, Ridge. Serenson wants you sent to Magroth."

Ridge snorted. His crime hadn't been *that* severe. Only convicts went to the Magroth Crystal Mines, convicts who would have otherwise been marched out to the firing squad. Very few thought the sentence of life in the mines with no chance of parole was an improvement.

The general pulled a sheet of paper out of the top of Ridge's file and laid it on the desk. "You leave in the morning."

"I—what?" For the first time, real unease settled into the pit of his stomach. He had left his blessed dragon figurine dangling in the cockpit of his flier, but maybe he should have brought it along, or at least rubbed its belly for luck that morning. "That's not very damned funny, sir."

The general's humorless gray eyes bored into Ridge like overzealous drills. "The king agrees."

The king? The king wouldn't send him to his death. He was too valuable to the war effort. Ridge started to shake his head, but halted, realization coming as his gaze dropped to the typed sheet of paper. Orders. They weren't sending him as a criminal, but as an officer. A contingent of men guarded the secret mines, the location known only to those high up in command—and those who had been stationed there.

"You want me to guard miners, sir? That's the infantry's job and one for a bunch of enlisted men." Sure, there had to be a few officers there to run administration, but there couldn't possibly be a posting for a colonel. "Or are you demoting me along with this... reassignment?" Ridge almost gagged on the last word. Reassigned! Him? All he knew how to do was fly and shoot; that's all he had done since graduating from flight school. He was only vaguely aware of the location of the mines, but knew they were in the mountains, hundreds of miles from the coast, from the front lines.

"Demotion? No, not a demotion. Read the orders, Ridge." Ort smiled for the first time in the meeting, the kind of smile a bully wears after pummeling some scrawny kid on the brisk-ball court.

"The king and I talked about this at great length this morning."

Ridge picked up the sheet and skimmed. Yes, a reassignment. To the position... He lowered the sheet. "Fortress *commander*?"

"I believe that's what it says, yes." Ort was still smiling. Ridge preferred his scowl.

"That's... that's a position for a general." Or at least someone with experience leading battalions of troops, not to mention the administration background a man should have. All Ridge had commanded were squadrons of smart, cocky officers not unlike him. What was he supposed to do with a bunch of infantry soldiers? Not to mention the gods knew how many murdering prisoners that roamed the tunnels?

"In times of war, it's not uncommon for less experienced officers to be forced to work in positions above their pay grade."

"What happened to the current commander?" Ridge muttered, imagining some poor general with a miner's pickaxe driven into his forehead.

"General Bockenhaimer is due to retire this winter. He'll be extremely grateful to be relieved early."

"I'll bet."

Ridge stared down at the orders, his eyes blurring. He barely managed to check the date. A one-year assignment. Who would command his team while he was gone? Who would pilot his flier? He had always thought... he had been led to assume—no, people had told him, damn it—he was indispensable out there. The war wasn't over—if anything, this year had seen more fighting than any of the previous four. How could they send him off to some remote gods-forgotten outpost in the mountains?

"I know this is hard for you to stomach, Ridge, but I actually believe it's for the best."

Ridge shook his head. It was all he could do. For once, he had no words, no quip with which to respond.

"You're an amazing pilot, Ridge. You know that. Everyone knows that. But there's more to being an officer than shooting things. This will force you to mature as a soldier and as a man." Ort hitched a shoulder. "Or it'll kill you."

Ridge snorted.

Ort waved a hand. "You have your orders. Dismissed."

Ridge left the chair, giving it and the harbor out the window a long look before he headed for the door. Grounded. For a year. How was he going to survive?

"Oh, and Colonel?" the general said as Ridge walked for the door.

Ridge paused, hoping this had all been a joke designed to teach him a lesson. "Yes?"

"Pack warm clothes. Autumn is just about over in the mountains." The general's smile returned. "And Magroth is at twelve thousand feet."

A lesson, indeed.

* * *

Sardelle woke with a start, her heart pounding out of her chest. Nothing except blackness surrounded her. Scrapes and scuffs reached her ears, and memories rushed over her: the sounds of the explosion, being ordered to the safety chamber, climbing into one of the mage shelters and activating it, then gasping in terror as the rock crashed down all around her, obliterating her world.

She patted around, feeling for the smooth walls of the sphere, but they had disappeared. Only rough, cold rock met her probing fingers. The scrapes were getting louder. Her colleagues coming to help? But they would burn away the rock or move it by magical means, not scrape through it with pickaxes, wouldn't they? Maybe the sorcerers of the Circle were too busy fighting back their attackers and had sent mundane workers.

Sardelle?

The telepathic query filled her mind with relief. Jaxi. Had her soulblade been buried in the rock somewhere as well? There hadn't been time to run and grab the sword when the mountain had started quaking.

I'm here.

Thank the gods. You've been hibernating for so long. You can't believe how lonely it's been. There's a limit to how many conversations you can start with rocks.

I assume that means you're buried too. The soft scrapes were getting closer, and a pinprick of light pierced the darkness a few feet away.

Deeper than you. You left me in the basement training rooms, remember?

Of course I remember. That was just this morning. As I recall, you were enjoying having that handsome young apprentice oil your blade.

Sardelle waited, expecting a retort, but a long silence filled her mind—and the pinprick of light grew larger. When Jaxi finally responded, it was a soft, *Sardelle?*

Yes... ?

It wasn't this morning.

When, then?

Three hundred years ago.

She snorted. *That's funny, Jaxi. Very funny. How long has it really been?*

Those army sappers were utterly effective in collapsing the mountain. They were shielded somehow, and our people didn't sense them. For that... we died. En masse. The mage shelter saved your life, but it was programmed not to take you out of stasis until favorable conditions returned to the outside. In this case, oxygen and a way for a human being to escape without being crushed.

That part, Sardelle believed. She remembered Jetia sending out the telepathic announcement—more of a mental shriek of fear—about the sappers seconds before the explosions had gone off, before the rocks had started crumbling. But... three hundred years?

If it makes you feel better, I've been conscious for all of those years, watching this mountain and hoping someone with mage powers would wander by, so I could call out for the person to retrieve me. I did manage to mind link with a couple of shepherds and prospectors, but they found my presence in their heads alarming, if you can imagine that. They ran off the mountain shrieking. Little matter. I estimate I'm under a thousand meters of solid rock. There would be no way for a mundane to reach me. Even you... I would appreciate it if you would find a way to get me out, but moving that much rock would be too much for you without me.

Is that so? Sardelle managed to lace the thought with indignation, though it was more a habitual reaction to Jaxi's teasing than a true objection. And this *had* to be teasing. Unlike with most sorcerers, who preserved their souls after they had lived many decades, Jaxi had died young of a rare disease, choosing to infuse her essence in the soulblade before passing. Despite having had several wielders and existing in the sword for hundreds of years, Jaxi retained her teenage sense of humor, often playing pranks on Sardelle.

Not this time, my friend.

I don't—

You'll see in a moment. You better pay attention to your surroundings. The world has changed. Our people were destroyed, and those who remain fear anything that smells of magic. A while back, at the base of the mountain, I saw a girl who had been accused of being a witch weighted down with stones and drowned in a lake. Do not use your powers where they can be observed.

Sardelle wanted to argue, wanted to catch Jaxi in a lie. Mostly she wanted for everything to be all right, for all of her kith and kin to have survived and for this all to be a joke. The scrapes had continued, and more light—the flickering of candle or perhaps lantern flames—seeped into her niche. Her eyes couldn't yet tell her who was out there, so she stretched out with her senses... and knew right away the two men clawing at the rock with picks and shovels were strangers. Though she was often off on missions, she knew all the sorcerers and mundanes who worked in Galmok Mountain, the seat of culture, government, and teaching for those with the gift.

Voices reached Sardelle's ears, rough and slightly accented.

"... see something, Tace?"

"Not sure. Maybe a room? There's a gap in the rocks up here."

"Maybe there's a crystal." Rock shifted, pebbles raining down a slope. "That would be cracking—they haven't found one all year. We'll get a pint if we bring one up. The general might even invite us for dinner."

They shared chortles at that notion.

Some of the words and pronunciation have changed over the

generations, but you're fortunate the language is the same. You'll be able to communicate with them without entering their minds. Jaxi was silent for a moment, but Sardelle sensed the unease through their link. *Actually... I'd stay out of their minds altogether if I were you.*

Telepathic intrusion without invitation is forbidden except in emergencies, Sardelle thought. The mantra was one of the early ones in the Texts of the Referatu, something Jaxi surely knew as well as she.

If being buried alive in rubble for centuries doesn't count as an emergency, I'll cede myself to a doddering geriatric to be used as a cane for the rest of my existence.

Sardelle sighed. *I'll... consider your point.*

Finally enough rock fell away that Sardelle could make out the men. Her saviors, whether they knew it or not.

They don't. This is your opportunity for escape, but you'll have to be very careful.

I'm not leaving without you.

A lantern lifted to the hole, one that was now more than a foot wide. A moment later, a man's face came into view, his skin caked with grime, a matted mustache and beard hanging to his chest, his greasy dark hair held back from his eyes by a dusty bandana.

"There's something in here," he said to his comrade. "I see cloth, and, er..."

"Greetings," Sardelle said. "Tace, was it?"

Surprise widened the man's eyes, and he stumbled out of view. An auspicious beginning.

"What was that?" his comrade asked.

"There's a girl in there," Tace blurted.

"You tugging on my shovel? There's no girls down here."

"I'm a woman," Sardelle said, "and I'd be obliged if you dug me the rest of the way out of here." She glimpsed a tunnel behind the men. She could handle the rock barricade in her own way, but Jaxi's warning trumpeted in her mind. *They fear anything that smells of magic.*

"A woman," Tace whispered. "A woman down here."

"How'd she get in there?"

"I don't care." More rocks fell away as the men worked at them with renewed vigor. "There ain't no soldiers 'cept back at the cages. They ain't gonna hear nothing. She can be ours."

And with those words—and the burst of lust that emanated from Tace like heat from an inferno—Sardelle came to understand Jaxi's warning.

"What if she's uglier than your grandma?"

"Don't care. Last time I tried to get with a girl, that nasty Big Bretta drove me out of the barracks like I was diseased. This is a prayer answered."

A prayer? What kind of man prayed to what kind of god for a woman to rape? Or maybe the deluded miner thought she would willingly jump into his arms because he had dug her out? No, he wasn't even thinking that—he was simply consumed with lust like a man digging toward a golden vein. She hadn't delved into his thoughts—and wasn't a gifted enough telepath to do so without alerting him anyway—but his emotions were on the surface, so strong she would have had to erect a barrier around herself to keep from sensing them.

More rock fell away. If she stepped to the front of the niche the mage shelter had left when it dissipated, she could have reached the men, had them pull her out, but she hung back, considering her options. Handling a would-be rapist wasn't a difficult matter if she could use her powers, but dare she? There were only the two men in the tunnel, but she sensed others in a maze of mines that snaked around inside the mountain. She wouldn't kill these two to keep them from divulging her presence. That was the sort of usage of power that had scared the mundanes into the sneak attack that had brought this mountain down.

Sardelle swam around Tace's overpowering emotions, trying to get a sense of the second man's state of mind. Might he be more reasonable? Someone to whom she could appeal? Her hope was squashed by her first brush with him. A darkness hovered about him, and she had the impression of a different sort of lust, of someone who liked to hurt, to cut with knives, to see pain on another's face. He would kill his comrade Tace as happily as work with him, if he could get away with it, and he would kill her too.

Sardelle drew back, her heart racing from the chilling contact. She snapped up her barriers to repel further brushes with their emotions.

I told you. Jax sounded sad rather than triumphant.

Enough rocks had been pulled away that the men could reach her now. They raised their lanterns for a good look. Sardelle stepped into the light, more because she wanted to scout the tunnel—and an escape route—than get closer to either of them. They smelled of sweat and grime, and even someone without the gift could have read the lechery on their faces. They were both large men, men who had been toiling here a long time and who had grown strong because of it. Through accident or design, they were blocking the narrow tunnel.

"It *is* a girl," Tace whispered, eyeing her from head to foot.

Sardelle had been dressed for the president's birthday celebration that morning—not that morning, but a morning hundreds of years in the past, she corrected, for she was gradually coming to believe Jaxi. She wore sandals and a dress fitting for a gala, not for tramping through tunnels. Her black hair hung about her shoulders, instead of being back in the braid she usually wore for work. Her pale green silk dress didn't show a lot of skin, but it did hug the contours of her body, and she realized the delicate collar had been ripped at some point in her mad race for safety. Both men's eyes locked onto that pale exposed flesh.

Tace grinned and stepped forward, reaching for her arm. Sardelle sensed Jaxi in the back of her mind, like a panther coiled to spring. The soulblade would attack their minds if she didn't find a way to defend herself.

Though rushed, Sardelle called upon a simple trick she had learned from a field healer, one she had used before when caught in difficult situations. She gave them rashes.

Their discomfort took a moment to register, and Sardelle feared she would have to use a more direct attack. Tace hauled her out of the rocks, and he pushed her against the cold stone wall, pressing his body against hers. He reached for his belt, but then he paused, a confused expression twisting his face. Behind him, his comrade was leaning on his pick with one hand and scratching his balls with the other.

Sardelle wanted to shrink away from Tace's hot breath washing her face, but she held her composure and merely raised an eyebrow. His hips shifted and the hand that had been about to unfasten his belt drifted lower, as he too suffered an overpowering itch.

The pickaxe the other man had been holding clanked to the ground, and he twisted and bucked, both of his hands now occupied. Tace's hands went back to his belt, but not with any intention of dropping his trousers to molest her. He stepped back, alternately scratching and investigating what was happening down there. Both men hobbled to the closest lantern for a better look, their trousers around their ankles.

At first, Sardelle only took a couple of steps, easing away slowly and silently, not wanting them to notice. When they didn't, she turned her walk into a jog, taking care not to let the sandals slap on the stone floor. She was already wishing she had worn her work leathers to the president's birthday, huge gala or not. The tunnel was dark and uneven, but her senses guided her, and she didn't conjure a light. She guessed that any other miners she met down there might be of similar mindsets to those two.

Good guess.

What is this place, Jaxi? Sardelle could handle a couple of dark-souled brutes, but what if... what if this was a representation of what the world had become? Her people's beautiful community destroyed, to be replaced with this? Her people... Her *friends*. Had they all died in that demolition? Tedzu, Malik, Yewlith? Her brother? Her parents? Even if they hadn't, they would have died in the years since. Was she all alone in the world now?

I'm here. For once, there was nothing flippant in Jaxi's response. She sent a feeling of compassion and support through their link. Sardelle appreciated it and wished it were enough. It wasn't. She was glad for the empty darkness of the tunnel, for tears were streaking down her cheeks and dripping from her chin.

It's been a mine for the last fifty years or so, and it's also a prison, Jaxi explained. *As to the world beyond this mountain? I don't know. I can't sense that far.*

I understand.

If it was a prison, maybe that meant some sort of sane person was in charge, someone she could talk to about... about what, she wasn't sure. How would she explain how she had come to be in the prison in the first place? And how could she escape and leave Jaxi buried under tons of rock? For that matter, how could she escape without investigating further and seeing if something remained of her people? Of her friends? Wasn't it possible that if she had made it to protection, others had too? Jaxi might simply not sense them because they were in the hibernation induced by the shelters.

I've checked. Hundreds of times. Trust me, I've checked. It's been a long, boring three centuries. I've also read all the books in the very dusty, very seldom-used prison library. If you ever need a summary of the titles, let me know.

Sardelle didn't appreciate the humor, not then. *When I was in the mage shelter, could you tell I was alive?*

Yes.

Sardelle struggled to find logic to refute Jaxi's certainty as to the others' passings. She didn't want to give up her hope. *We're linked. Maybe that was why you could sense me and—*

No.

Oh.

Light appeared ahead, lanterns hanging from nails in wooden supports. The dirt and rock that had been heaped against the walls in the area where the two men had accosted her was cleared here, and iron tracks ran along the ground, with ore carts here and there. More sections of track were stacked along one wall, the route waiting to be extended.

Sardelle slowed down, sensing more people ahead. Soon, the banging of carts and scraping of dirt reached her ears. With lanterns lighting this section, sneaking past miners would be difficult. That Tace had mentioned cages. Some sort of lift or tram system? He had also mentioned a guard. A guard could take her to whoever was in charge.

Someone jogged past an intersection ahead. Sardelle leaned against the wall between two lanterns, hoping the shadows hid her. Maybe she ought to wait in the darkness somewhere until the shift ended. But no, that wasn't an option. Sooner or later, her two rash victims were going to stop scratching themselves and seek medical attention, and she hadn't passed any branches in the tunnels.

She crept forward again. The bangs stopped, and it grew silent ahead. Had a lunch break been called? Maybe she would luck out.

Sardelle reached the corner and peeked around it. It wasn't an intersection, but an open chamber with lanterns hanging from a high ceiling as well as from the walls. Two men stood guard on either side of a metal cage on rails, a mesh door on the front side. The rails, as well as a cable attached to the top disappeared into a shaft angling upward at a diagonal. To the right of Sardelle's tunnel, at the back of the chamber, a big metal contraption with wheels and pulleys was bolted into the stone floor. A tram system. She had found her way out if she could get past those guards, or should she try talking to them?

Based on their tidy hair cuts, shaven faces, and clean uniforms—gray trousers with silver piping and navy blue jackets—they *looked* more likely to be reasonable than the thugs, but evil could walk in many guises. And it made her nervous that she didn't *recognize* those uniforms. They weren't the dark greens of the Iskandian Guard, the soldiers she had once worked with to defend the continent. More than that, she didn't recognize their weapons. Oh, she had seen things like the daggers they had sheathed at their waists and the studded maces on short chains hanging from their utility belts, but they bore firearms as well. Not the clumsy matchlock muskets she was familiar with—weapons many soldiers eschewed in favor of longbows or crossbows—but sleek black weapons the likes of which she had never seen. There was no ramrod attached to the top, nor were the men wearing powder containers, as far as she could see.

They've replaced powder and musket balls with bullets that contain the charges within, Jaxi informed her. *Each rifle can hold six rounds, and that lever on the bottom is for loading them into the chamber. They can fire rapidly, one shot every half second or so.*

Sardelle was fortunate the guards were talking to each other in low voices, and not paying much attention to the tunnels that emptied into the chamber, for she had been staring at them for a long moment. Even without Jaxi's explanation, the firearms—the *rifles*—would have told her what she hadn't wanted to believe. This wasn't her century anymore.

Sorry.

I know. Sardelle blinked, fighting back tears again. This wasn't the time. She would find a place to cry for her lost friends—her lost *everything*—later.

She was on the verge of stepping out of the tunnel, when the guards stopped talking, one halting in the middle of the sentence. They stared down one of the passages, not Sardelle's. There were men gathering behind a bend down there, but she didn't think the guards could see them from their position. Were the miners up to something? She thought about warning the guards—maybe that would buy her some appreciation from them—but she was too late.

A boom came, not from the tunnel with the men, but from one to the left of the cage. The ground shivered beneath Sardelle's feet. Black smoke poured from the passage, while the men who had been gathering down the other tunnel charged from around the bend.

Sardelle opened her mouth to shout a warning, but the guards were already reacting. They stepped back into the mouth of the tram shaft for cover, then, each man facing toward one threat, dropped to one knee, their rifles coming up to aim. Nothing came out of the smoky passage, but the guard facing the advancing men started firing. Sardelle, sensing the bursts of pain as the bullets found targets, had a chilling demonstration of the rapid-fire capabilities of the weapons. Even so, three of the charging men reached the guards, and the skirmish switched to hand-to-hand combat. The brawny miners wielded their pickaxes and shovels with fury and power, but it soon became clear that the soldiers were well trained. They kept the tram cage at their backs, so their attackers couldn't maneuver behind them, and they swung the maces with precise, compact strokes, deflecting the picks and shovels, then smashing the studded metal heads into ribcages and jaws. The three miners soon lay unmoving on the ground.

Other people had crept toward the chamber from the other tunnels, though nobody had come as close to it as Sardelle had. They seemed curious and hopeful rather than antagonistic. Harmlessly watching the show in case something happened in the miners' favor? A warning twanged her senses. They weren't *all* harmless.

"Look out," Sardelle called to alert them to a new assailant back in the direction of the smoke, the one who had originally lit the explosive.

A long cylinder with flame dancing at the end of a fuse sailed out of the tunnel, landing in front of the tram. One soldier fired at the man who had thrown it while the other stamped out the spitting fuse, as calmly as if he were grinding out a cigar stub.

All right, so they probably hadn't needed her warning.

One of the soldiers knelt to check the throats of the unconscious men. The other stared at her—she didn't try to hide, there being no point since she had given away her position, but she didn't step fully around the corner yet either. She wanted to see what their reaction to her was first.

"What are you doing down here, woman?"

Not exactly a thank you.

Sardelle was about to respond, but the second guard had taken out a knife and, without so much as a hesitation for a prayer or apology to whatever gods the miners worshipped, slit one of the unconscious men's throats.

"What are you doing?" Sardelle blurted, even as the soldier shifted to dispatch a second miner. "They're no threat now. Why kill them?"

The guard wielding the bloody dagger barely glanced at her. The other soldier strode toward her. "You people made your choice when you picked lives of crime, and these idiots made their final choice just now. There's no leniency here. We'd have to deal with that kind of thing every day if we were lenient." He jerked a thumb toward the men—toward the *bodies*, their life's blood flowing out onto the dark stone. Unlike Tace and his buddy, these miners were thin—too thin—with gaunt faces and hollowed cheekbones. They wouldn't have been a match for the soldiers under any circumstances.

Belatedly, his words sank in. You people. He thought she was one of them, one of the miners. Sardelle braced herself against the corner, ready to defend herself again if she had to. Would he try to slit *her* throat, as he had the others?

The soldier hung his mace on his belt and carried the rifle at his side rather than aiming at her, so she let him approach without reacting. She didn't sense kindly thoughts from him, but she didn't get the feeling that he meant to hurt her either.

"Come on, woman. You're not supposed to be down here. You know that." He gripped her arm and pulled her into the chamber, then frowned at her dress and sandals. "Or don't you? Did you come in with the prisoners yesterday? Didn't you get the orientation?"

Orientation, as if this were some educational campus where people were directed how to find their classes and the dormitories. But if it could explain her presence down here, she would go with it. "No. No orientation."

The second soldier stalked down one of the tunnels, his dagger still in his grip as he went to check on the people they had already shot.

The man gripping her arm shook his head. "This way. Randask, I'm taking this one up to the women's area. I'll report this mess to the captain, who can report it to the general, who can sit in his office and drink his vodka and not care a yak's butt, like usual. You going to be all right down here?"

"Yeah." The man walked back into the chamber, his dagger awash in blood. Sardelle had a hard time tearing her eyes from it. He walked into the opposite tunnel, though she could sense that the man who had thrown the explosive was dead. "The peepers have gone back to work."

Yes, the watchers Sardelle had noticed earlier had drifted back down their tunnels. Clangs started up again in the distance. There wouldn't be another attack for a while. She wondered what had prompted this one.

Desperation, Jaxi suggested. *Misery. They have nothing to lose.*

Do we?

I can't speak for you, but I live in hope that my situation will improve. At the very least, perhaps some new books will be dropped off in the prison library.

"This way." The guard ushered Sardelle into the cage, then shut and latched the door. He hadn't let go of her arm yet, as if she would run off and return to those awful tunnels. She suffered the grip, though couldn't help but dwell on the fact that yesterday—no, three hundred years ago—few men or women would have presumed to touch her without invitation, even some of the military commanders she had worked with for years. It wasn't so much that she was aloof or in the habit of reprimanding people who did so, but the ungifted had always regarded the gifted with respect—or, in some cases, perhaps more than she had realized, fear and wariness.

The second soldier walked over to the machine and pulled a lever. Clanks sounded, and the cage started moving, being pulled up the rails into darkness. Sardelle twisted her head to squint up the track. A distant light waited, little more than a pinprick. As the cage rose, she could feel herself being pulled farther and farther from Jaxi. Their link was strong enough that they could communicate across a lot of miles—since being joined with the soulblade, she had never been far enough away to truly test their range—but the symbolism made the problem feel more dramatic than it was. Nothing was truly changing, and yet... she felt like she was abandoning her only friend left in the world.

Don't worry, came the dry response. *You wouldn't be going far.*

Right, Jaxi had said this was a prison. Walking out the front door or gate or whatever they had up there wouldn't be an option. She trusted that she could evade whatever security they had and escape though.

Not unless you've learned to fly. The Ice Blades are as high as they ever were, and the road over the pass was destroyed when these people's ancestors took down half the mountain. Also, the first snows of winter have come.

Oh. But the guard had mentioned new prisoners arriving. *How do these people get in and out?*

Weather permitting, they fly.

They fly? Sardelle was glad for the darkness, so the soldier wouldn't see the way her mouth had dropped open.

They have ships that sail the airways, held up by giant balloons, and they also have small, maneuverable mechanical craft designed after the dragons of eld. As I've been telling you, the world has changed.

"How'd you get down here, anyway?" the soldier asked, disturbing the images she had been trying to form.

Sardelle shrugged. "Just came down."

"Huh."

She caught a hint of irritation in that single syllable. A point of pride? Since she had implied she had somehow gotten past him, or perhaps one of his fellow guards? They *did* seem a competent bunch; she could see where a suggestion of laxness would rankle. So long as he didn't start thinking of magical reasons she might have slipped past.

The tram seemed to be making decent speed, with a hint of cold fresh air whispering into the cage, but they had only made it halfway up. Sardelle wondered how deep into the mountain their tunnels reached. Maybe there was some way she could convince them to angle toward Jaxi's resting place. With pickaxes and shovels, it would probably take ages, but she had to try.

"You mentioned taking me to a women's area," Sardelle said, "but I actually need to see the person in charge." She hoped that wasn't the vodka-swilling general he had mentioned. "Can you take me to him or her?"

The soldier snorted. "The general doesn't see prisoners."

"Ever?"

"Ever."

Chapter 2

Sardelle stepped out of the cage and stopped so quickly the soldier nearly tripped over her. Icy wind buffeted her, whipping at her dress and raising gooseflesh on her arms. She gaped at the black stone fortress around her, around the tiny valley where merchants had once sold cheese and crops in the summer and where a wide road and bridge had led over the river and to the back gate leading into Galmok Mountain. The Goat Peak River was still there, half iced over as it meandered through the large courtyard within the fortress walls, but there was nothing inviting about it or the valley anymore. The crenellations and cannon-like weapons on the walls were as forbidding as the Ice Blades themselves, the snow covered peaks rising in all four directions around the valley, scraping the sky as they towered another five thousand feet above the already lofty valley. Most of the peaks hadn't changed, but Galmok... She stared in horror. It looked like a volcano rather than the majestic mountain it had once been, its upper walls slumped inward with a misshapen bowl where the peak had once been.

The soldier shoved her. "Get going, girl."

Sardelle wrenched her gaze from the view and stumbled down a path that hadn't been there the last time she had been outside. Just yesterday, her mind wanted to add, though she had accepted by now that it had *not* been yesterday. Aside from the three centuries that had passed, it had been summer when she had entered Galmok and warm enough for her dress. Now she wrapped her arms around herself as she picked her route, the trail following the tramline down toward the center of the fortress. There were other holes in the mountain, other tram tracks plunging into the darkness. What were they mining for?

Crystal? Hadn't one of her attackers said that? She couldn't imagine what sort of crystal they had found in there, though she did recall gold and silver veins in the area. A smelter set up on the far side of the fortress seemed to suggest the likelihood of precious metal mining.

Another push nearly made her stumble. "You act like you haven't seen this all before. I've got a report to put together. Walk faster." He pointed at a large stone building with laundry hanging on a line, whipping in the breeze as it dried in the meager sun.

"That's where we're going?" Even as Sardelle asked, a pair of women strode out of another building and headed for the one with the laundry lines. They wore heavy wool dresses and socks, scarves, hats, and fur jackets as they carried baskets of linens.

"Yes," the soldier said, drawing out the syllable as if he were talking to an imbecile.

Sardelle sighed and headed in the indicated direction. At least there were women here. She ought to be able to get information from them, one way or another. Maybe, given time, she could figure out a way to arrange a meeting with that general.

She walked over a bridge, but paused at the top, realizing her unfriendly guide had fallen behind. He had stopped to stare into the western sky. A strange flying craft was banking around Bandit Mountain and angling toward the fortress. Flying. She hadn't quite believed it when Jaxi had mentioned it, but the bronze metallic craft clearly wasn't a bird. With wings outstretched and something on the tips that resembled talons, it did vaguely resemble a dragon, at least the ones Sardelle had seen illustrated in books, the creatures having been extinct for a thousand years or more now. Some sort of rotating fan buzzed, keeping the contraption aloft.

A propeller, Jaxi said dryly.

Hush, just because you've been reading books these past centuries, doesn't mean I have. What's powering it?

The soldier muttering to himself distracted Sardelle, and she didn't hear the answer.

"What's this about?" the man asked. "Supplies and prisoners came in yesterday. Shouldn't be anything due for two weeks."

Whatever it is, it could be an escape chance for you.

I'm not leaving without you, Jaxi.

I'm not going to suffocate or die here. You can come back when you can.

The fortress didn't look like it would be any easier to sneak into than it would be to sneak out of. Besides, where would she go? This was—had been—home.

There is that. A mental sigh accompanied Jaxi's comment.

The flying contraption banked again. It was circling the valley like an osprey searching for a fish to snatch out of a lake. None of the soldiers on the ramparts were racing for the cannons, so Sardelle assumed it was a friendly aircraft, though everyone was watching it draw closer with curiosity. It angled for the wide, flat roof of the biggest building in the fortress, a two-story structure backing up to one of the walls. A flat roof was a strange choice for mountains that received many feet of snow every year—the other buildings had steeply pitched tops, as one would expect—but as the craft lowered, she realized that particular spot must have been designed for landing, though she couldn't imagine how it might be done. An osprey might be able to fold its wings in and alight on a perch, but a manmade craft wouldn't have that ability, surely. It seemed to be designed for going straight ahead, needing those wide banking turns to switch direction. But some sort of thrusters rotated down from the wings, allowing the bronze contraption to slow down without falling out of the sky. Soon it was hovering over the building, and then it lowered, the bottom half disappearing from her sight.

And I thought the rifles were impressive.

Jaxi didn't respond. Maybe she was investigating the craft.

A few soldiers jogged out of the second story of that big building and headed up the stairs to the roof. Their presence seemed to remind her guard of his duty, for he joined her on the bridge, pointing to the laundry building again.

"Let's go. We'll find out soon enough who's visiting."

Though curious about the flying machine, Sardelle couldn't imagine that a visitor would change anything for her, so she walked off without arguing. Maybe the pilot would stay overnight and she might have a chance to examine the craft. It wasn't her priority though.

A woman walked out of the laundry building as Sardelle and the soldier were walking up. The scent of soap and starch drifted through the doorway. The woman's figure was almost stout and brawny enough to be a man. She had a basket balanced on a broad hip and started to walk off the path around the pair, but the soldier stopped her with a hand.

"One-forty-three, isn't it?" he asked.

Sardelle blinked. What?

The number meant something to the woman, for she nodded. "Yeah."

"Looks like you lost someone." The soldier pushed Sardelle toward the woman.

"Never seen her before."

"I think she came in yesterday."

"Then why wasn't she here an hour before dawn to report for work, like everyone else?"

"No idea," the soldier said. "Found her down on the bottom level of the mine."

The woman gave an exasperated huff and looked Sardelle up and down like she might be a lost toddler. A particularly dumb lost toddler. "Seven gods, girl, you trying to get yourself killed? Or worse?"

What was worse than being killed? Sardelle thought of Tace and his crony and answered her own question.

"What is this?" The woman plucked at Sardelle's sleeve. "Where are your work clothes? You've got to be freezing. What's your number?"

Feeling lost and bewildered, Sardelle broke her oath as a sorceress and skimmed the surface of the woman's thoughts. Numbers. People were called by numbers rather than names. She didn't have to dig deep to find a memory of this woman—Dhasi before she had become One-forty-three—stepping off a supply ship with two other women and two-dozen men and being assigned her number.

"They told me, but I forgot," Sardelle said. She could have

made one up, but what happened if someone already had it? She hugged herself, thinking of sticking her hands under her armpits. What were the odds this conversation could be moved indoors? Her toes were freezing, and the rest of her wasn't much warmer.

"You forgot." One-forty-three—Sardelle hated to think of her as a number, but didn't want to get in trouble for one day calling her by a name that had never been shared—threw up her hands, dropped the basket, and turned for the door. "Wait here. I'll get the roster and try to figure out where she's supposed to be." She stomped back inside. Heat as well as soap odors drifted out, and Sardelle wouldn't have minded following her.

She glanced at the soldier, wondering if he had been irked by the woman, who was presumably a prisoner, the same as the miners below, giving him an order. The soldier was busy though, eyeing Sardelle's chest. She grimaced. Unfortunately, the sunlight showed off the sleek if dusty dress and the curves beneath it all too well, far more effectively than the lanterns in the mines. She had never thought herself a great beauty, but if the beefy laundry lady was representative of the women here, and if the men had as little contact with the outside world as she suspected, she supposed she could see the interest. See it, but not condone it. She watched the soldier through slitted eyes, wondering if another rash breakout would be in order.

Be careful, Jaxi warned. *These people might be brutes, but they're not dumb. And it doesn't take much for them to start talking of witches.*

That girl you mentioned who was thrown in the lake... was she gifted?

If she had been, do you think she would have let herself drown? My understanding from their books is that there are occasionally people born with talent, but that they either get hunted down or learn quickly to hide their quirks. They don't receive any training, not like they did in our day, so they rarely develop much more than a sixth sense.

The soldier touched Sardelle's sleeve, lifting his eyes to meet hers. "You with someone yet, woman?"

"*With* someone?" They all agreed she had just been pushed off the supply ship the day before. She didn't have a name-number—

or a clue—so how could she be *with* someone already?

"I'm in room seventy-two in the barracks, second floor." He nodded toward a building across the square. "Think on it. You're going to have trouble around here if you're not someone's girl."

To punctuate this point, a woman carrying a basket on her hip walked toward the laundry building, a woman who was quite obviously pregnant, very pregnant. Sardelle stared. She couldn't imagine having a child in this environment. She hadn't even seen any children. Was it allowed? Or did they...? She gulped. They wouldn't kill the babies, would they? They couldn't be held accountable for the crimes of their parents.

"She wasn't with someone," the soldier said after the pregnant woman had passed them and gone inside. "Heard it was rough on her."

"You people didn't think to stop it?"

The soldier shrugged. "Lot more of you all than there are of us. We can't be everywhere." That shrug said he didn't care very much about the fact either. "Better to be with a soldier. The prisoners usually don't bother you much if you are."

Usually? Much?

"I'll think about it," Sardelle managed to say rather than punching him. Although, at least with a punch, she wouldn't have to worry about anyone accusing her of witchcraft.

"Good." He smiled and repeated, "Room seventy-two. Tell the night guard you're here to see me, Rolff, and they'll let you in."

"This sort of thing is common, is it?"

For soldiers in the Iskandian Guard, there had been a regulation against molesting prisoners, but she had no idea what was permitted here, or even whose army she was dealing with. Most of those she had seen so far had the pale skin and brown to black hair of the natives of the Iskandian continent, but that didn't mean governments hadn't come and gone over the centuries.

The soldier looked away, shrugged, then looked back. "Nobody cares here."

Ah, so there *was* a regulation. It just wasn't being enforced. Well, that knowledge didn't help her much.

"I'd be doing you a favor," he said. "Trust me."

Sure, he just wanted to help *her*. How considerate.

He stepped closer, laying his hand on her arm. "I'm not so bad, promise. You'll think about it? You said that, right?"

Might want to take him up on the offer.

Jaxi!

What? He's not so bad looking, and he was a good fighter. Bet he's all muscle under that uniform.

This is what I get for agreeing to link with a teenaged soul, one who never got past her horny period before channeling herself into our sword. "Yes," she told the soldier, who was now stroking her arm. "I said that."

Where *was* that laundry lady anyway? She spotted a pair of uniformed men descending the stairs from the building and walking in their direction. Good, a distraction.

"There's your guest," Sardelle said, nodding toward the men, hoping Rolff would stop fondling her arm if an officer was walking past. Of course, she could only hope the newcomers were officers. With the soldiers wearing fur parkas in addition to their uniform jackets, she couldn't see insignia, not that she could have deciphered it anyway.

Her soldier stepped back from her at the men's approach though, dropping his arm, no, jerking it behind his back. "I can't believe it," he whispered. "Do you know who that is?"

Please, she didn't know who *anyone* was. "No."

He gaped at her, but only for a second before focusing on the two men again. "That's Colonel Ridgewalker Zirkander."

Ridgewalker? How cocky. Maybe he had given the name to himself.

"What's he doing here?" the soldier breathed, his voice scarcely more than a whisper as the two visitors drew nearer. The younger of the pair, one who kept trying to get the other to let him carry the duffle bag slung over his shoulder, was talking and pointing toward a building past the laundry facility, but the path would take them by Sardelle and Rolff—with six inches of snow in the courtyard, the cleared sidewalks were the only logical options. Good. She hoped one of them would ask what

Rolff was doing away from his post, which might result in him leaving her alone. Didn't he have some dead miners to report, anyway?

As they walked, the colonel had his head bent toward the younger man, listening to whatever information he was being given. He commented on something and grinned. The young soldier or maybe officer—he had a more academic look about him than the sturdy Rolff—blinked in surprise, then rushed to nod and smile back, though he didn't seem to know if that was quite the right response. Smiles and humor probably weren't commonplace around here. The young officer looked to be in his twenties and had the earnest eager-to-please face of a dog hoping for a treat. The colonel was closer to Sardelle's age, probably older, though there wasn't any gray in what she could see of his short brown hair—a fur cap canted at a roguish angle that she doubted was regulation hid most of it. He was on the tall side with a lean athletic build the parka didn't quite hide. He had a handsome face, a scar on his chin notwithstanding, and dark brown eyes that glinted with humor to match the grin that hadn't entirely faded.

Maybe you can get his *room number.*

Jaxi!

What? He's closer to your age than this puppy. Or are you holding out for the general? He doesn't sound promising.

Before Sardelle could give Jaxi a mental slap on the cheek, the colonel glanced in her direction. The glance became a second look, a startled one. For a moment, she thought he might recognize her somehow—her name and face were—had been—well known, at least among the soldiers she had assisted. For all she knew, she was in a book somewhere. But no, that didn't seem to be recognition on his face, just surprise.

He frowned at Rolff who came into an attention stance so alert and erect that he was quivering. He snapped his fist up for a salute.

"Corporal, why is this woman standing outside in so little clothing?" the colonel asked. "It's twenty degrees out."

"It's... she..."

Sardelle almost felt sorry for Rolff, no doubt groping for a way to explain her unexpected presence. Almost.

After a few more stutters, he settled on, "She's a prisoner, sir!"

The humor that had warmed the colonel's brown eyes earlier had evaporated. "How does *that* answer my question?" His frown shifted to the young officer at his side, who lifted his hands defensively.

"I've never seen her before, sir."

"We found her in the mines," Rolff said. "She wasn't even supposed to be there. The women work up here." Rolff flung a hand toward the laundry room—the door had opened, and the laundry lady stood there. She couldn't have heard more than the last couple of sentences, but she caught the gist and waved her clipboard.

"I got two new girls yesterday and no word about a third."

Sardelle thought about saying something, but she didn't have a cover story worked out that could explain the confusion around her appearance. She was starting to worry that between everyone's babbling, someone would figure out she hadn't come off that supply ship yesterday, but the colonel had a distasteful look on his face at what, coming in new, he must judge as incompetence. Sardelle raised a single eyebrow—the winter she had come home to teach, that expression had made her students stammer with the certainty that they had done something wrong.

The colonel didn't stammer, but he *did* look exasperated. He dropped his duffle bag, unbuttoned his parka, and handed it to her.

"Corporal, get this woman some appropriate clothing. Captain, I want her report on my desk within the hour." He grabbed his duffle bag and hefted it over his shoulder again. "I'll find my office on my own."

"But, but, sir!" The captain took a step after him, then paused, turned toward Sardelle, and held out a beseeching hand. "I don't know her number, sir!"

"Not my problem," the colonel called back. He muttered something else that sounded like, "What's a damned number?"

but Sardelle couldn't be sure of the words.

Grateful for the parka, she tugged it on. Her teeth were starting to chatter. It was still warm inside, with a clean, masculine scent permeating the lining. After standing out in the cold, it was all she could do not to start snuggling with the fur.

Corporal Rolff scratched his head. "Colonel Zirkander has a desk here?"

"He does now," the captain said.

"*Why?*"

"He's relieving General Bockenhaimer as fort commander."

Rolff mouthed another why but didn't voice it. Whatever Zirkander was known for, it apparently wasn't commanding forts. At first, Sardelle found this new situation promising—unlike everyone else she had met here, the man seemed to have a conscience—but when the captain jogged off to look for a report that didn't exist, reality batted her relief away. This new colonel already sounded like he was going to be more efficient than the old general. Before, she might have wriggled through a crack, but now? How was she going to explain her presence? And if she couldn't, what then? Would they assume her some kind of spy? Even in her day, spies had been shot. She had better start talking to people and come up with a plausible story, because she had a feeling she would be called into that office before the day was out.

* * *

A dusty directory that hadn't been updated since the *last* general was commander led Ridge to an administration building, where he headed to the second floor, searching for Bockenhaimer's office. The roar of engines started up on the other side of the fort. The pilot must expect it wouldn't take the general long to pack and catch his ride out of this place. Ridge paused at a window to gaze out, the lump that had been in his throat the whole ride out returning as he watched the man go through his safety check.

"It's just a year," he told himself. "A year in the deepest level of hell," he added, his eyes drawn to the forbidding mountains fencing in the fortress on all sides.

He had only spoken to five people thus far, and he could already tell the place was a mess. Did he have it in him to fix that mess? Just because he had returned from enough successful missions to get promoted regularly didn't mean he had the experience for this kind of job. He had already made an idiot of himself, gawking at that woman in the courtyard. He supposed women could be murderers the same as men, but he hadn't expected to find any here, and certainly not one he would have ambled up to in a bar and bought a drink. Admittedly, she didn't seem the bar type. Too calm. Too serene. Those pale blue eyes... they had been attractive, yes, especially in contrast to that raven hair, but they had seemed far too elegant for the dives he frequented. Not that that would have kept him from buying her that drink if she *had* shown up in one.

"Yeah, Ridge. Drool over the prisoners here. That'll look good on your report." He shook his head and resumed his climb.

A lieutenant carrying a stack of papers was coming out of a doorway, and judging by the quizzical expression on his face, he had heard Ridge talking to himself. Wonderful.

"The general's office?" he asked.

"End of the hall, sir." The lieutenant pointed, then glanced at a clock on the wall. "Though I don't know if he'll be, uhm."

"In?"

"Oh, he's in." The lieutenant looked like he wanted to say more, but shut his mouth and repeated, "End of the hall, sir."

"Thanks."

Ridge dropped his duffle bag by the door, knocked, and smoothed his uniform. He told himself he didn't particularly care what some retiring general thought of him, but foresaw being reprimanded for the missing parka. At this time of year, it had to be part of the official uniform up here. The cold seemed to bite right through the wooden walls of the building and creep up from the floor. For the second time, he wondered what judge had convicted that woman and sent her up here in a summer dress.

A long moment had passed, so he knocked again. He shrugged and opened the door. The snores met his ears at the same time as the scent of alcohol and stale vomit met his nose. Well, that explained some things.

The white-haired man leaning back in his chair, his head on the rest, his boots up on his desk, didn't look like he would have been awake—or sober—even if Ridge had arrived at dawn. A tipped over metal flask rested beside the boots, and several glass vodka bottles occupied the waste bin. A couple of suspicious stains in the corner implied the floor had been vomited on a few times—and poorly cleaned after the fact. In fact, a clean circle next to a potted tree made him think someone had simply pushed the stand over to cover up one such recent mess.

Ridge cleared his throat. "General?"

Only snores answered him.

Ridge walked around the desk, said, "General?" again, and gently shook the man's shoulder.

Bockenhaimer lurched upright, eyes leaping open as he tore a pistol from his belt. Ridge caught his wrist before he could aim it anywhere vital.

"General Bockenhaimer? I'm your replacement."

The general was scowling down at Ridge's grip, looking like he was still contemplating shooting this intruder, if he could only figure out how, but his bloodshot eyes lurched toward Ridge when the words sank in. "Replacement?" he whispered.

"Colonel Zirkander, sir." Ridge pulled out his orders and the general's discharge papers, unfolded them with one hand—that pistol was loaded and cocked, so he wasn't quite ready to release his grip on the general's wrist—and laid them on the desk. "Your retirement went through a couple of months early. I'm your replacement."

"Zirkander, the pilot?" The general's grip finally relaxed. He moved to return the pistol to his holster, and Ridge let him.

"Yes, sir." He waited for Bockenhaimer to point out that neither pilots nor colonels had the experience necessary to command army installations, but the general merely leaned forward to squint at the papers. "Retirement?" He leaned closer, a delighted smile stretching his lips. "Retirement!"

Ridge resisted the urge to roll his eyes. He wondered if the general had been a drunk before they shipped him out here—could this place have been a punishment for him as well?—or if commanding a remote prison full of felons had driven him to drink.

"Yes, sir," Ridge said. "If you could tell me about the S.O.P. here and give me a few—"

Bockenhaimer jumped to his feet, wobbled—Ridge caught him and held him upright despite being surprised—and lunged for the window. "Is that my flier? I can leave today?"

"Yes, sir. But I'd appreciate it if you—"

The general threw open the window and waved to the pilot. "Wait for me, son. I'm already packed!"

Oddly, the wobbling didn't slow Bockenhaimer down much when he ran around the desk and out the door. Ridge's mouth was still hanging open when the general appeared in the courtyard below, a bag tucked under his arm as he raced along the cleared sidewalks.

"That's not exactly how the change-of-command ceremonies I've seen usually go." Ridge hadn't been expecting a parade and a marching band, not in this remote hole, but a briefing would have been nice.

He removed his fur cap and pushed a hand through his hair, surveying his new office. He wondered how long it would take to get rid of the alcohol odor. He also wondered how long that poor potted plant in the corner had been dead. Hadn't that young captain been the general's aide? He couldn't have had some private come in to make sure the place was cleaned? Maybe the staff was too busy guarding the prisoners, and the officers had to wield their own brooms here.

Ridge was looking for the fort's operations manuals when a knock came at the door.

"Sir?" Captain Heriton, the officer who had met him at the flier, leaned in, an apprehensive look on his face. His pale hair and pimples made him look about fifteen instead of the twenty-five or more he must be.

"Yes?"

"It's about that woman... she said she was dropped off yesterday—we got a big load of new convicts—and that she doesn't remember the number she was issued."

"The number?"

"Yes, sir. The prisoners are issued numbers instead of being called by name. Keeps down the in-fighting. Some of them are prisoners of war and pirates, and there are a few former soldiers, and some of those clansmen from up in the north hills. It's easier if they start out with new identities here. The general didn't brief you?" The captain glanced toward the window—the flier had already taken off. "I guess he did leave abruptly."

"Abruptly, yes, that's a word." Not the word Ridge would have used, but he couldn't bring himself to badmouth the general yet, not until he had spent a couple of weeks here and gotten a true feel for where he had landed. "You don't happen to know where the operations manuals are, do you?"

"They should be in here somewhere, sir." The captain started to lean back into the hall.

"The woman's report, Captain," Ridge said dryly. He knew the man hadn't found it, but wasn't ready to let some prisoner wander around without being sorted or collated or whatever it was that was supposed to happen here.

"Er, yes, sir. I'm not sure where to look."

"How about under her name? I imagine she could supply you with that."

"She did, sir. And I tried looking, but her folder wasn't with the batch of files that came in yesterday."

"Perhaps already placed alphabetically?" Ridge suggested. This kid never would have made it onto his squad. Even when he wasn't speaking, his eyes darted around nervously. Waffly. Was that a word? He wasn't sure. Maybe he would have the kid look it up after he found the missing report.

"Uhm, the archive rooms are not exactly alphabetically categorized. They're more... well, the system was already in place when I arrived."

Ridge stood up. "Show me."

The captain's eyebrows rose. Ridge had a feeling the general had never asked to see the archives. He also had a feeling prisoners with missing files weren't all that uncommon.

"Yes, sir. This way."

Ridge followed the slender officer down two flights of stairs to an icy basement that had him wishing someone would have brought his parka back. Cobwebs draped old wooden filing cabinets along with newer metal ones. Dust-caked folders sat atop a lot of the cabinets, either left for later storage or taken out and not returned. A few tables in the middle held boxes with more files. If Ridge hadn't known better, based on the dust collection and the number of cabinets, he would have guessed the prison camp to be hundreds of years old. If all of those storage units were full of records, this place had to be going through people at an alarming rate. There weren't *that* many barracks buildings up there, and while rummaging for the manuals, Ridge had uncovered the most recent supply receipts. Food and gear was being brought in for seven hundred and ten prisoners and one hundred soldiers. There had to be thousands of files smothered in the dust before him.

"Captain."

"Yes, sir?" The wariness in the young man's voice wasn't heartening, but Ridge pressed on anyway.

"My job is to get this fort running smoothly this winter and increase output." Actually his orders said very little about his "job," but as a pilot, he knew how crucial the crystals buried in this mountain were. He wouldn't sit on his butt here for the next year and drink himself into a stupor while lackadaisical work went on—or didn't—in the tunnels below. "Can you guess what your job is going to be this winter?"

"Sir?" More wariness.

Ridge smiled and thumped the man on the back to try and take some of the sting out of his next words. "Organizing this room. Alphabetically. With the people who are still here in those cabinets and the deceased or departed there." Did any of them ever "depart," he wondered? From what he had heard, this was an assignment of life without possibility of parole.

The captain's narrow shoulders slumped. "Yes, sir."

"You can recruit helpers."

Those shoulders slumped further. "No, I can't, sir. All the men are needed to guard the prisoners. That's why this building is so lightly staffed. Most of those offices upstairs are empty. There are only a few of us running operations, and that's why there's never time for projects." He glanced at Ridge, then straightened. "But I'll find time, sir."

"Good. I'll be looking into the mines and figuring out if something can be done to ease the burden there as well. Am I right in that most of the problem is the miners trying to kill our people and escape?"

"Yes, sir. Mostly in the spring and summer, since there's no place to go in the winter, but some of them just lose their brains and go crazy and attack."

"I'll see what can be done," Ridge repeated.

The captain gave him a curious, almost hopeful look, and saluted.

Maybe Ridge shouldn't have promised anything. Who did he think he was that he could change such a system for the better? Well, surely he couldn't do any *worse* than Bockenhaimer had done.

"Yes, sir," the captain said. "I'll get started on this today."

"Send that woman to my office first. I'll fill out a temporary report for her until you find the one that came in."

"Oh, I can do that, sir. There's no need for you to waste your time on a prisoner."

"*You* are going to be busy in *here*." Ridge smiled and spread a hand toward the basement.

"Er, yes, sir." To his credit, the captain's shoulders didn't slump this time.

Ridge headed up the stairs, glad the captain hadn't protested further, telling him that interviewing prisoners was too menial a task for the fort commander. It *was*, he admitted, the sort of thing some young lieutenant could and should do. So why was *he* volunteering for it?

"Just want to make sure I get my parka back," he muttered.

CHAPTER 3

SARDELLE WALKED UP THE STAIRS in the administration building, Corporal Rolff clomping behind her, his boots ringing on the wooden floors. She felt less uncomfortable walking in front of him now that she was wearing a heavy ankle-length wool dress, boots, cap, and scruffier version of the colonel's parka—it seemed to be the official women's uniform here. Even without the shield of less revealing clothing, Rolff hadn't made any more mentions of his room number, not since the colonel's appearance.

"That's the general's, er, colonel's door." Rolff pointed past her to the end of the hall.

Sardelle had already rehearsed her story, so all she could do was keep walking and take a deep breath, trying to calm her nerves. Strange that reporting to some military commander could make her nervous after so many years of being outside of and, in a way, above such organizations.

Not here.

I know, Jaxi. I understand the situation thoroughly.

I'm just reminding you so you remember to act properly contrite and subdued in your meeting. Also, don't give him a rash.

Sardelle kept her snort inward, not wanting Rolff to think her odd—or wonder if she was having conversations with herself in her head. That was probably considered an indicator of witchy ways here.

The Itchy Brothers are seeing the medic right now in another building, Jaxi informed her. *I hope your name doesn't come up.*

It shouldn't since they don't know my name.

You've made enough of an impression that Woman in the Green Dress is all they'll have to say.

It'll be fine. Someone will diagnose it as a sexually transmitted disease. *I'm surprised they even went to the medic. You'd think that would be embarrassing for them.*

Sardelle supposed it would be immature of her to wish she were standing outside the door of that medic's office, so she could listen to the two explaining how they had both come to have the same rash on their genitals.

Oh, I'm already listening in. Want the details?

That's all right. I better focus on this meeting. Sardelle stopped before the door, actually a couple of paces before the door. A waste bin and crate full of empty alcohol bottles made it difficult to draw closer. She shifted the colonel's parka, draping it over her left arm, so she could knock with her right, but she paused when a long scrape, followed by a thud and a thump came from inside.

A cream.

Sardelle blinked at Jaxi's comment, at first believing it had something to do with the noises in the office. *What?*

They're being prescribed a cream. And a suggestion that they stay out of each other's pants.

Sardelle laughed before she could catch herself, though she turned it into a cough.

"He won't want to wait all day," Rolff said.

"I just wasn't sure about those noises." Two more heavy thumps sounded, and Sardelle pointed at the door. "Are you sure he's not doing battle with someone in there?" Or beating the tar out of some wayward private?

"Nobody here would pick a fight with him." Rolff leaned past her and knocked three times.

The noises inside stopped, and a "Yeah?" floated out the door.

Sardelle didn't know whether to take that as an invitation or not, but she *had* been instructed to report promptly. She turned the knob, stepped past the bottles, and poked her head around the door.

Colonel Zirkander was balanced in the air, one boot on the desk and one boot halfway up floor-to-ceiling bookcases built into a sidewall. He held a feather duster in one hand while he prodded at fat tomes that looked like they had been resting undisturbed on that top shelf for decades. He had shed some of his winter clothing, and the sleeves of his gray shirt were rolled up, revealing the ropy muscles of his forearms and... a lot of fresh dirt smudges. Dust—and was that a cobweb?—smeared his short brown hair, as if he had been sticking his head under beds that hadn't seen a maid in years. Or maybe a big faded brown couch, Sardelle amended, considering the office's furnishings. Whatever state they had been in before, they weren't dusty now. The floor gleamed, courtesy of a damp mop, bucket, and broom and dustpan leaning against the wall next to the door. A stack of folded rags and a jug of floor polish suggested the next task on the list.

"Uhm, sir?" Rolff asked, though he seemed stunned at finding his commanding officer cleaning, and the words came out quietly.

"Hah." The colonel, who hadn't stopped dusting and organizing books at their arrival, pulled a thick tome off the shelf. "Found you."

Rolff stepped inside, came to attention, and saluted. "Sir, I've brought the prisoner as requested, sir."

The colonel waved at him with the feather duster instead of returning the salute, which would have been hard given the fullness of his hands. "Good, thanks."

Sardelle bit back a smile at the corporal's puzzled face. He clearly didn't know how to react to a commanding officer that didn't seem to care about military decorum and pomp.

"Shall I stand guard outside, sir?" Rolff asked.

"Do you have a job you're supposed to be doing right now?" The colonel hopped down, grabbed a dust cloth, and wiped off the book.

"I was on guard shift in Level Thirteen when this all started, sir."

"Better get back to that then. I'll hope my roguish smile and charismatic ways are enough to keep—" he glanced at a folder on the desk, "—Sardelle from pummeling me into submission."

Colonel Zirkander smiled—roguishly—at both of them, but Sardelle imagined herself the lone recipient and found herself gazing back, admiring his lively face, dust smudges and all. His dark brown eyes had been so serious in the courtyard, but she sensed that this warm twinkle was more typical of him.

"Er, yes, sir," Rolff said, clearly more flustered than beguiled by the colonel's roguish smile.

Sardelle tore her gaze away from Zirkander's face, lest he notice her long stare. She eyed the folder instead. It had her name—first name real and last name made up—on the front above several blank lines. The information to be filled in during this interview? Was he going to trust her to tell him the truth? And had the missing folder simply been dismissed as some clerk's error? She hoped so.

The door shut, though the clank of glass floated through along with an *oof*.

The colonel shrugged, his expression a little sheepish. "I was going to toss those bottles out the window, but couldn't be sure anyone would clean up the mess before someone cut their foot. Not on this installation anyway."

With the corporal gone, Sardelle could only assume the words were for her, though he was blowing dust off the cover of the book instead of looking at her.

"Is that why you're cleaning your own office?" she asked, figuring she should chat with him if he was interested in it. Anything she could do to establish a rapport. "All the officers I've ever met had minions to handle such things."

"Apparently all the minions here are busy guarding prisoners. I realized the only way I was going to find what I was looking for was going to be to clean up around here. Also, the green-fuzz-covered vomit stains on the floor were disturbing me. I'm sure it was my imagination, but I thought I could see them moving out of the corner of my eye every time I looked away." Seemingly satisfied with his handiwork, he laid the book on the desk next to her folder. *Magroth Crystal Mines: Regulations and Standard Operation Procedures.*

You read that one, Jaxi?

Oddly, the title didn't entice me to delve in.

"Have you met many officers?" The colonel cocked his head, giving her a curious look.

Er, right. Her cover story didn't mention any time spent with the military and certainly not how she had, as *sherastu*—mage advisor—sat at tables with clan leaders and generals. She was going to have to be careful with what she said. "I've been... questioned by a few." Speaking of roguish smiles, she tried to give him one.

He stared at her. So much for roguish. She had been told more often that her smiles were enigmatic or distracted rather than playful or mischievous.

Don't try to change your personality, or you're sure to get caught in the lies. Pirates come with all manner of... mannerisms.

Sardelle acknowledged this advice with a mental wave.

"Right." Colonel Zirkander recovered and tapped the folder. "I just need you for a few minutes, if you don't mind. I want to get a temporary file made for you until my captain finds your real one."

Sardelle had been thinking that he was oddly polite for a commander talking to a prisoner, but her mind lurched at his last words. "Did he already look?"

"Yes, but let's just say I've seen the archives room, and I'm not surprised files are missing. I've tasked him with cleaning and organizing it though, so we'll find your record. We'll find everyone's record and make sure all the names—numbers—match up with faces. The way things are now, I don't know how they even order supplies with any accuracy here."

Sardelle caught herself breathing more rapidly and forced the airflow to slow down. It was too early to panic. Even if they never found her record, that wouldn't necessarily condemn her. It could have been left behind a seat on the airship that had supposedly brought her in, right? Surely these things happened.

Why don't you just make a fake record?

Jaxi's thought surprised her, but then she wondered why she hadn't thought of it herself already.

Because you're an honest and forthright person who doesn't think in deceitful scheming ways. Better get over that.

Thanks for the tip.

Creating a false record wouldn't be a stretch of her powers, so long as she knew where the blank records were stored and where to float it off to when she was done. Maybe...

Sardelle realized the colonel was watching her. Waiting for a response? He hadn't asked a question, had he? She reviewed what he had said. "I haven't been here long, but it does seem a touch chaotic. And in regard to the supplies, I did notice that some of the miners are well-fed and others look malnourished and scrawny." Like those disillusioned sods who had attacked the guards.

Zirkander's eyes sharpened. "Do they?" He took out a pen and a tiny spiral notebook and scribbled something on a page already filled with a list. "It's probably survival of the strongest and meanest down there, right now. All right. Have a seat, will you?" He tossed the notebook aside and, mid-gesture, noticed there wasn't a chair in front of the desk. In fact, aside from the couch and the colonel's chair, there weren't any other seats in the room. "Er, guess the general didn't invite people in for meetings often."

He considered the couch for a moment—there was room for three or four to sit on it—but shook his head, then gestured her to his chair. "Ms. Sordenta."

It took Sardelle a second to remember that was the last name she had given. She stepped around the desk and sat in the wooden chair, the armrests and back spindles more comfortable than she would have guessed from looking at it. Zirkander grabbed the folder and a pen, then perched on the armrest of the couch. Ah, too intimate a piece of furniture to share with a prisoner? Logically, Sardelle agreed with the professionalism of the choice, though the part of her that didn't want to play prisoner to his fort commander would have preferred to sit with him on it.

Looks like you're not going to get his room number after all.

Hush, Jaxi.

Zirkander scribbled something on the corner of the paper stapled to the front of the file. "All right, full name is Sardelle Sordenta, yes? We have the spelling right?" He held up the paper so she could see.

Strange that something so minor as a fictitious last name bothered her, but it did. Still, she nodded and said, "Yes." She would have to lie about a lot more than her name to survive here.

"Date of birth?" he asked.

She froze. It was such an obvious question, but, in making up her elaborate pirate past, she hadn't thought of it. *Quick, Jaxi, what year is it now?*

"Balsoth fourteenth... " *873,* came Jaxi's answer. "839," she finished, hastily doing the math.

Hastily or not, Zirkander noticed the pause. He gazed at her for a long moment, before copying down her answer. Sardelle had been keeping her senses ratcheted down since dealing with those thugs in the mine, but she eased up a touch now, needing to know if he thought she was lying. And right away she sensed that he did and that he was disappointed. For some reason, that stung. What had he expected? Honesty from someone who, by default, had to be a criminal?

"Birthplace?" he prompted.

"Cairn Springs." That at least was true. She had been born at the base of these very mountains, about a hundred miles to the south.

"The Cairn Springs that was buried beneath a lava flow forty years ago?"

Er. "Yes. Near there, obviously not at the site of the old village. I was born in a rural area." *Jaxi! You didn't mention that my birthplace was gone?*

I didn't know. That's too far away for me to sense.

Something that big wasn't covered in a book?

Most of the books here are at least fifty years old. I don't think reading is a big pastime among the prisoners. Or the soldiers.

"We were shepherds," Sardelle went on—the colonel was writing down her lies, so she might as well go on with her story, "—a very boring lifestyle for a young person. That's why I left— to find a little excitement. That and the arranged marriage. I wasn't ready to settle down. I went off to the coast and got a job on a merchant ship." She actually could answer questions about sea life, if he asked. She had traveled with the fleet often to defend the country from enemy warships. "After a year, we were caught by pirates. I was given the option of walking the plank or joining the crew. I'm not very brave. I joined. They treated me decently, I suppose. The first year was tough, but eventually I became one of them."

Zirkander had stopped writing. He had one boot up on the couch, his elbow on his knee, and his chin resting on his fist. Waiting for her to finish this fabricated story and see if she gave away anything useful in the telling? Yes. She didn't need her empathetic senses to tell that.

"Are you done?" he asked.

"I have another five years I can go over. But, ah, you don't seem to be recording the details."

"No. I was busy debating whether I should ask you to tie a clove hitch or if that would simply be embarrassing."

Sardelle *could* tie a clove hitch. Bastard.

I sense something.

My idiocy?

No. Outside. In the sky.

Sardelle looked toward the window, the sky visible beyond the freshly cleaned panes. From their vantage point, all she could see were clouds rolling in off Goat Peak. But a shout arose in the courtyard. No, not the courtyard—it was coming from one of the watchtowers on the ramparts.

Zirkander jumped to his feet, tossing the folder on the desk, and strode to the window. Footsteps thundered in the hallway.

"Gen— Colonel Zirkander!" someone shouted two seconds before the door burst open. Two privates Sardelle hadn't seen before charged into the room. "Sir, there's an airship in the northern sky. It's not one of ours!"

"All right. Report to Sergeant Homish and get whatever security measures are around for the fortress in place. I'll come up to take a look."

Sardelle had been reaching out with her senses, trying to get a feel for the airship, so she wasn't shielding herself from the emotions in the room, the excitement and anticipation from the privates and the disgust from Zirkander, who felt he should have been reading the operations manual rather than dithering around with a prisoner. And then he was gone, jogging through the doorway and down the hall, and his emotions faded from her consciousness. Once again, she felt chagrinned that she had disappointed him. Why she cared, she didn't know, but she had the urge to show him that she wasn't some useless prisoner, that spending time with her hadn't been a waste.

How are you going to do that? Jaxi's question held wariness.

Maybe everyone on the enemy ship will develop rashes, causing them to crash it into the side of the mountain.

I don't think your range is that good, Jaxi thought dryly.

We'll see.

Since the colonel hadn't left a guard or ordered her to remain in the office, Sardelle jogged down the hallway after him. In the courtyard, people were standing and gazing toward the sky, toward an airship that was little more than a speck lurking in the clouds near Goat Peak. Whoever had spotted it must have had a spyglass to identify whatever markings it had, to be certain it didn't belong to this army.

Up on the ramparts, soldiers were jogging into towers and to cannons. Cannons! They weren't thinking of firing those, were they? The calendar might not say winter yet, but piles of snow blanketed the steep mountain walls in all directions.

Sardelle spotted Zirkander and ran across the courtyard to the steps leading up to the wall. At first, no one stopped her—or even noticed her, their eyes toward the distant airship—but a soldier on the walkway grabbed her arm before she could race past him. The halt to her momentum spun her around, startling her, and she almost launched a mental attack. She caught herself a split second before she would have hurled him away from her.

"Where do you think you're going, woman?" the soldier demanded.

"I'm in the middle of a meeting with the colonel." Sardelle tugged at her arm, but the man had a grip like a vise.

"A meeting. Sure you are."

She glanced over her shoulder. Zirkander was standing on the northern wall next to a cannon, pointing and talking to a young soldier who stood on the other side. There wasn't time to convince this buffoon to let her go. With a subtle tug from her mind, she unfastened his belt. The weight of the dagger and other pouches on it pulled it down with impressive speed, along with his trousers. It was enough to startle him into loosening his grip. Sardelle wrenched her arm free and sprinted toward the colonel.

"Stop that woman," the soldier called after her, amidst an impressive stream of curses.

At the corner, someone turned and grabbed for her. On the narrow walkway, she couldn't dodge far enough to the side, and he would have caught her, except she loosened the mortar in the stone beneath his feet. It wobbled, drawing his eye for a split second. She ducked his grasp and ran around the corner, coming to an abrupt halt before the colonel.

"The cannons," she panted, out of breath from the sprint. "You can't fire them, not this time of year." She pointed at a cornice on the nearest mountain. "Could start an avalanche."

Zirkander looked at her for several breaths before responding—why did she get the feeling he was trying to scrutinize her?

Probably wondering if you're a spy.

After my horrible lying? A real spy would be much smoother.

"In my experience," the colonel said, "an explosion has to be set off on or in close proximity to the snowpack to cause an avalanche, but if we need to fire, we will be careful." Something squeaked behind him on the walkway, and he pointed over his shoulder without looking. A pair of soldiers was wheeling out something that reminded Sardelle of the harpoon launchers on whaling ships.

As the soldier she had unbuckled charged up behind her—his trousers securely fastened again—she felt sheepish. Of course a professional soldier would have experience blowing things up—explosives seemed to be far more common in this century than in hers.

A big hand clamped onto her shoulder. "I'm sorry, sir. I had… an equipment malfunction and didn't catch her before she wiggled by."

The soldier started to drag Sardelle backward, but Zirkander lifted a hand. "It's fine, Sergeant. She can stay. She was informing me about the conditions in the mines."

The soldier's face scrunched up. "Like a spy?"

"Something like that."

Sardelle read the double meaning in the colonel's slitted eyes. She did her best to look calm and serene... and definitely not guilty. But he had to be wondering who she was after that botched background sharing. The way he kept gazing at her—appraising her—made her want to squirm. Fortunately, the soldier next to him spoke, and Zirkander looked away.

"In your experience, sir?" The young man couldn't have been more than twenty, and he wore a hopeful expression as he prompted the colonel. Though the men were preparing to defend the fortress, nobody appeared that worried by the airship's appearance. Maybe this happened frequently.

"I might have started a few avalanches," Zirkander said.

"In your flier? With explosives?"

"Bring me a beer later, and I'll tell you some stories."

"Deal, sir!" The young soldier hustled over to help the men with the harpoon launcher.

"Perk of having your name in the papers next to all sorts of war-related exploits," Zirkander said. "You never have to buy your own alcohol."

Sardelle was the only one close enough to hear him, so the comment must have been for her, but the casualness surprised her. One minute he seemed to have her pegged for some kind of spy, and the next he was chatting with her?

Maybe he wants to keep you confused.

I get the feeling he confuses a lot of people.

"I much prefer being the one attacking to the one defending though." Zirkander lifted a spyglass. "He's just hovering out there. Scouting mission?"

He seemed to be talking to himself, but Sardelle decided to respond. "Do they come around often?"

The more he talked to her, the more trouble he should have ordering her execution later.

I wouldn't bet on it. Judging by the so-called witch drownings I witnessed, when it comes to magic, these people will kill their own kin without a second thought.

Sardelle focused on Zirkander's response instead of Jaxi's commentary.

"They *shouldn't*," he said. "This place is supposed to be a top military secret." Zirkander lowered the spyglass and gave her an appraising look again, though his gaze soon shifted over her shoulder. "Captain," he called to the man jogging up behind her. It was the aide who had been introducing him to the fort earlier. And wasn't he the one who had been tasked with organizing the archives?

If they were on his mind, Sardelle might be able to poke into his thoughts and find out where the room was located and where the empty forms were kept so she could fill one out for herself. She grimaced at the idea of, for the second time today, slipping into someone's mind. There was the risk he would feel it too. She decided to simply open herself up for the moment. Maybe they would discuss the archives and the thoughts would float to the tops of their minds where they might be easily accessed.

"Yes, sir?" the captain asked.

"This happen before?" Zirkander pointed at the airship.

"No, sir. As long as I've been here, no enemy ships have appeared in our airspace. Audacious of them—they're hundreds of miles from the nearest ocean. I wonder where they slipped in past our patrols."

"I wonder that too." Zirkander's jaw tightened.

He wanted to be out there. By now Sardelle had gathered that he was a pilot, and she could have guessed at his thoughts without trying to sense them. She did, however, catch a strong vision from him, an image of a dragon-shaped flying machine, not unlike the one that had dropped him off. But this one was his, and it wasn't alone as it cruised through the air. He led a squadron of other fliers along the shores of Northern Iskandoth—Sardelle had been along those fjords and gray sandy beaches enough times to recognize them, though she had never seen them from above. Zirkander remembered attacking an airship like this one off the coast, blowing up its engine, and bringing it down.

It should have reassured her that she and the colonel were essentially on the same side, having both fought to defend the continent of Iskandia—even if the people called it something different now—but it sank in for the first time that he must also be the descendant of those who had blown up her mountain... annihilated her people.

Zirkander frowned over at her. He couldn't have guessed her thoughts, but maybe he had sensed her skimming the surface of his mind?

She pointed at the airship. "Are your weapons able to reach them from here?"

"No chance," the captain said. "Neither the cannons nor the rocket launchers has that kind of range."

Rocket launchers? Sardelle had never heard of such a thing, but, now that she looked, could see that something more sophisticated than a harpoon lay nestled in the artillery weapon's cradle. She caught Zirkander and the captain looking at her and then at each other.

"Ms. Sordenta," Zirkander said, "I think it's time for you to return to whatever work you've been assigned to do here. We'll take care of the intruders."

"I understand," Sardelle said. It would be suspicious if she tried to find an excuse to stay up there.

She walked slowly back to the courtyard though and with hearing that might have been slightly augmented with magic, she caught a few more sentences on her way back to the stairs.

"Find her record, Captain. And find some of the people who arrived on the supply ship yesterday. If nobody remembers her..."

"Think she's a spy, sir?"

"We'll see."

I may have to escape and come back for you, Jaxi. Sardelle paused at the bottom of the stairs, not sure where to go. She hadn't been *assigned* to any work yet, so how was she supposed to go do it?

I understand. And Jaxi did, but she couldn't hide the sadness at the thought of being left behind, and it tore into Sardelle's heart.

There was more at stake too. If the enemy—were these still the Cofah who had troubled the continent in her day?—destroyed this fortress or collapsed the mountains around it, would she ever be able to return? If the mines were shut down, who could possibly help her reach Jaxi? For that matter, who would help her find the belongings—relics—of her people? If she was truly the last of her kind, wasn't it her responsibility to save and preserve some sign of her heritage?

Sardelle dropped her forehead into her hand. So much lost, and she was worried about being thought a spy? What did it even matter?

The captain jogged down the stairs, thoughts of the archive building floating at the top of his mind. Without looking up, Sardelle plucked the location from his mind as well as the layout. He frowned at her when he reached the bottom of the stairs, but all he did was point toward the laundry building.

"One-forty-three will assign you tasks. She's in charge of the women's area."

"I understand," Sardelle said.

Sewing or doing laundry, that would be the perfect time to let her mind wander. She refused to tinker with the memories of those who had arrived yesterday, assuming she could even locate them before the captain questioned them. Creating a record for herself would have to be enough. She gazed up to the rampart where Zirkander had the spyglass out again. With luck, this unprecedented enemy appearance would keep him busy, and he would forget about her.

* * *

Ridge walked through the mines, following a stocky infantry lieutenant for a guide, while two of his hulking soldiers trailed behind, each wearing enough armament to assault a fortress on his own. Ridge felt like a pansy for having bodyguards, but Captain Heriton had nearly pitched over sideways when his new commanding officer had suggested he would take a stroll on his own. After receiving a belated report about an attack on one of the lower levels that morning, Ridge had allowed the escort. Besides, his mind was more on the Cofah airship than this inspection. The craft had left without coming closer or doing anything else, but Ridge had a feeling it would be back. He knew a preliminary scouting mission when he saw it. He didn't know how long they had been searching for the crystal mines, but now that they had found them, there would be trouble. It was no secret what powered the dragon fliers—and that there wasn't an equivalent energy source out there. Maybe someday there would be, but not yet. And without the fliers, his people would have a hard time defending the continent against a superior naval force.

Ridge had written a report, but there was nowhere to send it, not until the next supply ship came in two weeks. Someone had mentioned a pass over the mountains but that it was only accessible during the summer months. How helpful.

"What're they staring at?" the lieutenant muttered, looking back and forth uneasily.

Ridge's group was walking down a wide corridor, and a squad of miners was approaching from the opposite end, on their way off shift, their dirty clothes and weary faces implied. An armed soldier following the workers watched his flock carefully, not saluting—he held his rifle in both hands—but giving Ridge a respectful nod. The miners were staring at Ridge's little troop.

"It's either me or you, Lieutenant," he responded. "You tell me, am I the pretty one or are you?"

The lieutenant cast a glum look over his shoulder. His nose had been broken a time or two in his career—or perhaps before it. "Definitely you, sir."

The miners slowed down, and a few muttered to each other. They wouldn't think to attack him with so many armed men present, would they? All they had for weapons were pickaxes and shovels. Yes, those heavy picks could do damage, but only in close quarters. Of course, in the tunnel, Ridge's group would have to pass within close quarters.

"This is why the general never came down here," the lieutenant muttered, resting a hand on the butt of his pistol. He must have read danger in the troop as well.

The first miner, a scruffy bedraggled man wearing a bloodstained shirt and a bandana around his throat, stepped toward the center of the passage. He removed a sweat-stained cap, pressed it to his chest with one hand, and raised the other—it was devoid of picks or other weapons.

"Colonel Zirkander, sir?" he asked.

"Yes?" Ridge had only been in the fort for a few hours; he hadn't realized the news of his arrival had preceded him down here.

"I, uh, we want you to know… " He waved at his grimy comrades. "We've heard about your fighting out there in the skies. Sometimes someone who can read catches hold of a newspaper, and there's a former pilot down here that tells some stories about your early flights—he claims to have met you, but I'm not sure that's the truth. Still, real entertaining stories. We appreciate them. And that you're out there, fighting for our country." The miner eyed the infantrymen, who had their fingers on the triggers of their rifles. "We just thought you should know."

It was a moment before Ridge could come up with an answer. He'd had the king's subjects thank him for his service before, and received his share of hero worship from young pilots, but he hadn't expected felons to care about their country or those defending it.

Ridge stepped away from the lieutenant, met the man in the middle of the tunnel, and stuck out his hand. "Thank you… "

"One-fourteen," the miner supplied, gripping his hand.

Ridge raised his eyebrows. "And the name your mama gave you?"

The miner blinked a few times. "Kal."

"Thank you, Kal." Ridge walked down the line and shook more hands and got more names and numbers and was surprised at the shyness, considering all the broken noses and missing teeth in the group. "How're you all being treated down here? Tough but fair? Getting enough food?"

With the questions, he opened himself up to a volcano of grievances, but he listened without making too many promises.

If the fort was attacked in the future, he needed these men—*all* of the men—to stay put in the mines and not make trouble. That would be asking a lot—he had been a prisoner of war once, and he had used the first diversion he could to escape—but Ridge might need to siphon more of his soldiers into defense.

As he continued his tour, he crossed a lot of apathetic miners who didn't care a yak's back teats about the change of command or him, but he came across even more who knew who he was and seemed to think something special of it. He would use any advantage he could to win over the prisoners. He also found the "pilot" the first miner had mentioned. Ridge had never met him and through a few private questions learned the kid had been kicked out of the flight academy for fighting after three months. Not that surprising. These were all rough men. Ridge didn't doubt for a moment that their deeds had rightfully earned them places here. Fortunately, none of them asked him for parole—he doubted he had the power to grant that even if he wanted to. When he asked what they did want, most of the requests were ridiculously simple, and he promised to look into them. If a rockslide table, a dartboard, and some pictures of near-naked women would improve morale, he had no problem acquiring them.

A private caught up with Ridge and his entourage somewhere toward the end of the tour. "Sir? Someone was killed up top. You may want to look in on it."

"Show me," Ridge said.

How many deaths was that for the day? They were far too common here.

Though nobody had made a threatening move toward Ridge, his escort followed him to the tram.

"What sort of killing was this?" he asked the private as the cage creaked and groaned, heading for the fading light at the end of the passage. Twilight had either come, or the sky had darkened further with clouds.

"A woman was hung for being a witch."

Ridge's stomach lurched. The prisoner he had been talking with? Sardelle? She was out of place here, but he didn't think it had anything to do with witchcraft. He had her pegged as a spy—if a poor one—or, more likely, someone who had sneaked in to try and get a crystal. One could be sold on the black market for a great deal. Or she might even be an academic who wanted a sample for research—the gods knew the military had a stranglehold on the crystals. He knew that university professors had come to the airbase before, with bags full of microscopes and tools, wanting to study them. Few had ever had a close up view, for neither the king nor the commandant wanted information getting out where the country's enemies might pick it up. Perhaps Sardelle was one of those curious professors who wouldn't take no for an answer.

Or was it that he simply didn't *want* her to be some hardened criminal who truly deserved to be here? It wasn't as if a spy or a thief was much better. A thief might be turned away with a moderate level of punishment, especially if she didn't succeed in stealing anything. A spy though… Ridge closed his eyes. He would be forced to shoot a spy.

A moot point if she had already been hung, he reminded himself with another lurch to his stomach. "Do you know the name—number—of the woman who was hung?"

"No, sir," the private said.

Ridge resisted the urge to describe her for the private. The cage was nearing the top of its ride, the darkening sky visible in earnest now. All around the fortress, the pathway and rampart lanterns had been lit, though they did little to drive back the encroaching night. It was definitely snowing, thick swirling flakes that would make visibility difficult for anyone flying. Good. He hoped the airship would be forced out of the mountains and into skies where it would be spotted and shot down.

"This way, sir." The private opened the cage and walked into the snow. "It's in the women's barracks."

Ridge strode after the private and found himself outpacing the man, then turning to crunch through the old snow in the courtyard rather than following the walkways—with fresh powder on the ground, they weren't that cleared anymore anyway. He had found maps of the fortress and the mines before his tour and memorized them as well as he could. This was either a shortcut to the barracks or he was heading for the munitions building. Either way, the private noticed he had lost his C.O. and jogged across the snow after him.

Fortunately, Ridge's memory proved accurate. He pushed open the front door and gave the traditional, "Male on the floor," warning call, though the private's furrowed brow made him think nobody here bothered. Maybe female prisoners were supposed to be used to random men walking into their sleeping and bathing building. From what he had skimmed of the operations manual, courtesies to inmates weren't important enough to be mentioned.

"Third door, sir," the private said.

Ridge could have guessed that by the knot of women standing outside, staring in, gesturing and speaking. Most had removed their heavy outer clothing and appeared to be off-shift for the night. Sardelle wasn't among them.

"Sergeant Benok gave orders that the body not be disturbed," the private said.

"Good," Ridge said, though he wasn't any sort of forensics expert. He certainly wasn't a witchcraft expert.

"Move aside," the private barked to the women, despite the fact that they had already been doing so.

Ridge gave them a more cordial, "Thank you, ladies," though all he wanted to do was charge into the room to check...

It wasn't Sardelle. He told himself that his relief was uncalled for—someone was still dead, choked to death by a rope made from torn and braided linens, dangling from a water pipe crossing the ceiling. The woman's head drooped forward, her snarled brown hair falling into her lean face. It didn't quite hide the swollen lip and lump on the side of her cheek. She wore the heavy wool dress common to the female prisoners, and it covered most of her skin, but tattoos of knots and anchors crossed her knuckles, and more sailing-related artwork disappeared under her sleeves. The tip of one of her pinky fingers had been cut off at some point in her life, leaving a shiny pink stump. Her feet almost touched the floor, and Ridge guessed her six feet tall. *This* woman he would have believed was a pirate before ending up here.

"Her name?" he asked of the observers.

"Six-ten."

"Her *name*?" Ridge repeated.

"Oh. Uhm." The women glanced at each other.

"Big Bretta," someone said from the back of the crowd.

"Thank you. Private, what led you, or your sergeant, to believe this hanging was a result of witchcraft?"

"The sergeant found some things in her bunk, a collection of people's hair and some crude dolls carved from scraps of wood. It looked like she got caught trying to put hexes on someone."

"She was on the shift with us in the kitchens this morning," someone said in the crowd. "Then she didn't show up this afternoon."

"I'm the one who found her," another woman said. "Came in to collect the towels for washing and 'bout screamed my head off. Then the soldiers came and took over."

"First one tried to say it was suicide," came an indignant addition. "Big Bretta wasn't that type. She used to defend us from the bas— those that thought they could walk in here and have their way."

"People don't usually punch themselves in the face before committing suicide," Ridge said. "Assuming nothing's been moved, there's no stool or ladder or anything she could have used to climb up there and drop either. Private, where's the sergeant who sent you to find me? And who usually handles murder investigations?" Usually on an installation this small, Ridge wouldn't expect there to be much crime—certainly not many murders—but given the background of his workforce, he supposed it was inevitable.

"It was chow time so the sergeant went to dinner, sir. He said I could go too after I found you." The private shrugged. "Nobody investigates murders of prisoners. Bodies just get put in the crematorium, same as those who die in mine accidents."

"How efficient."

"Yes, sir. We would have done that with this one, but the

sergeant said I should ask you on account of her maybe being a witch and maybe having done some evils before someone got her. Maybe she was even the one who called out and let that enemy ship know where the mines are."

At some point in the conversation, Ridge's fingers had curled into a fist. He didn't want to punch the private—not exactly—but he felt like punching something. On the one hand, he understood that these people were just numbers to those in charge, numbers who had already been assigned a death sentence for their crimes, but on the other hand, they were here—they had chosen this miserable life and were helping their country find the resources it needed to fight a war. Didn't they deserve some respect for that? More, without those crystals, he never would have had a career, never could have flown. He owed them something surely.

Wind railed at the shutters of the small high windows on the outside wall, stirring Ridge from his thoughts. "I want an investigation."

"Of the witchcraft, sir?"

"I want to know who killed this woman." Ridge smiled without humor. "Maybe I'll let you stuff *him* in the crematorium."

"Him? How do you know it's a him?"

"As strong and capable as these ladies are—" Ridge waved toward the crowd, "—I doubt one of them hefted a six-foot-tall woman up and hung her from that pipe."

The private sucked on his cheek as he considered the dead woman. "All right, but, uhm, what if she was a witch, sir? It wouldn't be right to punish someone for getting rid of one of them."

Ridge had yet to meet anyone with magical powers, witchy or otherwise, and had always suspected most of the people killed for that were innocent, but if this Big Bretta *had* been casting spells on people... He shrugged. "Maybe not, but that's the point of an investigation. To determine the circumstances and to facilitate judging right and wrong."

"All right, but who, sir? Nobody here handles investigations, unless they're about machines or mining accidents."

Ridge was tempted to lead it himself, but running the fort

and mitigating the threats from without had to be a priority for him. He wasn't qualified anyway. "We've got a doctor or at least a medic here, right?"

"Yes, sir. Captain Orsom."

"Start with him. I want an examination and to know what happened *before* she was strung up there. He can report his findings to me, and I'll decide who to assign from there."

The private was scratching his head, wearing an I-don't-see-the-point expression, but he said, "Yes, sir." He trooped out of the building.

For all that Ridge had rebelled against the rules imposed by his own superiors during his life, he had to admit there were times when it was nice to simply give orders, knowing they would be obeyed, rather than discussed in a committee.

Ridge headed for the door as well. "We'll leave her until the doctor has a look," he told the women watching him, "then hold the funeral in the morning, if any of you want to say something before... " He trailed off, in part because he didn't know a euphemism for a cremation—burials, either at sea or in cemeteries, were more standard in the country—and in part because he spotted a new face at the back of the crowd.

Sardelle. She was carrying a half-filled laundry basket, so she hadn't been let off shift yet, but she must have stumbled onto the crowd and taken a look into the washroom. Her expression... Maybe because she was new here or less jaded than the others, she appeared stunned. No, horrified. And scared too.

Ridge thought to say something, offer some reassurance, but she was already backing away, her knuckles white where she gripped the laundry basket. She spun and raced out of the building.

Ridge didn't race after her—the private and all these female onlookers would find that odd or wonder if he suspected her of something—but he had been leaving anyway, so he strode down the hall at a good pace. He opened the door in time to get a blast of cold snow in his face, but also to see her dart into the laundry facility, a few buildings down. He had work to do, but he also felt this urge to go after her and comfort her somehow. Not that he had offered any hugs of condolence to the other women, women who had clearly known the victim. They hadn't seemed to need it though. They had been indignant but not scared or horrified. Most likely, they had seen all too much of this type of situation before. Sardelle was different.

"Yeah, and that's another problem you have, isn't it?" Ridge muttered.

The private walked out after him, giving him another curious look. *Yes, your new commanding officer talks to himself. Move along, kid. Move along.*

The private shuffled off. Maybe Ridge was too eccentric for this job. At least he didn't have to answer to anyone higher than him. As he considered everything that had happened in the few hours he had been here, everything that was now his responsibility, he wasn't sure if that was the boon he might have once thought it.

CHAPTER 4

SARDELLE DUMPED HER LOAD OF laundry in the big steam-powered washing machine—yet another contraption that hadn't existed in her time—and grabbed a pile of towels to fold. Dhasi, the woman in charge of the facility, had told Sardelle she had to stay late since she had started late. After seeing that poor woman strung up in the barracks, she was almost relieved. She would rather be working and have a distraction, rather than lying in her bunk and struggling to get the image out of her head.

Are you upset by the loss of the prisoner or the realization that it could be you?

Both, Jaxi. Sardelle resented the insinuation that she didn't care.

Sorry, I just wasn't sure which tack I should take with my comforting condolences.

I don't need comforting. Didn't she? She had been upset by the grisly death, but also by hearing the colonel say, "Maybe so" when his man had suggested that someone who killed a witch didn't deserve punishment. It hadn't exactly been a heartfelt judgment, but it was a reminder that she dare not let him or anyone else know about her power. And she feared this prison was a microcosm of the world as a whole these days. Would she find Jaxi and escape, only to learn that she would be hunted at every turn if she revealed her powers? Could she hide them forever? Her first training had been as a healer. How could she encounter sickness and injury and not step forward to help if she could? And if she did, would the one she saved then turn around and attack her for using magic? *All right, maybe I need a little comforting.*

He's coming.

What?

But Jaxi didn't answer.

A cold draft swept into the laundry facility. Sardelle peered past the vats of soapy water and drying racks toward the front door. Zirkander had walked in. Complete darkness had fallen beyond the windows, and there were only two other women left in the building, both staying warm over near the furnaces. Zirkander asked a question of one of them and was directed toward Sardelle's corner.

Uh oh. Jaxi, was I being suspicious when he saw me? He wouldn't think I had something to do with the death, would he? I hadn't even seen that woman before.

If anything, your mouth-hanging-open, caught-in-the-avalanche expression should suggest innocence.

Thanks. I think.

You're welcome. Don't forget to ask him to unbury me from this rubble.

As soon as I figure out how to do that without incriminating myself, I will.

Sardelle kept folding towels as Zirkander headed toward her, weaving past the vats and ducking rows of laundry drying before a fan. She didn't know whether she should pretend she hadn't noticed him or smile and invite him to take a seat on the wicker laundry hamper next to her. She ended up meeting his eyes and giving him a solemn nod.

"Good evening." He waved toward the towels. "Need a hand?"

"I don't know," Sardelle said, surprised by the offer. "Are you experienced?"

"Not at all. Back home, there's a place where I can drop off my entire duffle full of dirty drawers, and they'll have them ready the next day for a mere two nucros. By morning if I promise to bring Ms. Mortenstock mango turnovers from the Palm Flats run." Nothing in Zirkander's smile or tone said he found her suspicious, at least any more so than usual. That was one relief anyway. "I do think I could manage the geometric complexities of making those towel squares though."

Sardelle knew he had more important things to do—for that

matter, *she* had more important things to do—but she stepped aside, so there would be room for him beside her at the table. "If you're up to the challenge. Just know I'll be judging you."

His eyebrows rose. *"Really?"*

She blushed. She shouldn't be so familiar with him. It was his fault, she decided, for setting that tone.

"Not harshly. It's my first day, too, after all." Naturally she couldn't mention the magical contraption she had once delivered her own dirty drawers to, one that had washed, dried, and folded, without requiring turnovers or any other kind of compensation.

"You're kind," he murmured, then removed his cap and parka, draping them over a rack, and picked up a towel.

Zirkander, with his friendly tone and smile, had to be there to comfort her, though she couldn't guess why he would bother.

He's attracted to you, genius.

I doubt that. If anything, I'm a puzzle he's trying to solve, which is not a good thing for either of us. I shouldn't be encouraging him.

Right, and that's why you just shifted over to stand closer to him.

I was reaching for that towel, and have I mentioned how amazing it is that you can spy so effectively from under a mile of solid rock?

No, you don't mention how amazing I am nearly often enough. Listen, just because he's couth enough to look into your eyes instead of at your boobs doesn't mean he doesn't find you attractive. I'd use that if I were you. Make him like you so that if he **does** *discover your little secret...*

He'll feel particularly bad about shooting me?

"You seemed distraught about Bretta's death," Zirkander said. "Understandably so. I wanted to make sure you were all right."

"I was just surprised by the scene." He knew the woman's name? Sardelle hadn't. She felt like a fraud. "And thought of the pain she must have suffered before that ignoble end. There was a time when I trained to be a healer—a doctor—" she glanced at him when she made the correction, not sure if the word "healer" would still have a magical association in this time.

He gazed thoughtfully at her, but she didn't read any suspicion. "I think that might be one of the first true things you've told me."

She blushed again and grew quite focused on the towels. "I'm certain your captain will find my report and verify that I..."

"Belong here?"

Did she want to fight for that? To belong with all these cutthroats and rapists? "That there's nothing unusual about me or the circumstances that led me to come here."

Well, that was vague. No wonder he finds you an enigma.

Hush.

His eyebrows twitched. "I see." After a moment of silent folding, he spoke again. "I was thinking... This stack is getting high. Where do these go next?"

Sardelle pointed. "In that cart."

Huh. He was actually folding, not simply poking around while he spoke to her.

"I was thinking that since you're also concerned about the welfare of these people," Zirkander said, "that maybe you could keep your ears open and help with the investigation of Bretta's death. Nothing risky, but you could let me know if you hear anything that might not otherwise be said when I'm around. I've never considered myself overly gruff and intimidating, but soldiers tend to make like clams when officers wander past. I'm suspecting miners are the same way."

Sardelle watched him out of the corner of her eye. Was he trying to give her some small task so she wouldn't dwell on the woman's death? Or did he truly want this favor from her? Jaxi's advice aside, she ought to stay away from him—he saw all too clearly through her fibs. Just because she found him handsome—especially with his cap off and his hair tousled in such a way that made her wonder what it, and the rest of him, might look like when he climbed out of bed in the morning...—didn't mean he wasn't the most dangerous person here.

Despite that acknowledgment, she found herself asking, "So, you would want me to report in to you every morning with the latest gossip?"

"Well, the gossip related to this investigation. Or if you were to see or hear something that suggested someone or some persons within these walls *were* using witchcraft."

Sardelle's heart forgot to beat. He wanted *her* to let him know if anyone was using magic? She coughed to cover the strangled sound her throat wanted to make.

It must have sounded strangled—or distressed—anyway, for he put a gentle hand on her back and asked, "Are you all right?"

She managed a nod, though his touch flustered her further. *That's what you get for imagining him in bed.*

"I'm fine," she said. "I just—"

Zirkander withdrew his hand and waved it dismissively. "Never mind on the witchcraft. I wouldn't want you to get yourself in trouble on my account. They say that back in the old days, those people could read minds."

"Yeah," Sardelle managed, her voice hoarse.

"The last thing I would want is for you to be hurt because someone thought you were a spy." He considered the towel he was folding. "Perhaps this was a bad idea. Even the average prisoner here might get suspicious if you're always wandering up to my office."

"Given what I've seen, heard, and been propositioned with today, I'd guess they would think I was sleeping with you rather than spying for you."

This time, Zirkander made the strangled-distressed noise in his throat. She held back a smirk, though she was somewhat pleased to have broken his equanimity for once.

"That would also be less than ideal." He glanced toward the furnaces, probably wondering if the other two women had heard, but they had disappeared into the building somewhere or perhaps left for the day. The lanterns in their work area were out now.

"I'm not your type, eh?" Sardelle wasn't sure why she asked it, or why she was making light when the notion had disturbed him.

Jaxi smirked into her mind. *Because you want to know.*

"Oh, you're nice, but it wouldn't be appropriate for an officer—or, as I am now, a glorified prison guard—to take advantage of a prisoner, and whether that was happening or not, the appearance… " Ridge snorted. "You don't know how ironic this is, coming from me, with my record full of demerits, but they were always honorable demerits. I mean, I could argue that way. Ignoring the rules for the greater good. Or to irk annoying senior officers who deserved irking. I—oh, hells. Never mind. I guess it doesn't matter that much what these idiots think."

Well, you've succeeded in flustering him.

So I see.

Not quite sure whether "you're nice" answers your question though.

Sardelle sighed inwardly. *Me either.*

"So, just to be clear, I am or am not having coffee with you in your office tomorrow morning?"

Zirkander blinked and looked at her—he had been avoiding her eyes for most of the towel folding session. "Does that mean you'll share what you hear?"

"I will, but I feel it would be fair for me to receive a small favor from you as well. Since I will be making your job easier for you." Sardelle smiled.

He smiled too. It was warm and friendly as usual, but there was a keen intensity in his eyes, too, and she almost had the feeling that she had walked into a trap.

He wants an opportunity to observe you and figure out who and what you are. You've just agreed to see him every day. And you're also about to tell him something you want, something that might give him another puzzle piece.

You sound like you don't approve. I'm angling to get you out of here.

I know, but be careful. He's not dumb.

No, I've figured that out.

"Yes?" Zirkander prompted and went back to folding towels. Maybe he realized his eyes had given away too much.

"I would like to see a map of your mines."

"Would you?" He said it more like a statement than a question.

I've seen the map. If you're thinking you could find a spot to dig me out on your own, I'm nowhere near any of their tunnels.

I still want to see it for myself. I have an idea.

Yeah? It better be good. He's going to be suspicious of why you want to see the map.

"Yes, I've studied the civilization that used to live here, inside this mountain. I might have some insight into where you should be digging to find that which you seek." She almost laughed. Beyond a vague notion of "crystals," she had no idea what they were mining for—more than ore, she was certain of that now, because an enemy vessel wouldn't need to spy on a silver mine. But she suspected it had something to do with what her people had left behind.

Maybe he wants your magical laundry machine.

Funny.

Sardelle mentally pushed Jaxi away, wanting her full concentration, for he was studying her again.

"A half truth this time, I think," Zirkander said.

She gave him her best I'm-too-mature-for-these-games single eyebrow raise, though she doubted he bought it. "I won't answer that other than to say I'm beginning to think *you're* the telepath around here."

Sardelle smiled, but his eyes widened in surprise—no, anger. He grabbed her arm and stepped close, his chest brushing hers as he leaned down and whispered harshly, "Do *not* say such things."

He glanced about the facility again.

"I'm sorry," she whispered, stung by his anger. Even more, she was irritated with herself for turning their playful chat—their cat-and-mouse game—into something darker. "I meant it as a joke. That's all."

He stared down at her, and she could feel his deep breaths, the hardness of his chest beneath his shirt. She didn't ready any defenses, didn't think she would need to, but she was aware of the strength of his grip—of him. His dark eyes bored into hers, no longer playful or speculative, but intense, as if he *were* trying to read her every thought, as if by sheer will he could do so. She looked into his eyes, trying to show him that she hadn't been lying, not this time.

Zirkander glanced down, seemed to realize that he had a lock on her arm, and loosened his grip. He lifted his hand, fingers spread, and stepped back. "I overreacted." He faced the towel table again, though he grasped the edge, his hands still tense and tight. "I apologize. It's just that I've seen careers ruined because of such accusations."

Not his, or he wouldn't be here, but some close friend perhaps. "Once they've been made, no matter how dubious the source, well, you can't prove a negative, as they say."

Sardelle should have felt mad or at least disgruntled at being manhandled, but the haunted expression on his face made her want to give him a hug instead. "I understand." Before she could think better of it, she laid a hand on his, wanting to ease the tension there. "I shouldn't have said that."

Zirkander eyed her hand, his face inscrutable. Sardelle withdrew it, a little disappointed by his reaction, but she shouldn't have been so presumptuous.

He grabbed his parka and put it on. "I should go. I hope my small assistance with these towels has lightened your load somewhat." He smiled, though it didn't reach his eyes, and bowed slightly.

When he turned away, Sardelle asked, "Are we still—uhm, am I reporting to you in the morning?"

He hesitated for a long moment, and she expected a, "Never mind" out of his mouth. He glanced toward a dark window. "If you find something to report, I'll be in the office until nine."

As he walked away, she was certain he presumed she wouldn't find anything tonight, that he wouldn't have to see her again soon. He didn't want to see her. She didn't need telepathy to sense that in the stiff way he took his departure. Her stupid comment had changed something.

Too bad.

She wanted to see that map. She *would* find something to report.

***

He had almost kissed her. The memory from the night before still burned in his thoughts. What in all of the hells had he been thinking? She had made that joke, and after his initial reaction—*over*reaction—he had recognized the humor for what it was, but then he had been standing so close to her, staring into her eyes... and it had been as if he were some sexually starved inmate who couldn't control himself.

"I have not been out here *nearly* long enough to be that desperate to get with a woman." Ridge blew on his mug of steaming coffee, fresh from the little stove in the break room downstairs. "Though apparently I've been here long enough to start talking to myself."

At least his door was closed this time. None of his men should hear his solitary conversations.

Ridge took a sip and picked up his pen again. He had the operations manual and the personnel rosters out and was working on a list of things he hoped would improve efficiency and free up more men for defenses. At nine, he was heading to the mine entrances again, this time with an engineer. While he would like to think those people down there wouldn't take advantage of an enemy attack, not when they seemed to respect him for his exploits in the skies, he couldn't assume that. He wanted some heavy iron doors built over the tram shafts, doors that could be locked from the outside while his soldiers had to defend the fort. He had been up early and had sketched what he wanted for the engineer.

Actually, he had been up early—and late—thinking those sexually starved inmate thoughts. Though he forced himself to get his work done, his gaze drifted often toward the rolled up map leaning against the end of his desk. He had fished it out as soon as he'd gotten to his office, several hours before dawn, just in case. If she truly wanted to see it, she would come. He would have to make sure she wasn't lying, telling him some made-up fibs about Bretta's death, so she could gain access to the information. She wasn't a good liar, at least she didn't seem to be. He had to accept that she could be there, trying to gain access to his information by playing inept, or by playing *him*.

Agreeing to show her the map... even as he had done it, he had known he was bordering on treason. The map didn't mention anything about the crystals or where they had been found—he had another map that did that, which he would *not* show her—but it might give her something. Something she needed. What, he didn't know. That was why he had agreed to it. So he could watch her, see how she reacted, and try to make some guesses.

"Seven gods, Ridge, if she were a man, you would just interrogate her." He rubbed his temple, annoyed because he knew he was right, and more annoyed because he couldn't imagine doing it. He had only known her a day. How had she insinuated herself into his thoughts so? Maybe she was some master seductress. Except she had seemed surprised last night when he had gotten close, startled. If she had sensed when his anger vanished and other feelings arose, she hadn't shown it. That touch on his hand—the one that had sent an incendiary jolt of electricity through him—had been the purest innocence, an expression of concern. Surely a skilled seductress would have slid a hand around the back of his neck, pulled him down for a kiss, and—

He grunted. "I need an ice bath, not coffee."

A knock came at his door, and he cursed himself. He had been so busy thinking about *other* things that he hadn't heard anyone walking up. "Yeah?" he called, wondering if his visitor had heard him talking to himself. Wondering, too, if his visitor was she.

Captain Heriton poked his head in. "Sir, I'm never quite sure if that's an invitation to enter."

"I'm rarely doing anything in here that's so scintillating that I can't be interrupted."

"Yes, sir." Heriton pushed the door open wider, but paused again. "I'm not sure that was an invitation, either."

Ridge winked. "Maybe you'll have it figured out by the time I leave."

"I'm hoping I get to leave sooner, sir. Six months left on my orders." Heriton gazed wistfully out the window.

Understandable. "Come in, Captain. What do you have for me?"

Heriton glanced over his shoulder, shrugged, and came in with a stack of papers. "It's actually what you have for me, sir. Did I understand your memo correctly? You want these... reading lists to go out to the guards to be posted for... the miners?"

"That's right."

"Oh. I thought you might mean it for the soldiers."

"I trust *you* all have a good education already." Ridge waved toward the papers. "I'm trying to improve morale, offer some incentives for them to better themselves."

"Better themselves, sir? To what ends?"

"To work more efficiently for us."

"And, uh, reading the classics will cause that?"

"Call it the crazy colonel's experiment." Ridge was certain the gaming tables would be more popular, but if some of the prisoners *did* start reading... "Those who show an interest might prove themselves worthy of more responsibility. What I'm hoping these changes will ultimately do is give us some trustworthy individuals who might help us—or at least keep others from stabbing us in the back—should we need to funnel all of our resources into defending the fort." And if that didn't work, Ridge had his backup plan. The doors.

"Ah, I see, sir." Heriton did sound a tad less perplexed now. Or at least he had decided to go along with his eccentric C.O. He pointed to the bottom of a page. "And you want to give them a day off if they finish a book?"

"If they can summarize it sufficiently and answer questions that prove they read it. Those are hefty tomes, and those men don't have a lot of free time. There has to be some sort of incentive."

"I think I understand, sir. But, uhm, who's going to quiz the miners?"

"What's the matter, Captain? Haven't *you* read those? They're classics."

"I, uh, a couple."

Ridge grinned.

"I'll familiarize myself with them," Heriton said, though not without a daunted look in his eyes.

"Good. Dismissed."

"Thank you, sir. Oh, I almost forgot. You have another visitor." Heriton pushed open the door, revealing Sardelle standing in the hallway, her lush hair loose about her shoulders, her mouth curving into a tentative smile.

Last night, Ridge had been certain it would be better for his sanity if she didn't come today, but seeing her there made his soul soar. It also made his cheeks flush as his thoughts from the night before reared to the forefront of his mind again. Thank the gods that matronly prison dress didn't do anything to distract him further. Aware of the captain's eyes, Ridge managed to keep his face neutral.

"She *assures* me she's expected." Heriton raised his eyebrows.

"Yes, she's my insider on the magic investigation." Ridge chose the word magic instead of murder, understanding that nobody here seemed concerned about the deaths of miners. Magic, on the other hand, was surely something they could all understand investigating.

Heriton's brows rose higher. "Oh, really? Does that mean you don't need her report anymore?"

"No, I'm still waiting for you to produce it." Ridge smiled and waved the man out of his office.

Sardelle walked in, her own eyebrows raised. "Have *you* read all the books on that list?"

Ridge lifted his chin. "I've read many of them."

"Many? More than three?"

"No less than five, I assure you."

She snorted, then a speculative expression bloomed on her face. "A day off for anyone who can summarize a book? For *each* book?"

"That's the deal I put out, yes."

"When's the test?"

"After a day of laundry duty, you're ready to take off?"

"Oh, more than ready." Sardelle rubbed her hands together. "Do you have a copy of the list? I'm ready now. I'll even constrain myself to the ones you've read."

"How do you know you've read the ones I've read? There are more than a hundred books on that list." All the classics they had in the meager prison library had gone onto the list. Some of them were as dusty and old as the mountain itself. "I don't believe you've read them all."

"I've read enough for a day off. Or five."

"Fine." Ridge pulled his master copy of the sheet out of a file in the bottom desk drawer. "How about *Denhoft's Theories on Aerodynamic and Aerostatic Flight?*"

Sardelle clasped her hands behind her back. "Written approximately four hundred years ago, the text dealt largely with theory rather than proven scientific experiment. Denhoft theorized that there were two types of flying machines that could allow for lift to overcome gravity..."

Ridge had to consciously keep his mouth from falling open in surprise as she continued on, offering a precise and accurate summary of the book. He asked a few questions in the end, and she answered them satisfactorily, though with a few hesitations.

"History is more my specialty," she said before he could compliment her. "I read a lot of the ones in that left row in school."

Ridge had only read two of them. He started with the ones he knew. She was more animated and confident in her summaries of those books, adding opinions and gesturing with her hands as she described the rise and fall of the imperial dynasties that had claimed this continent before the original tribes had rebelled, declaring themselves an independent sovereign nation and fighting off any aggressors who sought to impose upon them again.

After summarizing the books he knew—and five others he didn't—she leaned forward again. "Oh, Dusmovan. Have you read his book? It's a fictional tale, but it's incredibly detailed, showing the archaeologist's journey to discover what came of the dragons. He hunted all over the world for fossils that would help explain their sudden passing from our world."

Ridge lifted a hand. It did sound interesting, and he would put it on his own reading list—on the off chance this job gave him any free time—but... "You've already earned eight days off, and I believe you came here this morning on another matter?"

"Oh." Sardelle flushed, the red of her cheeks bringing out her blue eyes.

Ridge wouldn't have minded letting her continue on, but he had that meeting to get to. It had been a surprisingly enlightening interlude though. His earlier theory, that she might be some rogue professor here to hunt for crystals, or even other artifacts, returned to the front of his mind. Would a military spy be that versed in the classics? The classics of *his* continent? Not only that, but she was clearly passionate about history.

"By the way," Ridge said, "this school where you read these books... was it before or after you left your family's shepherd ways to become a pirate?"

Her cheeks dimpled when she smiled, a shy caught-me smile. "Before."

"I never knew a rural education to be so thorough. Your teacher should be commended."

The smile drooped, and something flashed in her eyes. Pain?

"Yes," Sardelle said more somberly. "She was inspiring."

Ridge debated whether to apologize for chancing across some painful past memory, but she spoke again first.

"The murder. It doesn't seem to have had anything to do with magic." Sardelle glanced at his eyes. "Or I should say, the woman, Bretta, had nothing to do with magic. I investigated the so-called magical tools that were, I believe, planted under the blanket in her bunk. According to *Braytok's Compendium of Sorcerers and Sorcerous Artifacts*, a book that isn't on your list but should be, since it could clear up confusion due to ignorance, tools for holding energy, souls, or for performing tasks or enhancing powers must be made from a sturdy enough material to contain energy, generally a metal alloy or diamond or other such gem. Hard rocks occasionally, but not wood. The book says it would combust at the first pouring of energy into it."

Ridge listened attentively, though it made him uncomfortable to hear her speak so openly of magic. That book she had mentioned... nobody outside of an academic setting would ever dare be caught with such a thing. Even then, it made people twitchy. It made *him* twitchy. He had never cared much until the Cofah had started importing those witches or wizards or whatever they called them, and putting them into the sky where he and his squadron started encountering them. Since then, he had lost... too much.

"Forgive my rambling," Sardelle said. Ridge wondered if she

had noticed a reaction in him. He hadn't meant to let anything show. "My point is that dolls made from twigs are hokum. Someone planted those in her bunk to arouse suspicion—or validate what he was going to do—and then sneaked into the barracks when few were around and killed her."

"Any ideas on who?"

Ridge didn't expect her to have learned who in the scant hours since they had last spoken, but when she swallowed and gazed out the window, he realized she did know. So, why the hesitation? He tried to read her face. It was a study of concentration. She seemed to be wrestling with herself.

"Are you afraid he'll come after you for revenge if you tell me?" Ridge asked.

"I'm afraid he might have genuinely thought she was a witch, and in your—our culture, well, that would have made killing Bretta justifiable, wouldn't it?"

Ridge leaned back, feeling the hardness of his chair against his shoulder blades. He had noticed her slip-up, and it put doubt into his assumptions all over again. More than that, he sensed she was lying.

"Who is it?" Ridge asked. "We'll hear from him and decide the rest." We? It was he, wasn't it? He would have to be judge and juror here. A fact that hadn't been mentioned on his orders.

"I don't know for sure," Sardelle said slowly. "Gossip and hearsay and who saw what, when, you understand."

"Yes..."

"But if you can find out if a man named Tace was missing from his shift yesterday afternoon when this happened, you might have your answer. He might have had help from a second man. I didn't hear the other name."

"Thank you." Ridge wrote the name down. For once a number would have been easier, but Captain Heriton ought to be intimately acquainted with the archives by now. Maybe he would recognize the man. "I'll find him and have him questioned."

Sardelle nodded curtly. Her gaze was still out the window. Ridge waited for her to inquire about the map—she must have seen it rolled up next to his desk, but something was bothering her. All the animation she had shown when reciting the book summaries had drained from her. He felt an urge to comfort her, the same urge that had taken him to the laundry room the night before. This time, he made himself remain where he was.

"Is there something else I should know?" he asked.

Sardelle shook her head and pulled her focus back to him. "No, it's just... a lamentable situation."

"Yes."

Ridge pointed his pen toward the map. "We made a deal. There's the map. There aren't many up-to-date copies around, so I trust you'll understand if I don't let it leave my office." Not to mention how many vomit stains and dust bunnies he'd had to clean up to find it wedged against the baseboard behind the couch.

"I understand." Sardelle still seemed subdued as she came forward and unrolled the map.

Ridge picked up his papers so she could lay it out on his desk.

She did so, using a couple of paperweights to pin down the corners and gazed at it for no more than thirty seconds before issuing an eloquent, "Huh."

Ridge wasn't sure what he had expected from her, but that wasn't it.

"Is that where the ore is?" Sardelle waved toward the section of the mountain where the levels and levels of tunnels snaked around.

Ridge didn't answer. He would let her look, but he wouldn't provide intelligence. He was already worried his generosity—or perhaps it was foolishness—would turn into a regret. He had allowed the map deal in the hope that he, in observing her, would learn more about *her* than she did about the facility.

"All the miners mumble about crystals," she added, looking up at him.

She seemed curious and faintly puzzled. An act? Wasn't she *here* for the crystals? Whether she was a spy or some kind of archaeological bandit, Ridge had assumed she had come for them. What else was of value in this mountain? Silver was worth something, but it wasn't that rare an ore. Even if she hadn't come for the crystals, he found it odd that she could discover a murderer's name overnight, but didn't know about something all of the miners knew about. Granted, the women remained up top and handled the domestic duties, but Ridge would be surprised if most of them didn't know what was in the mountain under them.

"The placement of the tunnels surprises you?" Maybe he could extract some information from her, though what he was fishing for he didn't truly know.

"According to the books, the people who lived here before… before they were destroyed, they had their home in this part of the mountain." Sardelle waved to a spot that was mostly off the map. "There were a few tunnels over here, I think, but they were more interested in, well, I suppose I don't know, but the old road leading to the pass exited from the other side of the mountain. That was the road more traveled. There wasn't much back here, except a few market stalls in the summers, and a private area for practicing… stuff."

It was all Ridge could do not to blurt out, asking what she was talking about. People who had lived here? Maybe *he* was the one who needed to go around talking to the miners. But no, he had perused a lot of the operating manual, and it didn't mention anything about former inhabitants. It specifically said the crystals were an unexplained phenomenon that had only ever been discovered in this mountain.

"In what book did you find this information? Because I'm certain it's not one of the ones on my list."

"No. Something I read at one point. I can't seem to recall the title."

After the morning's memory display, Ridge had a hard time believing she forgot much of anything. Did some university out there know more than the military did about its own secret? Or maybe someone in the military knew and had forgotten to mention it to Ridge before foisting the command on him. If so, that seemed rude.

"And who were these people who, according to your forgotten source, lived here?" Ridge asked.

Sardelle opened her mouth as if to spout the quick answer, but paused and searched his face for a moment before shrugging and saying, "The Referatu."

A chill ran through him. "The sorcerers." The sorcerers who had tried to take over the continent, to enslave everyone who didn't have their powers. He knew about the purging, about the war that had been fought against them three hundred years ago, but he had never heard that they had come out of a mountain base. Or that this had been it. True, he wasn't a huge academic, having never been interested in more than the military and flying as a kid, but he wasn't completely ignorant either. This was *not* common knowledge. So how did his little spy/thief know?

Sardelle spread her hands. "I assumed you knew. Or at least whoever started mining here knew."

Was she being honest, or was this another lie? His head was starting to hurt. It wasn't even nine in the morning yet; it was too early for headaches.

"These crystals," she said, "are they—"

Footsteps sounded in the hallway, fast, urgent footsteps.

"Sir!" The captain knocked on the door, but Ridge was already on his way to opening it and caught the man, fist raised in the air. "The airship is back," he blurted. "And it's coming closer this time."

Ridge cursed, grabbed his parka, and ran into the hallway, tugging it on as he went. "It's still snowing, isn't it? I thought that would keep them away."

"It is, sir. And it's not."

"Wonderful."

Chapter 5

LEFT ALONE IN THE COLONEL'S office, Sardelle debated whether to race outside after him or to take the moment to study the map further, in private. A glance had told her that the tunnels were several hundred meters from Jaxi's location—it was only dumb luck that those miners had stumbled upon her. The mage shelters had been located in the deepest part of her people's complex, farthest into the mountain core. A mistake, it had turned out, because so few had made it down there in time.

Only you.

I know. Sardelle touched the map, tracing the lower level tunnels with her fingers. *I think this is about where I was discovered, though this doesn't look like it's been updated to include the passage Tace and his cohort were working on.*

Thinking of them again made her wince. She had agreed to help Zirkander with his investigation on a whim, because she saw her opportunity to barter for a look at the map. She hadn't expected to find out Tace was the murderer or that Bretta was someone who had denied him sex in the past—and used her brawn to protect the other women from him as well. She certainly couldn't have foreseen the chain of events that would lead him to accuse Bretta of giving him his new and persistent rash. Sardelle might not regret defending herself, but she now wished she had found another way. At the least, she should have later sought the man out—from a distance—and healed what she had inflicted.

Unforeseen consequences. The elders had understood them well. That was why the Circle had never acted as judges over others and had insisted the Referatu be held accountable to the same laws as the people in the rest of the country. Until that handful of sorcerers had gone rogue, believing themselves above the law. They were the ones who had established the fear of magic in the population, a fear that had resulted in... Sardelle gazed out the window toward the mountain, her chest tightening with emotion she had been trying hard to distract herself from. But talking to Zirkander and realizing that no one even remembered the Referatu had been here... *A few unforeseen consequences, and I'm the last of my people.*

Perhaps noticing Sardelle wasn't thinking of anything constructive, Jaxi directed her back to their current consideration. *If you were to convince the miners to extend that shaft and angle downward approximately fourteen degrees, you would eventually reach my location.*

And how do I convince them of that?

Keep working on the colonel.

The colonel is busy with—

A boom sounded in the distance.

"I thought he wasn't going to use the cannons." But even as she spoke, Sardelle swept her senses out, along the walls and confirmed what her ears should have told her. The explosion had come from farther away. The airship, what else?

Leaving the map on the desk, Sardelle ran through the building and outside. Daylight had come to the mountains, but the heavy clouds and the continuing snow made it feel like perpetual twilight. She struggled to spot the airship and wouldn't have found it at all had she not seen a harpoon—no, Zirkander had called it a rocket—streak away from the rampart. It disappeared into the white sky, but by following its trajectory, she located the intruders. The enemy airship was up near the top of a snow-covered ridge, dropping explosives into the cornice she had noted the day before. Yesterday's fear returned in a surge.

The rocket exploded in the sky below the craft's wooden hull. Whatever force or shrapnel it hurled made the ship rock, tilting on its side for a moment, but the massive oblong balloon stabilized it. The captain must have had a good idea as to the rockets' range and was staying out of it.

Well, he didn't know *her* range.

Sardelle stepped into the shadows of a building and checked around to make sure nobody was watching her. The miners were down in the mountain, and all of the soldiers in the fort were busy grabbing weapons from the armory and running up to the wall to fight. This battle wouldn't be won with firearms though.

Hating that she had to think of herself first, that she dared not be discovered, Sardelle waited long painful seconds so she could time her attack with the soldiers' next one. While a second rocket was loaded and aimed, the airship dropped another bomb.

"Hurry," she whispered.

Finally, the rocket flew away. Sardelle forced herself to wait until it exploded, to see if it might be near enough that shrapnel would account for…

There. Orange light burst against the gray sky, the weapon exploding even closer to the airship than the first. Shrapnel reached the hull, though not enough to give it more than a few dents and dings.

"Good enough," she muttered. Sardelle drew energy from within and cut a long slash in that balloon.

The envelope was thicker than she realized—it might have held up to shrapnel even if the rockets had struck closer—but it wasn't a match for her power. She wasn't sure how long it would take to deflate, so she cut more holes, little snips and pricks that would appear as shrapnel damage later. With more time, she could have made sure the craft went down, but an ominous rumbling started up. It wasn't coming from the airship but from the mountain behind it. From the snow.

A buzzing wail erupted from a horn at the corner of the fort.

"Avalanche!" someone cried.

I was afraid of that.

Don't get caught, Jaxi warned. *Snow is just as impossible to dig out from under as rock.*

I know. I grew up around here, remember?

Sardelle ignored Jaxi's snarky retort. She took several deep breaths and flexed her hands, like an athlete getting ready for a race. Cutting a hole in a balloon was easy, but this?

With a soulblade in her hand, her power combined with Jaxi's, she might have handled it, but even then, she would have needed time to plan an attack. The snow was already falling, gathering speed, gathering more material as it tumbled down the steep slope. That high up, there were no trees to slow its momentum. Sardelle tried to create invisible barriers to slow it down, but it was like sticking her fingers into a dam to plug up holes as more and more burst open. Then that shelf of snow collapsed completely, rushing down too fast, too powerfully. All she could do was partially divert it away from the fortress, to angle it off to the side, but the installation was at the lowest point in the valley, and even a sorcerer couldn't defy gravity for long.

The tail end of it crushed into the east wall, knocking men down, devouring them. The rocket launcher disappeared, too, and—Sardelle gulped, and whispered a plaintive, "Noooo."— Zirkander, who had been trying to shove other men away, to push them toward the back side of the fort, was swallowed too. The wave of snow crested the towers and crashed halfway across the courtyard, burying that eastern wall and two of the tram entrances, before tumbling to a stop.

Only vaguely aware that the wounded airship was limping away—and losing altitude as it did so—Sardelle raced for the mountain of snow.

A shovel, Jaxi warned.

What?

You need a tool. Don't do anything—anything else—*that could get you noticed.*

It was good advice, even if she didn't want to heed it. Already she had hesitated, protecting herself instead of simply attacking. If she hadn't, she might have stopped that ship before it dropped that last explosive.

"Shovels," someone yelled. "Get those men out of there!"

Sardelle clambered up the slope with a surge of soldiers, all of them slipping on the ice and snow but desperate to save the men. "The colonel went down here," she yelled. "I was watching, I saw."

She didn't expect anyone to listen to her—Zirkander was the only one who treated her as anything other than a prisoner—but maybe the confidence in her voice convinced them. Three soldiers scrambled over to join her. She pointed, then grabbed a shovel from someone who had brought extras. She *had* seen Zirkander go down, the wave sweeping him from the wall, but she could also sense him beneath several feet of snow. He was alive and not badly hurt, but confused, trying to figure out which way was up, and how much air he had.

Sardelle dug. She had never been caught in an avalanche but had heard from others who had survived. The snow became like cement once it compacted above a person, impossible to dig through. A man had to be dug out by others. She flung snow to the side, planning to do just that.

"You're sure it was here?" one of the soldiers asked.

"Yes," Sardelle said without looking up from her task. They had only gone down two feet. They needed to descend at least four more, but she kept herself from explaining that. Someone would later remember such unlikely precision.

"Because the snow would have moved him," the soldier said.

"I know that. I've already factored it in. There's a... mathematical model that I've studied." There. That sounded plausible, didn't it? For all she knew, there truly was such a thing.

"Just keep digging, Bragt," another soldier said.

Sardelle's hands were already growing raw from the shoveling, but she didn't slow down. Two more feet. They ought to be close, ought to hear something soon. Zirkander should hear them soon and cry out, let them know they were close.

"Stay below," someone's voice came from across the fort. "Just stay down there. We'll let you know when it's safe to come out."

The soldier next to Sardelle grumbled, "If those prisoners get out and try to use this to their advantage..."

"I'll shoot them, no questions asked," another responded. "Sir! Are you down there? Can you hear us?"

A faint muffled groan came from within the jumbled slope of snow.

"I heard him," the soldier cried.

"He's here!"

Soon there were so many shovels digging in, that Sardelle

could barely see the snow. Someone grabbed her from behind and pushed her out of the way.

"We'll handle it, woman."

She stumbled and almost fell. She hadn't been digging slowly—there had been no reason to move her.

And you wanted him to see your face first? Jaxi raised a mental eyebrow. *To know you were responsible for pulling him out?*

No. That doesn't matter. Sardelle scowled at the back of the soldier who had replaced her. She was done delivering rashes, but he might look good with his belt unbuckled and his trousers around his ankles. *Maybe a little*, she admitted to Jaxi.

Better he not have reason to later dwell on your uncanny ability to find him.

A collective gasp sounded, then a sigh as a hand reached out. "It *is* the colonel."

Everyone had joined in to dig him out. Though she hadn't been here for long—and he hadn't been here for... even longer—Sardelle thought she knew Zirkander well enough to guess that he would be annoyed when he realized they had stopped searching for everyone else to focus on him.

The hand was followed by an arm, with no less than four people grasping it. They pulled, and Zirkander's head came next, snow sticking in his hair and frosting his eyebrows. With their help, he clawed himself out of the hole, then collapsed on the slope a few feet away from Sardelle. He dug something out of his pocket, a little wooden carving, and kissed it before returning it to its home.

"Are you all right, sir?" one soldier asked.

"Do you need to see the medic?"

"That was a brilliant shot with the rocket launcher, sir! Did you see? Their balloon was struck, and they were going down."

"Uh, yeah." Zirkander looked dazed, but he pushed the snow out of his hair and recovered enough to point at the slide area. "We have more men under there?"

"Yes, sir. Several others were up on the wall with you and—"

"Then don't stop digging, man. Get them out!"

"Yes, sir!"

The soldiers turned to consider the wide expanse of snow and hesitated. One spun back toward Sardelle. "She knew where the colonel went down."

"That's right. Did you see any others?"

This drew Zirkander's attention to Sardelle for the first time. She considered how helpful she dared be—how far would they believe her mathematical model? But then she shook her head. People's lives were at stake. To put her own safety ahead of theirs would be cowardly. She already had Bretta's death on her conscience.

Sardelle closed her eyes, seeing beneath the snow with her other senses, judging who had the least air and needed to be dug out soonest.

"One went down over in that area." She walked over and scraped an X in the snow, then backed away, happy to let them shovel. She glanced down at one of her palms. She would have a few blisters to heal when nobody was looking.

A hand reached out and caught her wrist before she could drop it. Zirkander had climbed to his feet, and he stood next to her. He arched his eyebrows at her raw palms. Ah, the wounds were worth it if they meant he knew she had helped dig.

"Nobody else knows about the days off I'm due," Sardelle said. "I had to make sure you got out."

"Of course. Very wise of you."

She eyed his pocket. "You have a lucky charm?"

Zirkander lifted his chin. "Yes, I do. Good thing too. I needed luck today."

Sardelle raised an eyebrow. She wouldn't have taken him for the superstitious sort.

He gave her a sidelong look. "It's not uncommon among pilots. We risk our lives every time we go out. When you've survived as many near misses as I have, you develop your rituals and beliefs, anything that might help things go right. You know it's illogical, but you don't want to tempt fate." He shrugged. "One of the kids in my squad kisses each of his flier's six guns before climbing into the cockpit, even if we're actively being fired upon at the time. Another sniffs spearmint oil because he claims it clears his head. I have a little carving my dad made for me. That's nothing crazy."

"I wasn't judging you, Colonel."

"You raised your eyebrow in that way of yours. I know what that look means by now."

Er, she hadn't realized it was such a signature expression for her. "Actually I think it's sweet that you have a keepsake that your father gave you."

"Uh huh."

"Sir," someone called from behind, his voice turning the word into a couple of extra syllables as he slipped trying to climb.

"Yes, Captain?" Zirkander released Sardelle's wrist.

The officer carried a leather bag. "Were you injured? Do you need treatment?"

"I'm fine. I wasn't down there long, but stay close. Others might not be so lucky." Zirkander pointed at Sardelle's shovel. "May I?"

The captain—the medic, she presumed—frowned. Sardelle wanted to tell him to lie down and relax as well, but he took her shovel and climbed up the slope to join the others.

A gun fired nearby, and Sardelle jumped. Smoke wafted from a rifle held by a soldier guarding one of the two mine shaft entrances that hadn't been buried by the snow.

"You *will* remain inside until the area out here is safe," he growled.

Zirkander looked back thoughtfully, then called a lieutenant over. "Tell any of those miners who want to come out and help dig that they can have the rest of the day off once we recover all of our people."

"Yes, sir."

"You, woman!" a soldier called from the snow pile. "Did you see where any others went under?"

Sardelle climbed onto the slope and looked around thoughtfully. She knew exactly where the rest of the people were and how many feet of snow was mounded on them, but she didn't want to appear too certain, on the off chance she could yet pass this off as keen observational skills and an understanding of mathematics.

She was in the process of marking another spot when a chill washed over her that had nothing to do with the falling snow. A presence swept down from the mountains, something she recognized but had not expected to feel here. She paused to gaze in the direction the airship had disappeared. She couldn't see anything except falling snow and the vague outline of the closest mountain, but she was certain she wasn't the only sorcerer out here.

***

Someone pressed a mug of steaming brown liquid into Ridge's hand. "Coffee?" he asked.

"Close, but stronger," Captain Heriton said. "You look like the survivor of an alligator death roll, sir."

Ridge tugged his blanket more tightly about him and didn't disagree. Any number of people had tried to get him to go inside and warm up, but he wouldn't retreat while people were still being dug out of the snow. Granted, those buried in the avalanche had been retrieved and only the mine entrances remained to be cleared. He sipped from the mug, then twitched an eyebrow at the captain. "Stronger, as in alcoholic?"

"I believe that's the secret ingredient, yes. It's a local drink."

Drinking on duty wasn't allowed, especially when it wasn't even noon yet, but the sweet liquid did have a bracing effect, warming him from the inside, something he could use at the moment. He doubted he had been buried in that snowdrift for more than ten minutes, but it had seemed an eternity. An eternity of dark lonely helplessness. When the scratches of the shovels had penetrated the snow, he could have danced and shrieked with delight, if he hadn't been pinned, facedown in the ice.

He knew he had Sardelle to thank for his swift retrieval, though he didn't know how she had managed to find him—and so many others since then. Oh, Ridge had seen her walking across the slope, scribbling equations in a notepad, and measuring from points on the wall that hadn't been devoured by snow, but he wasn't sure he believed the show. Oh, well. Who was he to complain if it saved him and his men?

After the last soldier had been pulled from the snow, Ridge had watched Sardelle retreat to the wall of a nearby building. She was gazing thoughtfully to the north. That was the direction in which the airship had disappeared, wasn't it? He had been busy being buried in snow and hadn't seen its final departure route. Someone had cheered him for striking it with that last rocket. Had he truly hit it? He hadn't thought the range nearly far enough. He had been firing out of wistfulness rather than logic, hoping one of the explosions would alarm the pilot and that he would crash into one of those towering peaks.

"Captain, what's the status on the airship?" Ridge asked.

"The balloon was ruptured with the last rocket. It flew off to the north and was losing altitude."

Ridge sucked in a breath. "Was it, now? Did anyone see it crash?"

Heriton shook his head. "The snowfall was too thick. She was high up there too. If it crashed at all, it probably sailed several miles before striking down."

"So it could be smeared all over the side of a mountain right now?"

"You're smiling, sir. You thinking to send a team out to look for survivors?"

"Survivors? I suppose they could be handy, but I was thinking more of repairing the ship and claiming it for the fort."

"To what end?"

"Gathering intel for one, but we're fish in a basket sitting here. If we had an aircraft, we could at least meet intruders on their own footing. Right now, it's too easy for them to avoid our ground weapons." And Ridge could fly again... Granted, an airship was clumsy and bloated when compared to his dragon flier, but it would help keep him sane if he could escape to the skies once in a while. On scouting missions, of course. Nothing so frivolous as random cloud hopping. "If headquarters had any idea the Cofah were out here, they would send a squadron to defend this place, but until we can get the word back to them, acquiring an enemy airship is the best we can do."

"What if they don't want to give it up?"

"Well, we'll have to determine that. If they crashed, they might be in bad shape. If they didn't crash, or if they're only slightly damaged, we can expect them to try again."

"That does seem likely." Heriton eyed the mountaintops. They were wreathed in clouds, but that didn't hide the amount of snow already up there, with more falling by the minute. Even now, more avalanches could be created from what was up there.

"I don't suppose there are any fliers hiding anywhere in the fort, are there?" Ridge would far prefer flying over to check on the airship, rather than marching, especially since they didn't know where it had gone down—or even if it had gone down—but he knew even as he asked, that finding a flier here was highly unlikely.

"No, sir. I think... I remember hearing about one that crashed into the other side of Galmok Mountain about ten years ago." The captain waved vaguely. "They couldn't get it flying again, so the crystal was salvaged, and it was left out there to rust."

A less than ideal option. "I'll check on the airship first."

Ridge turned away, already thinking of men he might steal away for a trek across the mountainside.

"*You*, sir?" Heriton asked, stopping him.

"I'm not doing anything particularly useful here." Ridge hefted the mug. "I think the fort can do without an alcohol-swilling, blanket-wrapped commander for a few hours."

"I don't think that's a good idea, sir. If they crashed, and if they survived, they're not going to be happy about their situation. I'm sure they're all armed. Why don't you let me fetch Sergeant Makt and his team?"

"Are any of them pilots?" Ridge knew they weren't—almost everyone here was infantry. He was the logical choice for salvaging an airship, if it could be salvaged, and knowing whether it could be made airworthy.

Heriton scowled. "No, sir, but—"

Ridge lifted a hand. "I'll be careful, Captain. Your concern for me is touching though."

"I just don't want to be left in charge," Heriton grumbled. "Running the base would interfere with my ability to finish organizing the archives."

Ridge smiled. "Your disgruntlement is noted. I'm going to change clothes and see if I can find some snowshoes. Send those infantry fellows up to my office anytime. I'm not above cowering behind hulking young men if trouble comes along."

Heriton looked at the snow-smothered fortress wall where the rocket launcher had once been. "Somehow, I don't believe that, sir."

Ridge waved, then headed across the courtyard toward his office. Now that he was determined to go, he wanted to leave as soon as possible, in the hope that they could hike out there and back before dark. A lot of years had passed since his cold-weather survival training at Fort Brisklebell—or Fort Brisk Balls, as the men called it.

A familiar raven-haired woman jogged over to walk next to him. "You're going out there? After the airship?"

"Were you eavesdropping?" Ridge asked.

Sardelle took a moment to consider her answer—she did that quite often—then said, "I was standing nearby when you were discussing your plans in a normal tone of voice in an open area."

"So... not eavesdropping?"

"Correct."

"If we had lowered our voices, would it then have been eavesdropping?" Ridge asked.

"Possibly." Sardelle looked up at him. They had almost reached his office building. "I'd like to go with you."

Ridge stopped with his hand on the doorknob. "What? Why?"

If anything, he would have expected her to use his absence to snoop around, perhaps examine that map more thoroughly.

"I believe it might be more dangerous than you think out there," Sardelle said.

"Oh?"

That made it seem even more unlikely that she would want to go.

"It's just a feeling." She shrugged. "A hunch. Don't you ever get hunches when you're out there flying?"

"Yes. I get hunches when dealing with inscrutable blue-eyed women too." Ridge laid a hand on her shoulder before she could comment. "Stay here where it's safe—" he glanced at the mountain of snow in the fort, "—safe-*ish*."

Sardelle's eyes narrowed with... determination? He couldn't quite read the emotion, but she didn't object further when he left her outside, so he could jog in and pack. Ridge decided that, despite what Heriton believed, he would indeed let those muscular infantry boys go first. He couldn't imagine why Sardelle wanted to go, but given that he had watched her point out the spot where every single man had been buried in the snow, he believed her hunches were worth worrying about.

Chapter 6

Gathering supplies was easy—Sardelle told the people who asked that she was doing it for Zirkander—even if all of the snowshoes had clearly been designed for men much larger than she. Getting out of the fort... that would be harder. There were more soldiers shoveling snow away from the mine entrances than there were standing watch on the ramparts, but there were still eyes in the towers overlooking the main gate, a big iron gate with hinges that squealed like a dying pig when opened.

That's probably intentional. To let everyone know when someone is trying to sneak out.

I'm sure I can quiet them. And unlock them. It's walking out under the noses of those guards that will be hard to do without being seen.

Seen and caught. You're not the most agile person on snowshoes.

Thank you, Jaxi.

Remember the ice dragon sculpting competition? Where you knocked over the table, along with all of the entries?

No.

Truly? I can refresh your memory if you wish, send the details of—

Not necessary. Sardelle stood at the corner of the administration building, watching as Zirkander and his team headed out. They wore snowshoes, carried trekking poles, and wore their weapons on their backs along with stuffed packs—they must believe they might have to spend the night out there.

Sardelle thought about trying to slip in at the end, but even with the snowfall, there was no way those alert soldiers wouldn't notice her. The gate clanged shut. She would give them ten minutes before following, long enough to walk away from the fort and enter the trees. Long enough for the men on watch to return to whatever card or dice games they might be playing.

They're not. They're standing by the windows attentively.

Truly?

Yes. They're depressingly faithful to their duties. Maybe they want to look good for the colonel.

Sardelle flexed her fingers inside her mittens and let her own senses drift toward the towers. One man stood in each of the ones closest to the gates. They were the main people she needed to worry about. She could either distract them or tweak their thoughts, so they wouldn't remember seeing her. That would require a delicate touch, though, and it would be difficult to do to two people at a time, not to mention the sketchy morality.

Just give them rashes.

That thought did cross my mind. But perhaps something less painful this time. Sardelle closed her eyes and examined the interiors of the towers. Both had stairs spiraling up to wooden floors at the top where the soldiers stood. The lower level of each tower held a big cast iron stove with neat stacks of firewood under the stairs. A little smoke might do for one, but for two? Too much of a coincidence. In the left tower, a hint of life other than that of the soldier's made her investigate between the floorboards. A family of rats staying warm for the winter. Perhaps they would enjoy a little exercise.

You're not a sorcerer, you're a prankster.

Sardelle snorted. *You say that as if you don't approve. I'm sure you're down there, roasting some chestnuts to snack on while you watch this.*

Possibly.

Sardelle closed the flue on the stove first. She waited until the soldier in that tower started crinkling his nose before sending the rats out from beneath the floor in the second. Soon, a family of six was scampering around the soldier's legs. He cursed and tried swatting at them with his sword before hunting around for a broom. In the other tower, the guard was jogging down the stairs to investigate the stove.

"Time to go," she murmured, and glanced around the courtyard to make sure there wasn't anyone inside looking her way. The snow, which was falling more heavily than ever, made it hard to tell. So long as it made things hard for other people too.

She strode across the packed snow, waved a hand to disengage the lock on the gate, and muffled the squeak of the hinges. After closing it behind her, she strode onto the trail Zirkander's team had left, her snowshoes tucked under her arm. Even with the unwieldy things attached to their boots, the soldiers had sunk down several inches in the fresh powder. Autumn calendar date or not, there had to be at least three feet already snuggled up to the fortress walls.

A quick check showed that the soldier in the stove tower had figured out the flue was the problem. His comrade was still chasing rats, but he would be back at his post shortly. Even with the trail broken, Sardelle floundered in the deep snow as she tried to reach the trees before witnesses showed up. The fortress occupied the only level land in the tiny valley, and she was already angling down a slope. Maybe she should have put her snowshoes on in the courtyard, but that would have been hard to explain if someone spotted her.

Half running and half floundering and flailing, Sardelle reached the first of the trees. She put several more of the ancient evergreens behind her before stopping to put on the snowshoes. She readjusted her pack and wiped sweat from her brow.

"I've gone a hundred meters, and I'm already thinking about a nap."

Hm? I'm sorry, I wasn't listening. Watching your friend run around after the rats is indeed entertaining.

The most excitement you've seen in three hundred years?

Sadly so. The world is dreadfully boring when you're not awake.

I'll take that as a compliment.

A cold wind whistled across the hillside, whipping at Sardelle's damp skin. She pulled her cap low over her eyes and wrapped her scarf up to her nose, then pushed away from the tree and headed down the trail. The soldiers would probably walk faster than she could, even breaking the trail. She didn't want to catch up with them anyway—explaining her presence and why she had disobeyed Zirkander wouldn't be fun. All she wanted was to be close enough to help if the sorcerer she had sensed attacked the team.

Are you sure you **want** *to help against someone who might be a distant relative?*

If he's Cofah, he's no relative of mine.

Not technically true. Their ancestors are the same as yours, back from the dragon-riding days when mages were flying around the world and colonizing it as easily as... well, as easily as they can do today in their airships, I suppose.

I know, Jaxi, but the Cofah were trying to take over our homeland three centuries ago, and that doesn't seem to have changed. Whoever is out there isn't anyone I have anything in common with.

Except magic. Would a day come when she would grow so lonely for her own kind, for those she could speak openly with about the mental arts, that she might seek out sorcerers on other continents, continents that had either never suffered a purge or could boast more survivors from that time period? If so, it wasn't today. She certainly wasn't going to stand aside and let Zirkander get hurt. He was... she didn't know what he was to her exactly, but she knew she didn't want to see him wounded—or worse.

Sardelle waited for a snarky comment, but Jaxi must have been distracted. Maybe she was trying to scout the mountain ahead to see if the airship had indeed crashed—with a sorcerer inside—or if it had escaped into the ether. Sardelle paid more attention to the forest around her, to the towering evergreens stretching toward the sky, the boughs heavy with fresh snow. Now and then an overburdened branch would drop its load, and the noise would make her jump. There were few other noises out there. Whatever animals lived in the hills had probably gone to ground when the avalanche roared through the mountains.

The path leveled, giving her legs a break—remaining upright while walking across an ever-steepening slope was not an easy task—but it turned to head through a narrow canyon too. She eyed the craggy gray walls and the high perches overhead, wondering if there were any mountain lions about. Because she was looking in that direction, she missed the movement behind a tree to the left of the canyon entrance.

A dark figure jumped out and grabbed her before she could

so much as think of defense. An arm wrapped around her waist, tugging her off-balance, and she tumbled against...

"Colonel Zirkander," she gasped, glad she had identified him before her wits had returned and she had launched some attack that would be hard to explain later.

The grip around her waist loosened, though he didn't let her go. "It *is* you. I didn't think it could be... how'd you get out?"

"Just waited for a moment when nobody was looking."

"I'm going to have to talk to those gate guards." Zirkander released her and propped her back upright on the trail—the snowshoes did make it difficult to maintain one's balance. He touched her pack. "You came prepared."

Sardelle decided not to remind him that she had grown up in the area, not when she had been caught mentioning a town that no longer existed. "Are you going to send me back?"

Zirkander looked back along the trail. If he said yes, turned her around, and swatted her on the backside to get her moving, what choice would she have but to do so?

"No. We've already encountered tracks out here."

"Human tracks?"

He nodded. "A couple of men went most of the way to the fort, presumably to see if the avalanche swallowed us whole or not."

"That means the ship *did* land then."

"Or crash. Come on. We'll find out." He headed into the little canyon.

"Thank you."

"And along the way, you can tell me why you're so eager to come along." Zirkander gave her a long look over his shoulder. "I doubt there are any archaeological dig sites out here."

Sardelle stumbled. She almost asked what made him think she was here as an archeologist, but she caught herself. If he thought she was some academic here to poke through stones, let him. That was a lot better than being a prisoner. Of course, she had already installed her forged record. It was only a matter of time before that captain stumbled across it.

Just worry about the now, **Jaxi** suggested. *And be wary of what's* ahead. For all we know, that sorcerer could be one of the ones padding about out here.

Good point.

They passed through the canyon without being jumped on by mountain lions, and a fit, young soldier veered out of the trees to join them on the opposite side. A nametag on his parka read *Oster*.

"Sir?" He looked at Sardelle.

"Our shadow," Zirkander said.

"She's coming?"

"She seems to be of that opinion."

Oster stared at the colonel, but didn't question him. Sardelle wondered if people would start to, behind his back if not to his face, because of her. She was still dressed in prisoner garb, if with a few extra layers she had piled on for this trek. Even if she had helped with the avalanche retrieval, the soldiers wouldn't necessarily trust her. She hoped the fact that Zirkander seemed to wouldn't make trouble for him.

"You find any more tracks, Corporal?" Zirkander asked.

"No, sir. The two sets over there walked out to the fort and then walked back the same way. They didn't have snowshoes, so it's possible we'll catch them if we hurry."

"Tell the sergeant to go ahead then. I'll catch up. You young warriors would probably like me out of the way for any fighting that comes up anyway."

The corporal hesitated. "We wouldn't want you getting sniped or—" he glanced at Sardelle, "—anything else, either, sir."

"I'll be fine." Zirkander pulled out the rifle strapped across his pack and held it in front of him. "I'm a fair shot, I'm told."

"Yes, sir." Oster saluted, then jogged down the trail ahead of them.

"I didn't know you could jog in snowshoes," Sardelle said.

"It takes practice."

She wagered Zirkander could have kept up with the younger men and was staying back because of her. She didn't know how she felt about that.

Like a burden?

Not until you mentioned it. Thanks, Jaxi.

Sardelle extended her senses around them as she walked—she hadn't been paying attention earlier, and Zirkander had snuck up on her with embarrassing ease. It wouldn't do to let anyone else approach. They were tramping down a slope toward a canyon, this one much larger than the other they had passed through. Large enough to hold a crashed airship. Something out there tickled the edge of her senses. Several people, and someone... The sorcerer? Working some magic? He or she didn't seem aware of her, but she pulled back anyway. The magic user seemed busy, but since she had sensed him probing the fortress, he might feel her presence as well.

She wanted to warn Zirkander, not only that the crashed ship and several people were at the other end of the canyon, but about the other sorcerer as well. How, though? She focused on the back of his head, wishing she could will whatever prejudices he had against magic users away. An impossibility, alas. She shook her head. She would have to simply try to help the soldiers when they encountered the airship crew.

Zirkander lifted a hand. "Wait here, please."

He removed his snowshoes, leaned his rifle against a cliff, and scrambled up the rock, the edges and crevices slick with ice and snow. She gaped as he went up forty feet, as if there were a rope there to assist him. Yes, he definitely could have kept up with the young soldiers.

At the top, he crouched, his back to a boulder, and peered toward the valley. The snow had slowed to a few intermittent flurries. "Yes, I thought I smelled smoke. They're here." He clenched his fist. "It doesn't look like they smashed into any trees, but there was definitely some damage done on the way down."

"You really want that ship, don't you?"

"Yes." Zirkander crawled back down, not quite as quickly as he had gone up, but he landed in the snow beside her without falling or appearing in danger of falling at any point. "Some astute bartender would doubtlessly pin this desire back to my childhood days when my father refused to buy a model airship for me."

Astute bartender? Is that what passed for a therapist in the army? "Why wouldn't he buy it for you?"

Zirkander strapped his snowshoes back on as he answered. "He said he didn't want to encourage me—I was already flight mad by five or six—but Mom said we didn't have the money for silly toys. I decided to make one of my own. Out of sticks. It was more of an air-raft." He nodded his readiness and started down the trail again.

"I'm sure it was cute," Sardelle said.

A shot fired in the distance. Zirkander cursed and started jogging. Sardelle did her best to keep up. More shots were fired, all from the direction of that canyon, and she thought he would tear off without her. But he glanced back, saw she was falling behind, and stopped to wait. His hand was clenched about his rifle, and he reminded her of a sled dog, straining at the traces, eager to charge off down the trail.

"You don't have to wait for me," Sardelle said. "I'll catch up. Or maybe hang back and stay out of trouble."

"Oddly, I don't believe you."

Good. She wanted him where she could keep an eye on him anyway. She would try to watch over the other soldiers as well, but Zirkander was... her best hope of freeing Jaxi.

Uh huh. I'm the reason you're trailing him across the mountain and through a blizzard.

Sardelle waved at the scattering of snowflakes. *This hardly constitutes a blizzard.*

Give it time. You should see the clouds coming in your direction.

She grimaced. Yet more news that would be useful to share with the others, but which she couldn't.

She extended her senses again, trying to get a feel for the situation ahead, to help their soldiers if she could. There were people at the other end of the canyon, but some had scattered. At this distance, she couldn't be certain if they were Zirkander's people or men from the ship. Oster was the only one she recognized. He was farther back, closer to her and Zirkander.

Trees and uneven terrain had forced the trail to twist and wind before it reached the mouth of the canyon, but they were finally entering it. A minute or two had passed since the last shot fired. She sensed...

"They're leaving." Sardelle clapped a hand over her mouth, worried she had given away something she shouldn't have been able to tell from her position.

But Zirkander nodded. "I see it."

The trees made it difficult to see much of anything, but ah, she needed to look up instead of ahead. That massive balloon was clearing the canopy. If she had damaged it once, maybe she could again, although the number of people she sensed on it was high. Over two dozen. Maybe more.

"She's not nearly as wounded as I had hoped," Zirkander said.

No, a sorcerer could make short work of repairs.

A few people moved about on the deck, beneath the shadow of the balloon. From Sardelle's angle, she could only see those closest to the railing, but she squinted, hoping to catch sight of the magic user, wanting a look at her opponent. What she saw was someone with a spyglass, standing next to someone with a rifle, looking down at them.

"Look out," she whispered, backing toward a tree—or trying. The oversized snowshoes tangled beneath her feet, and she tumbled to the ground in the middle of the trail, in clear sight for those on the ship.

A shot fired, and she flung an arm out, forming an invisible barrier in the air around her. A clunk-clang sounded, another bullet being chambered, and a second shot fired on the heels of the first. Belatedly, Sardelle realized it was Zirkander shooting, not those on the ship. In fact, one man had already disappeared from sight. The second, clutching his chest, toppled backward, falling from her view.

Zirkander leaned toward her, and she dropped her shield before he bumped into it. He picked her up and carried her behind a couple of thick trees before setting her on her feet.

"Thanks," Sardelle said. "I forgot I was wearing these clunky things."

"They're definitely awkward." He was standing beside her protectively, his arm around her back, but his gaze was toward the sky. Carried on the currents, the ship had already drifted out of view.

"I'm sorry you didn't get your salvage," she said. Or maybe not. What if she ripped the balloon again? Sure, there were no rockets to hide her sabotage, but with the trees blocking the view, who would know what had happened?

She closed her eyes, envisioning that balloon, and tried to cut a hole as she had before. This time, it didn't work. She sensed the why right away. There was a protective film about it, not unlike the barrier she had just thrown up. The sorcerer. He knew she was out there and wasn't going to be caught unaware again.

A screech came out of the depths of the canyon, eerie and hair-raising. Sardelle gulped. "Was that a cat?"

There had been mountain lions and wolves in the Ice Blades in her day, and she had heard both, but this sounded like something different. Something less… mortal.

"Almost sounds like a hawk," Zirkander said. "A really loud, creepier-than-a-haunted-battlefield hawk. Let's find the other men and get back to the fort. There's nothing left for us here."

The screech sounded again, closer this time. It reverberated from the canyon walls and seemed to hang on the breeze for an eternity. Something about it made Sardelle want to spring in the opposite direction and let those soldiers find their own way home. Zirkander didn't shy away though, and she strode after him.

She searched the valley with her senses, hoping to find the creature and identify it. Or maybe just find it so they could better avoid it. She sensed the men. They had been spread out, trying to sneak up on the ship as its crew finished repairs. They were angling back toward each other now, though two seemed to have lost their way in the snow and trees—or maybe they were intentionally looking for the source of those cries. Sardelle shuddered. She wouldn't.

Oddly, she couldn't find it even with her mage senses. The screech sounded one more time, so she knew the cat or hawk or whatever it was hadn't left the canyon, but she couldn't feel anything in the direction the noise had come from. Or where it had *seemed* to come from. The way it reverberated from the rocky walls made it hard to tell.

Two shots fired.

"They're not shooting at some animal, are they?" Zirkander didn't sound out of breath from their charge into the canyon.

Sardelle was too busy gulping air to respond.

"Unless the airship left some men behind," Zirkander added.

"I don't think so." Sardelle didn't sense any people in the canyon, other than those on the colonel's team. "It seemed pretty full," she added, when he glanced back at her. Minus the two men he had shot. They wouldn't be happy about that. She hoped the craft wasn't heading back to attack the fort. It had flown off in the opposite direction, but that might not mean anything.

"Colonel Zirkander?" came a call from their left. Boulders and the cliffs of the canyon wall were visible beyond the snowy trees, but Sardelle didn't see the speaker.

"Coming," Zirkander called. He veered off the trail. "They must think we're alone if they're shouting," he added more quietly. "But what are they shooting at then?"

The screech sounded again, as if to answer his question. It sounded like it was coming from the sky rather than the canyon floor, or maybe some precipice up the cliffs. Once again, Sardelle tried to find it, but the only life she sensed was that of the soldiers and of a few rodents and chipmunks, most burrowed beneath the snow. She counted four soldiers. Hadn't there been five before? Maybe she had been mistaken.

"How many men are out here with you?" Sardelle asked.

"Five."

Uh oh. Either someone had gotten separated from the group, or...

The parkas of two of the men came into view through the trees. If not for the contrast of the white ground, Sardelle might have missed them. It was growing dark, with the snow picking up again.

One of the soldiers lifted a solemn hand at their approach. "It's Nakkithor, sir."

"What happened, Sergeant?" Zirkander asked.

"We're not sure."

"We didn't see it," the second soldier said. "Nak was behind us, maybe ten meters back, at least that's what I thought. Then we heard his screams. We ran back and…"

Sardelle tried to see past Zirkander without leaving the trail he was breaking. The drifts hugging the trees to either side were above her waist. It took a moment before she located the man they were talking about. The soldier lay unmoving on the ground in a tiny clearing, his body half hidden by a tangle of thorny brambles on one edge. Dark crimson stains spattered the snow. She didn't have to take a closer look to know he was dead.

"I swear I saw something, some shadow running or flying away," the sergeant said. Sardelle squinted through the gloom to pick out the names on their parkas. Makt. "It was big and moving fast, whatever it was. I shot twice, then realized it might be you."

"I haven't managed to move that fast out here," Zirkander said, stopping beside the body. "It wasn't me."

"I thought I hit whatever it was, but it didn't cry out. It just disappeared behind the trees."

"Rav and Oster went to look," the second man, Eringroad, said. "See if they could find tracks or a sign that we'd hit it. As you can see, there's nothing around here except our snowshoe marks."

"Are you sure they're all our prints?" Zirkander asked. "The Cofah could have had snowshoes too."

"Fairly certain, sir. We saw the ship take off and searched around it. No one seemed to have been left behind."

"No *one*."

While the men debated, Sardelle mentally braced herself and walked up to the side of the body. She couldn't believe she hadn't sensed something that was big enough to kill a man, and to kill him swiftly it sounded like. His face had been ravaged by claws or—she thought of Zirkander's hawk guess—talons. The eyes were missing, gouged out, the holes so deep they revealed brain matter beneath them. The front of his parka was shredded, his flesh cut open, entrails torn free and slumped into the snow.

Sardelle took a long breath, glad the air was so fresh and cold. As a healer, she had seen death before, and all manner of wounds, but this was a particularly grisly display. Had she arrived earlier, maybe she could have saved him, but maybe not. He must have died quickly from those extensive wounds.

"Looks like the attack came from the air," Zirkander said. He wasn't unmoved by the death, she sensed, but his words came out calm and detached. This would be an analytical discussion, not an emotional one.

Makt glanced at him. "That's what I thought, sir. But I wasn't sure. I didn't want to sound stupid. I reckon there's eagles and other big raptors up here, but an eagle couldn't do this, could it? And even if it could, why would it?"

"Why, indeed?" Zirkander looked to Sardelle. Did he think she would have the answer? He couldn't possibly think she was somehow responsible, could he? Maybe he had figured out that her powers were more than academic. Or maybe he thought it suspicious that she had run after the group. "Are you all right?" he asked, flexing his mittened fingers toward the body.

Oh. Concern. Not suspicion. Not yet.

She looked at his hand but not at the body. She had seen enough. "I'm..." Fine? That seemed a ludicrous thing to proclaim with a mauled soldier at her feet. She simply nodded to finish her answer.

Snow crunched, heralding the return of the other two men, their rifles in their hands. They were shaking their heads before they reached the colonel.

"We didn't see anything."

"Not so much as a tuft of fur." Oster glanced at Makt. "Or a feather."

"It's getting dark though." The first man eyed the metal gray sky above the pines and firs. Thick flakes wafted down peacefully, unperturbed by the death below. "If there had been drops of blood out there, they would have been hard to pick out."

"Should we head back, sir?" Oster asked. "Even darker clouds are heading this way, and there's a lot of wind coming across the canyon up above. The airship had to fight to head off to the north."

Zirkander was staring down at the body, a fist pressed to his mouth. "Yes, there's nothing for us out here now."

Except a mystery. Sardelle couldn't believe something had slipped past her awareness. Something deadly. Was it possible the airship sorcerer had masked it somehow?

"Let's make a travois so we can haul him back," Zirkander said. "I'm not leaving his body out here to the animals."

"Yes, sir," Oster said. "Rav, you got an axe? Use those saplings to—"

A screech ripped through the forest.

It wasn't in the distance this time, but nearby, overhead. Sardelle searched the clouds, her hand balled into a fist, ready to unleash an attack. Even in the small clearing, the trees fenced them in, and little of the dark sky was visible.

"Cover," Zirkander barked.

The soldiers split into twos and lunged behind trees, then knelt, their rifles pointing to the sky. Zirkander started for a tree of his own, but saw Sardelle wasn't moving and grabbed her. Just as he was pulling her away, she glimpsed massive outstretched wings high overhead, the dark shape seeming more shadow than substance against the snow and clouds.

"There," she cried at the same time as two rifles fired.

Zirkander pushed her toward a pair of trees. "Stay between them," he ordered, even as he took two steps in the other direction and raised his own firearm to the sky.

The bird—no, it was far too large to call it a bird—had swooped out of sight almost as soon as they had spotted it, but it came back around, higher. Even with the poor visibility, Sardelle would have expected the men's bullets to hit it, but the creature never flinched, never altered its flight path. It was climbing higher and higher. Readying for a dive.

She still couldn't sense it, and that perplexed her but didn't keep her from preparing an attack of her own. Shots rang out from all of the rifles. The massive bird pulled in its wings to dive, like an osprey arrowing into a lake for a fish, except its target was Zirkander. Sardelle pulled wind from the coming storm, channeled it, and slammed it into the plummeting creature. It was flung to the side, hurled into a stout pine.

Sardelle blew out a quick relieved breath. She had feared that since she couldn't sense it, she wouldn't be able to strike it, as if it were some kind of illusion. The great bird—it had the markings of a barred owl, not a hawk, but it was nearly as tall as a man—recovered before it hit the ground, thrusting its wings out to beat at the air, to pull itself back into the night sky.

All through this, the soldiers were firing, their spent casings leaping from their rifles and burning holes into the snow all around them. The creature climbed back into the sky, not fleeing from the barrage but preparing to dive again.

"Who hit it?" one soldier shouted. "Where did you aim to make it fly sideways?"

"We've *all* hit it," another responded. "The bullets are bouncing off—I saw mine strike and veer off as if that thing were solid metal."

"Someone hurt it though—it crashed for a moment. If we could all target that spot."

"That wasn't a bullet, you idiot. That was the wind."

Technically true.

Jaxi! What is this thing? Someone's familiar? Someone's extremely enhanced familiar?

I believe you're looking at a Dakrovian shaman's animal companion.

Dakrovian! From the jungles in the southern hemisphere? That's thousands of miles from Cofah.

Jaxi offered a mental shrug. *Perhaps they went recruiting.*

"Sir! Look out. It's dropping again."

"I see it." Zirkander jumped to his feet and ran toward Sardelle's trees.

He ducked around the biggest one and fished into his ammo pouch to reload his rifle.

Nobody except the dead soldier remained in the tiny clearing, but that didn't keep the giant owl from diving down again. Though Sardelle knew she risked what little of her confusing cover story remained by using magic, she hurled another funnel of wind at it. The bullets weren't doing anything. *Someone* had to drive it away.

But the bird somehow sensed her attack and dodged. The blast of wind barely ruffled its feathers. It dropped to within two feet of the ground, then impossibly turned the dive into an upward swoop, pulling out at the last moment. No, not pulling out, and not turning upward. It streaked horizontally, paralleling the ground, its dive taking it toward the trees two of the soldiers hid behind.

"Look out!" someone yelled.

More shots rang out, though the soldiers must have realized by then that they couldn't hurt it. Zirkander yanked out a foot-long dagger and charged toward the creature. The soldiers leaped to the side, avoiding the owl's attack in time, but only because the stout firs slowed their avian attacker. One ran around a tree and clubbed the owl in the wing as it shifted from flying to standing, its spread talons enough to keep it from sinking into the snow. The soldier's attack did nothing to hurt it. It flung its wing out, the tip catching him and hurling him ten feet.

Zirkander ran at it from behind, fast enough, even with the snowshoes, to surprise it. He leaped onto its back and tried to sink his long dagger into its neck. As with the bullets, the blade bounced off. Its head spun around a hundred and eighty degrees. That must have been alarming—it was suddenly staring right at Zirkander—but he attacked it without hesitation, this time aiming for one of its great yellow eyes.

Sardelle had her own hand raised, trying to think of some attack she dared make while Zirkander was right on top of it, but she paused, hoping he had guessed right and that the eye represented some vulnerability.

The blade started to sink in. At least she thought it did—it was hard to tell. At the first touch, the owl shook its head vigorously. Zirkander didn't let go of the weapon. He tried to push it in deeper, but was thrown free. He landed hard on his back. The creature jumped after him, seeming to rear up to an impossible height as it spread its wings.

Sardelle tried to find its heart, to wrap the fingers of her mind around it to stop it from beating, but again her senses told her nothing was there. A soldier ran out, an axe in his hand, as if that would do what the bullets hadn't. The bird ignored the man and attacked Zirkander, plunging downward with its beak.

Sardelle cursed, knowing she would be too late as she tore a heavy branch from the tree above the owl, hoping to bring it down onto the creature's head. Zirkander had already rolled to the side and leaped up, not as helpless as he had appeared.

The branch landed, flinging snow everywhere, and surprised him as much as the creature. He recovered first and hurled his dagger. The weapon struck the owl's eye, but in throwing the attack, he exposed himself an instant too long. A talon flashed up, striking like lightning as it ripped into his parka. Zirkander leaped back, but blood sprayed the snow around him.

Sardelle growled, prepared to drop an entire tree on the bird's head, and to the hells with what anyone saw, but it was flinging its head about and screeching now. The dagger was stuck in its eye. For a moment, she thought it might be a killing blow, or at least a seriously wounding one, but the creature used a talon to bat it away. The weapon landed point first in the snow. The owl leaped into the air, raking the axe-wielding soldier with its talons, too, before it flapped its wings and climbed out of reach again.

"Sir, Rav, are you all right?" Makt ran out from behind the trees on the other side of the clearing.

"Just a scratch," Zirkander said.

Sure, a scratch that had left blood all over the snow. Sardelle started toward him, but the owl screeched again. It wasn't done with them. It was circling and rising again, preparing for another dive.

"Let's get out of here." Zirkander pointed to the rocky canyon wall. "Are there any caves or fissures in that cliff?"

"Don't know, sir."

"Go, look. There's nothing for us to gain by fighting this thing."

And everything to lose.

"Yes, sir."

"It's starting another dive," one of the men said.

"Go, go." Zirkander waved the men forward and reached

back toward Sardelle.

She had thought to linger, to try dropping a tree on it when the men were out of sight, but Zirkander was like a sheep dog, gathering his flock. Nothing in his expression said he would let her loiter.

She hustled after him. A tree probably wouldn't kill that creature anyway. Not unless she could ram the trunk through its eye.

The owl swooped again when it reached the ground, trying to dart through the forest after them. Zirkander and the soldiers weaved into the thickest areas. Even the powerful creature couldn't rip trees aside with its talons. It returned to the sky, tracking them from above. There was a bare stretch near the cliff wall. They would have to be careful crossing it.

"There's a big crack." Someone pointed.

"Might be a cave."

"Another hole over there. Impossible to tell without looking."

"It's too dark to tell either way. That's just a big shadow, I think."

Zirkander looked up. Yes, the creature was up there, banking and turning, flying back and forth. Waiting.

Sardelle skimmed the craggy rocks with her mind. That spot was too shallow, that one too narrow to get into, that one large enough that the owl could follow. A dozen meters to the left, there were two little caves that should work, each with just enough space for two or three men to squeeze into.

"Down there." Sardelle pointed. "I've studied geology. Those are Brackenforth Fissures. They'll be narrow but deep."

One of the soldiers snorted. "Is she joking?"

"It's going to dive again." Oster stabbed his rifle toward the black sky.

Sardelle ran toward the caves she knew were deep enough. Zirkander cursed and ran after her, yelling, "Find hiding," to the soldiers.

"I ought to tackle you," he growled, his voice right behind her. He could have. She definitely wasn't fast on the snowshoes.

"Not a good time." Sardelle waved to the sky without pausing, then climbed up the cliff face. She tried to anyway. She couldn't manage with the big, clumsy shoes on. She bent, unbuckling them as fast as she could, and hurled another buffet of wind at the owl as she did so. It was already diving, choosing her as a target since she had been foolish enough to run out first.

Rifles fired. Those soldiers never gave up. Fortunately, Sardelle's attack clipped the owl's side this time, diverting it a few meters. Its screech filled their ears, as it nearly slammed into the rocks at the base of the cliff.

Sardelle scrambled up without glancing at it, aiming for the first little cave, the smaller of the two. Zirkander was right beside her, shadowing her, protecting her. She slipped twice, her mittens falling away from the icy rocks when she tried to grab them, but Zirkander caught her both times, holding her up until she found a new grip.

The creature recovered from its near crash, rising again, readying itself for another dive. The soldiers were farther down the cliff—they had gone for the caves directly in front of the area where they had come out of the trees. Sardelle hoped they found sufficient cover there.

"Here," she said, and squeezed through a crack. It smelled of mildew and cold but nothing more ominous. She had already checked to make sure nothing was making a den inside. She crawled to the back—which was all of six feet from the front—and tried to make herself small so Zirkander would have room.

His rifle clunked against the rock, and clothing rasped and ripped. His body blocked the mouth of the cave as he grunted, trying to wedge himself in, and full darkness filled the small space.

"Can you make it?" Sardelle asked. She had thought it would be big enough, but he was taller and broader of shoulder than she was. Reluctantly, she said, "There's another fissure a few feet up if you can't." She didn't want to spend the night alone in the cave.

More like, you don't want to spend the night alone in the cave without his company.

Hush. This is about keeping everyone alive, nothing more.

Uh huh.

This space isn't big enough for anything more anyway. Not that Sardelle seriously thought Zirkander would contemplate "anything more" even if this *were* the time and the place. She was his little puzzle to be solved, nothing more. If he was protecting her, it was simply because he would do that for any woman.

"I'm in." Zirkander leaned out. "Find a place, Rav! It's coming."

Sardelle checked the others. They had found a cave big enough for three, but they weren't able to fit the other soldier inside.

"Trying, sir!" came the distant call.

Zirkander wriggled his rifle back out. He was poised like a panther on a tree branch, muscles bunched, ready to spring. Sardelle resisted the urge to tell him he couldn't do anything to drive off the owl. He wouldn't appreciate it. She couldn't do anything either, if she couldn't see it, which she couldn't from the back of the cave. Even when she *could* see it, she hadn't been able to do much. She needed to dig out books on those jungle shamans when she got home.

Home?

Well, back. They're buried down there somewhere, right?

Possibly, though I do hope you'll make my retrieval your priority.

We'll see.

"There's room over here," Zirkander yelled.

Sardelle crept forward, found a rock to stand on, and tried to see past his shoulder. If she could locate the owl, she could attack it with wind again. She could—

"He got in." Zirkander turned and bumped into her.

She fell off the rock and grabbed the nearest thing—his shoulder. "Sorry," she said, stepping down. "I was trying to see out."

"And here I thought you were overcome by the euphoria of surviving and wanted to fling your arms around me for a kiss."

"I..." Did he *want* that? No, his tone was dry. A joke, nothing more. "Look out," she cried as a shadow blotted out the night forest behind him.

The dreadful screech filled the tiny cave, hammering Sardelle's eardrums. She stumbled back, pulling Zirkander with her. He needed no urging. Talons scraped and tore at the rock around the entrance. He pressed himself against the back of the fissure, grunting as he shifted about to face the entrance, positioning himself so he was between her and the creature.

With its wings tucked in, the owl wasn't much bigger than the men. If it could climb in...

Sardelle gulped, terrified she had led them to a trap rather than a haven. She summoned her energy to batter at it again, but one of its talons slipped, and it disappeared amid a flurry of wing beats. It soon returned, beating at the mouth of the cave. Sardelle examined the top of the cliff above her. The snow-covered top of the cliff. She nudged a drift over the edge. It wouldn't hurt the owl, but maybe...

Big clumps of snow rained down on it. The creature shrieked and disappeared from view.

"I do not like that noise," Sardelle said. She hoped the others' cave entrances were narrow enough that the owl would have no chance at getting to them.

"Now I know what my mother meant all the times she used the term ear-drilling to me," Zirkander said.

"In relation to what?"

"My learning to play the trombone one summer. *I* thought I sounded fabulous."

Sardelle smiled despite their situation. She had no idea how they were going to escape that owl, but couldn't think of anyone else she would rather be trapped with at the moment.

Chapter 7

"Sir?" came a distant call.

Ridge left Sardelle—he had been smashing her anyway—and returned to the front of the cave, grunting as his foot caught on rock. Their shelter lacked a flat floor. "We're fine, Rav," he called back. "Everyone there make it?"

"We're all in, but, uhm, the owl... it's sitting out there waiting in a tree branch."

"With luck, it'll get bored of waiting and leave."

The soldier's "Yes, sir" sounded encouraged, but the follow-up of, "What if it doesn't?" was a little more plaintive.

"We'll figure it out in the morning," Ridge called. Dropping his voice, he asked, "Owls are nocturnal, right?"

"Regular owls, yes," Sardelle said. "I'm less certain about magical ones."

Ridge digested that. "So it *is* magical. I didn't think it could be natural, but I've never heard of anything like this."

After a pause, Sardelle asked, "It wasn't in the operations manual?"

"No."

"I'm guessing it belonged to someone on that ship."

"A ship that is now free to go back and harass the fort without me there." Ridge slapped the wall with his hand. Damned fool's errand, that's what this had been. He had lost a man, and now the fort might be in danger again.

"I'm sorry," Sardelle said softly.

"Not your fault." Ridge hadn't figured out yet why she had come out here—or how in all the levels of all the hells she had managed to sneak out past his men—but she hadn't been a burden. She had pushed herself to keep up and hadn't complained about the pace. She had even been right about the cave. He snorted.

Brackenforth Fissures. He would have to look that up when he got back to the fort—*if* there was a fort to return to. He growled at himself. All this because he had wanted the airship. What had he thought would happen? That the crew would all be dead, and he could simply salvage it for himself? At the least, he had hoped they wouldn't be able to put up much of a fight. But that ship had been well manned, and it was uncanny how quickly the Cofah had repaired it. He wondered…

"So if someone on that ship has a giant magical owl, does that then mean that said person has magical powers of his own?" Ridge didn't know when he had started to think of Sardelle as his guide to all things arcane, but she had read at least one book on the topic, and that was one more book than he had read.

"His or her own, yes," Sardelle said. "It would take someone with an alarming amount of power to command such a beast." Concern laced her words. Thus far, she had faced everything with a calm demeanor. This was the first time she had sounded worried.

And that worried *him*. What he had assumed was a simple Cofah scouting mission looked like it was much more. A well-equipped ship that had apparently come with the mission to bury the fort—and the mining operation—beneath snow and rock.

Frigid wind whistled through the canyon. It was going to be a stormy night. He hoped the owl got cold. And knocked off its branch by a gust.

Clothing rubbed against rock as Sardelle shifted positions. She patted around, grunting a couple of times as she hit rocks, and settled on the ground between the entrance and the back wall. It was the widest spot in their little prison. "I don't seem to have picked out a very comfortable cave."

"I'm not sure any cave would be comfortable on a night like tonight." Ridge waved toward the snow—it was falling sideways now, driven by the wind. "The temperature's going to drop. Too bad the owl wasn't considerate enough to let us gather some firewood on the way in."

"Yes, I've heard magical owls are very rude."

"That's in that book you were quoting, eh?"

"Actually, no. I was joking. I know very little about magical owls, I'm afraid."

"Hm." Ridge debated between sitting down beside her and standing there, keeping watch. What he was keeping watch over, he didn't know—with the increased snowfall, he couldn't see the owl, or much of anything. He just felt like he should be vigilant. He had already done enough wrong tonight. His chest ached though, reminding him of the scratches—as if the icy air creeping through the torn parka and shirt weren't enough of a reminder. He ought to dig out bandages. And antiseptic. For all he knew, magical owl claws could give a man rabies.

"How's your injury?" Sardelle asked. "Do you want me to bandage it?"

Odd, it was almost as if she knew what he had been thinking. Maybe she had simply seen him touch his chest, though he didn't remember doing so. "It does sting a little. I was debating whether one could get an infection from magical critters."

"If its talons were dirty, well, dirt's dirt. Better on the outside than in your cuts." Sardelle shifted about, opening her pack probably. "I grabbed one of the first-aid kits from the room that had the snowshoes. Do you want to sit down?"

"Not only did you sneak out of my fort, but you fully supplied yourself for the road before doing so. I'm definitely going to have a talk with my men when we get back." Though he felt a little disgruntled at this failing—every failing of a soldier was a reflection of his commanding officer, after all—he patted his way over to her and sat down. It *did* feel good to slump against the wall, to rest.

"It's not their fault," Sardelle said.

"No? You're just so amazingly talented in the art of stealth that they can't be blamed?"

"Something like that. Hm, what I did *not* bring is a candle or a match. I don't suppose you have something in your pack? This would be easier with light."

Ridge dragged his gear over. He took off his mittens to unbuckle the straps and dipped into an outer pouch to fish out a small travel lantern and his box of fire-starters.

"I can do that." Sardelle found the equipment in his hands. She had taken off her gloves as well, and the touch of her skin against his was... nice. "You can relax and be the patient."

"Careful. If you demonstrate a good bedside manner, I'll let the medic put you to work in the infirmary."

"That would actually be a suitable position for me." Yes, she had mentioned training to be a doctor once, hadn't she?

"You wouldn't miss folding towels in the laundry room?"

"Not particularly." Flint rasped, and sparks fluttered down to land on the soft fuzz from the fire-starting kit. The soft orange light revealed her face, none-the-worse for the afternoon's activities. She blew on the sparks, producing a flame, and lit the lantern. "This cave is small enough that this flame and our body heat might keep us warm for the night."

"Our body heat, huh?"

She smiled at him. "Yes. Now take your shirt off, please."

"Uhh." Ridge could feel the coldness of the rock wall behind him even through his parka. "How about I just lift it up a little? When you're ready to get started." And not a second before. It probably wasn't manly to complain about the weather, but now that he had stopped running and climbing and leaping onto the backs of giant birds, he was cooling down, his sweat chilling his skin.

"You're not shy, are you?" Sardelle opened a dark bottle of the bromine concoction that came with the kit and gave it a dubious sniff.

"In tropical climates, not at all. Even in temperate climates, I might wander about shirtless, but here... I haven't quite acclimated to the icicles dangling from my nostrils in the mornings yet." Ridge pushed back the parka, unfastened his uniform jacket, and went so far as to tug his shirt out of his trousers, but he wasn't exposing any flesh until she was hovering over him with a swab of antiseptic in one hand and bandages in the other. Already, cold whispered up his back from having his shirt loosened.

"I suppose that means I needn't worry about you wishing to engage in... convivial activities with me tonight then, activities that might require the shedding of clothing." Sardelle shifted toward him, her rag now doused. "Shirt up, please."

"No, you needn't worry about that." Ridge supposed her comment proved that his earlier thought was unlikely. She wasn't there to seduce him for information. He probably shouldn't feel disappointed by that. "Although, for the record, men don't need to expose a whole lot of skin to get *convivial*."

"I suppose that's true. Shirt up," she repeated.

Ridge reached for the hem, but hesitated, nibbling thoughtfully on the inside of his cheek.

"Problem?" Sardelle asked.

"Just wondering if I need to rub my dragon before enduring this."

"Uhm, pardon?"

"You know, my little charm." Ridge eyed her doused rag. "Or maybe *you* should rub my dragon."

"Perhaps later," she murmured.

He was probably safe so long as she didn't dig needles and suture thread out. Ridge tugged up the shirt, grimacing where the blood had dried, and the wool stuck to his skin.

"These don't look like they need stitches," Sardelle said, "but you'll have scars."

Ridge thought to grunt that it wouldn't be the first time, but he actually didn't have that many war wounds. The only time he had crashed, it had been in the ocean, and he had come out unbloodied. "I'll survive, so long as that owl is gone in the morning."

"I hope it does prove nocturnal, or that it at least misses its master and feels compelled to go find him. Her. Whomever."

"Me too."

Sardelle's left hand rested on his chest while she gently wiped his wounds with the rag in her right. Ridge could feel the warmth of her fingers against his skin, in contrast to the coolness of the damp cloth. He hadn't been thinking of *convivial* activities until she had mentioned it, but now that she had—and that she was bent low and touching his chest—he had a hard time pushing his mind away from the topic. The wind was shrieking outside, with a half inch of snow already crusted on the ledge. It seemed the perfect time to cuddle with a woman. All right, cuddling wasn't *quite* what he had in mind. Anything more—and even that—would still be inappropriate. For all that she had helped them, helped *him*, he didn't truly know if she was friend or foe. Still, he noticed that she had been touching his chest for a while and had brushed over the same wounds more than once. Was it possible she was enjoying the ministrations? He had stopped feeling any sting. In fact, he was feeling that if she didn't stop soon, he would wrap his arm around her and pull her against his chest, kiss her—

"Where did you get the scar on your chin?" Sardelle leaned back, set the rag down, and screwed the cap back on the bottle.

Ridge had to clear his throat before he found his voice. "It's an old one—got it as a kid. I'm surprised it still shows."

She raised her brows.

"It was a gift from a street tough, one twice my size. He was always picking on me. I was terrified of him, but finally got tired of getting pushed around. I offered him a pie if he would teach me how to fight."

"A pie?" The corners of her lips lifted into a smile. Even her smiles seemed serene. He wondered if she ever lost that equanimity. Such as in the throes of passion.

Ridge cleared his throat again. Down, boy. "I was about nine at the time. I didn't have any money or anything valuable, but Mom always baked to distract herself when Dad was out of town. At the time, there were three pies cooling in the window."

"And this bully agreed to your price?"

"He did. Lesson One was on how to take pain." Ridge touched the old scar, still vividly remembering that board with the nails on it hammering him in the face. "I think this tough enjoyed the lessons even more than he had enjoyed picking on me. I did get better at defending myself, even if I didn't learn how to bring down others until my army training. Even though I'd been accepted into the officer academy and flight school already, they make you go through the same first year of training that every grunt endures. Guess they want you to be able to fight your way home if you get shot down in enemy territory."

He realized he had wandered off topic. By now, Sardelle was holding the roll of bandage, probably waiting for him to stop yammering so she could continue her work. She merely smiled again and said, "You fight well, Colonel."

"Thanks." Ridge lifted a shoulder. He hadn't been hoping for compliments. "You might as well call me Ridge. For good or ill, I've given up on thinking of you as a prisoner."

A hint of wariness entered her eyes, and she lowered them to study the bandage roll. She picked at it, pulling out the end. He thought she might ask what he *did* think of her as, but her next question was, "Ridge... walker, isn't it? I had wondered..."

"Who gave me such a kooky name?" Ridge smirked. He got that a lot.

"Cocky was actually the descriptor that came to mind when I first heard it."

His smirk widened. He got that a lot too. "Either way, I have my dad to thank for it. He was—still is—a world explorer and spent a lot of time in the Dresdark Mountains, mapping the jungles and looking for, oh, I don't know. He told Mom he would come home with piles of gold someday. He never did. Didn't seem to bother him. He was delighted to show off his new maps. He made a bit of money selling them to universities and *real* treasure hunters. Anyway, he doesn't do it much anymore, but he always took his gear for climbing mountains. He's been up some of the highest ones. He thought I would follow in his footsteps."

Ridge knew he was telling her anything and everything about himself. He probably shouldn't be, though he doubted anything bad could come of sharing his distant past. If she were asking about military secrets, he would be much more wary. He ought to ask *her* a few things about herself, but he suspected he would only get lies. Again. Strange how he could come to care about a woman in two days, especially one who he should probably be considering an enemy. Or maybe it wasn't that strange. She had been trying to help all along. He smirked, remembering her charging up to make sure he didn't use the cannons for fear of burying the fort. And she *had* been responsible for recovering him and his men from the real avalanche. Amazingly, nobody had died in that event. Some of the buried men *would* have died, would have run out of air, if they had been waiting for the digging soldiers to randomly chance across them. However she had done it, her assistance had saved the lives of men he was responsible for.

"Do you want to sit up so I can wrap this around you?" Sardelle lifted the bandages.

Bandages, right. He had almost forgotten.

Ridge pushed himself up, which brought them closer together. He noticed the sprinkling of freckles across her nose and cheeks. He especially found himself noticing her lips, which pursed with concentration as she leaned close to encircle him with the bandage. He held his shirt up for her, wondering if she was admiring the view at all, or if this was simply one of thousands of chests she had seen as a healer. He liked to think his more nicely muscled and appealing than most, but he was doubtlessly biased. Whatever her background with chests, she seemed to be deep in thought as she wrapped his. She didn't notice when her black hair brushed his skin, creating the most delightful sensation. He wagered it would be soft to run his hands through. Too bad she was busy debating… who knew what? Maybe whether or not she should spill her secrets to him tonight. He wondered if *he* would have any luck seducing *her*. And wheedling out those secrets? Honestly, he would rather just have sex. Except he had promised her he wouldn't make any advances on her. Damn, what had he been thinking? And why was his mind running sprints from ear to ear? Searching for a justification to slip his hand behind her head and kiss her?

Sardelle tucked the bandage in and looked up, meeting his eyes for the first time. He struggled to smooth his face into something attentive, or at least not lustful. Though the way her face was tilted toward him, her hand lingering on his waist… was it possible she was thinking of more than first aid?

"Will I live, Doc?" Ridge asked.

"For the night at least. I can't make any promises as to the morning."

She had clearly meant it as a light comment, but it struck him to the core, instantly bringing an old quotation to mind. "The gods promise tomorrow to no man," he murmured.

"Barisky," she said.

Ridge chuckled. Of course she would know the author. Had it only been that morning she was summarizing the classics for him?

He didn't know how she would react, but he lifted a hand and brushed his knuckles against her hair. Despite enduring snow and killer owls, it was as soft as he had imagined. He leaned forward, watching her face for signs of rejection. Her eyes widened slightly, but she didn't pull away. Her lips parted, and that was all the invitation he needed.

* * *

Sardelle had been hoping for the kiss but not truly expecting it. That close, with nothing but a cocoon of rock and snow around them, she had sensed his emotions even when she had tried not to, and she had felt his response to her touch. She had also sensed that moment when he decided to act upon his response. His lips were warm, his taste even warmer. She leaned into him, happy to spend the night kissing, though it already saddened her to know how his feelings would change when he learned the truth.

A problem for tomorrow. Or maybe the snow would bury them, and this would be all they had. Might as well enjoy it.

She slipped her arms around his waist and under his shirt, enjoying the warmth of his skin, the hard ridges of muscle over his ribs. She had been identified as a gifted one young and had grown to adulthood within the Circle, wearing the robes of a sorceress. The only men who had ever dared approach her were other magic users, those who found her perfectly normal, not some strange being to be worshipped—or feared—and those men had rarely had the muscular frames of soldiers. Some of her sisters in the arts had donned costumes and gone out to find their lovers, but Sardelle had never had a taste for that, not for relationships that had no hope for a future.

So, what was different this time?

With his easy-going nature and quick smile, and the serious passion to his duty that lay beneath it all, Zirkander—*Ridge*—had made her care, made her want to protect him and to be protected by him. To be a team. Also, he kissed like a god, and she melted into his arms, the heat from his lips flowing through her nerves like wildfire.

He leaned back, drawing her down with him. Their lips parted for a moment, and Sardelle whispered, "Colonel—Ridge—are you trying to get convivial with me?"

"When I said I wouldn't?" His breath warmed her cheek; his dark eyes gleamed with humor. "Of course not. I just want to show my appreciation for your fine bandaging job."

She was lying on those bandages now. She wouldn't think it would be comfortable for him, but he was the one pulling her down. "I see. Very thoughtful."

His warm hand slid beneath her parka, massaging her back. "Can we go back to kissing now?"

"Yes." Sardelle wished she weren't wearing the thick wool dress, that his hands were tracing bare skin. But their breaths fogged the air, and cold air whispered in through the entrance. Taking off clothing didn't seem wise.

Perhaps Ridge sensed her problem, for he shifted onto his side, laid her on her back, and leaned in, protecting her from the draft. Her thick parka took the edge off the rocks, and, as his hands drifted across her body and his kisses deepened, she grew less and less aware of the cold. Everywhere he touched aroused heat, and by the time his hand found bare skin, she was breathing hard, charged with passion, cognizant of nothing but his lips, his tongue, his fingers, his hard body pressed against hers.

Sardelle had thought they might simply spend the evening kissing, whiling away the time while the storm raged, but she knew as soon as they started that she wanted more. His roaming hands and his deft tongue made her want... everything. Very little air separated them now, and she was certain he wanted everything too.

She slid one hand from his back, down to his lean waist,

enjoying the sensations as she stroked the rippling muscles of his abdomen, the dusting of hair tickling her fingers. She lowered her hand to his belt, but his lips pulled away from hers, and he whispered, "Don't."

A surge of disappointment filled her—had she read him wrong?

"Not yet," Ridge added and gave her a lazy smile. He kissed her again, leaving her breathless before his lips moved to her throat, then collarbone. She curled her fingers into his thick, short hair as he drifted lower, nipping and teasing her through the dress.

"Ridge," she whispered, having some notion of telling him there needed to be less clothing involved, winter be damned, but her thoughts tangled, and she couldn't get out more. All she knew was she didn't want him to stop.

His hand slid up her thigh, pushing the fabric of her dress up to her waist. Cold air nipped at her legs, but the contrast of the heat of his hand only made her shudder with pleasure. His mouth drifted lower, and his idea of showing his appreciation made her eyes roll back in her head. She was soon panting, digging her fists into the parka's fur lining, and calling his name. He refused to rush, though she urged him to when she could find the breath. That only made him grin up at her, his eyes crinkling, though the intensity infusing their depths never faded. He watched her as the stubble on his jaw rasped against her inner thigh, wanting to make sure she was enjoying his caresses. She wasn't sure why he cared, but knew he did, and she arched toward him, the knowledge and his touch filling her with waves of fiery euphoria.

When his lips returned to hers, they were hot and hungry, incensed with his own delayed need. She wrapped her arms and legs around him, wanting to please him as much as he had her. She ran her hand across his stomach, finding his belt again. He didn't stop her this time.

"Are you comfortable enough?" Ridge whispered between kisses.

She nodded. A thousand rocks could have been gouging her in the back, and she wouldn't have responded differently. He pulled her over anyway, putting his back to the rough ground. Part of her wanted to object—he had already suffered enough wounds for the day—but his hands found her hips, stroking her bare skin as he guided her onto him, and all conscious thought fled her mind. She gasped as he filled her, her hands finding his shoulders, fingers digging in, holding on as they rocked into each other. She wanted the moment to last forever, but passion built, sweeping through her, demanding release like an avalanche poised on a mountainside. The urgency of his kisses, the fire in his eyes, she knew he felt it too. They crashed together a final time, and ecstasy burst from within, coursing through her veins.

Shuddering, Sardelle dropped against his chest. She buried her face in the inviting warmth of his neck, inhaling the masculine scent of him, sweat and gun smoke, and the forest.

He nuzzled the side of her face and murmured, "You're amazing."

Her? What had *she* done? He had been everything. She wasn't sure she was ready to confess that, so she chose the lighter option. "Does that mean your wounds didn't bother you overmuch?"

"Didn't even notice 'em." His voice was muzzy. His hands still stroked her absently, but he seemed on the verge of sleep. "You must be a good doctor."

Sardelle *had* infused that awful tincture with a little magic to ensure the gouges would heal well, so she accepted this praise more easily. "I'll agree with that."

Ridge chuckled softly. She laid her head on his shoulder. The lantern had gone out at some point, and she was glad, for tears pricked her eyes. The night had been more than she expected. More than a way to while away the time. For both of them. Even if she hadn't sensed his feelings, his touch had shown that he cared. Her tears were because at some point, she either had to hurt him with the truth or walk away before he found out. Taking either action felt insurmountable.

Sardelle told herself to go to sleep, that she was ruining the moment by worrying. Best to enjoy this while she could. She kissed him one last time and snuggled into his drowsy embrace.

Chapter 8

THE OWL WAS GONE IN the morning. Ridge probably would have discovered this himself eventually, but he was still snuggled under the parkas with Sardelle when the shout came from outside. He sat up and shivered at the cold air that blasted him. His poor soldiers had doubtlessly had a less enjoyable night than he, so he wouldn't complain.

"Morning?" Sardelle murmured, her tousled locks flopped over her face.

"Yes." He pushed her hair back and kissed her.

She smiled and returned it, lifting a tender hand to stroke the side of his face. His heart danced at this simple gesture, trusting it meant that she was in no rush to rise, in no rush to forget their night together.

Reluctantly, he extricated himself. As much as he would have enjoyed spending more time with her, time he knew they wouldn't—*shouldn't*—have together once they returned to the fort, his duty compelled him to return as quickly as possible. The storm had passed, and a clear blue sky was brightening in the east. His men would be worried about him, just as he worried that the airship had swooped back in that direction after leaving that damned owl behind.

Ridge fastened his clothing, shivering. He didn't remember being cold last night, but maybe that was understandable. Body heat, indeed.

"I suppose no one will bring us coffee," Sardelle murmured, her clothing rustling as she, too, got ready.

"Not until we get back. Though I don't know if you'd like the stuff Lieutenant Kaosh makes. It's sludgy."

"Then I won't feel jealous that I'll not likely be invited to breakfast."

She didn't sound stung, but the words made him wince nonetheless. Yes, as far as the rest of the fort knew, she was a prisoner, someone he definitely shouldn't be sleeping with, and even if she wasn't truly a prisoner, he probably still shouldn't be sleeping with her. Last night, he had been too busy launching campaigns from his trousers to remember that fact. If she would just *tell* him who she was and what she wanted...

But no, if she could, she would have. He had sensed that a few times, when she had been gazing at him, *almost* saying something.

"We'll figure something out," he mumbled, though he couldn't imagine what.

Shifting rock outside of their cave let him escape from the moment without further promises.

"Sir?"

"Yes, Rav. We're fine."

Ridge was glad he and Sardelle were fully clothed—she even had her pack on already—when the soldier peered inside, though he had a feeling the fact that he had spent the night in a cave alone with her would be all around the fort within an hour of their return. At which point all sorts of speculation would occur. Oh, well. He had more important things to worry about than fort gossip. Besides, it wasn't until the news made its way back to his commanding officer that he truly had to worry.

"Owl's gone," Rav said.

"Yes, time to get back." Ridge grabbed his pack and rifle, but hesitated before trooping out. Rav had climbed down out of view, so he paused to give Sardelle a one-armed hug and murmur, "I'll find a way to get some coffee to you. Any other breakfast requests?"

She kissed him on the cheek—it couldn't feel that nice with a day's beard growth poking out of it, but she didn't seem to mind. "Those mango pastries sound good."

"I'm afraid I would have to take you back to civilization to find one of those. A basic pastry might be doable."

"I'll look forward to it."

Ridge squeezed her one more time, knowing it would be the last for a while, then climbed out of the hole. The soldiers were all waiting at the bottom, their packs and snowshoes on. Belatedly, it occurred to him to wonder if he had any lipstick smears across his face or bite marks on his neck. No, Sardelle hadn't been wearing any makeup—where would she get it in that pit of a fortress?—and she had been enthusiastic, but still on the refined side, and worried about putting weight on his wounds. As if he would have noticed. She probably wouldn't bite him until their *second* night in a cave.

That thought had Ridge grinning, but he managed to rein it in by the time he reached the bottom. The first question he got was whether they should try to dig Nakkithor's body out of the snow, and that sobered him right up. He and Sardelle helped retrieve the dead soldier and build a travois, then Ridge led the way out of the canyon. The snow had blurred their trail but not swallowed it whole, though he could have found his way regardless. He might not have all the combat assets these infantrymen did, but he didn't get lost, not even when he was upside down, streaking away from an airship with cannonballs flying by on either side.

It doubtlessly marked him as crazy, but the memory of that battle filled him with nostalgia and a longing for home. He wondered if Sardelle would like his little cabin on the lake. Not that she would ever visit it… She would finish whatever she had come here for and then disappear, sneaking out past the guards as easily as she had the last time. And if she took something from the mines, it would be treason if he let her go without trying to stop her. At the least, it would be ineptitude. He had never thought his record was in danger of being stamped with either label. A first time for everything. Unless he locked her up until she talked. That would be a lovely reward for last night.

The fortress came into view more quickly than he expected, or maybe his thoughts had kept him busy and he hadn't noticed the trek. Men had been working to clear the east wall, so one couldn't simply run down the hill of snow and into the courtyard, but it would be some time before evidence of the avalanche was completely gone.

The gate opened before they arrived, and Ridge found

Captain Heriton waiting in the courtyard, along with a couple of burly soldiers and a scruffy prisoner with shifty eyes.

"Uh oh," Sardelle murmured behind him.

Before Ridge could ask for clarification, the prisoner thrust his arm toward her. "She's the one."

Captain Heriton nodded slowly, as if he had known all along. Ridge met Sardelle's eyes and found concern there. Was her secret about to come out?

"What is this, Captain?" Ridge asked, his palms suddenly damp inside his mittens. If her secret turned her from an uncertainty to a known enemy, what would he do?

"This is the man you had us detain, the one who supposedly killed the woman in the washroom."

"He denies it?"

"No, he admits it since he claims she was a witch and had put a curse on him, on his loins specifically. He's had a rash ever since. He assumed she had done it because he'd tried to coerce her into a sexual relationship. She threatened him apparently." Heriton wriggled his fingers, as if these details were dismissible, but his eyes sharpened as he launched into the rest of his explanation. "In interviewing him, I discovered that your... friend—" the captain extended a hand toward Sardelle, "—was also a suspect, albeit one this prisoner couldn't reach to interrogate since she's so often been with you. But it seems she was also present when this man developed his rash. He had just found her down in a mine shaft."

"Not a shaft," the shifty-eyed prisoner said. "She was *in* the rocks. It was odder than a three-legged parrot. We had to dig her out. Rescued her. She wasn't grateful like you'd expect though. Crazy woman ran past us while we were bent over."

"Because of... a rash?" Ridge asked.

The man nodded, crossed his legs, and dropped his hands protectively over his crotch. "Most painful itchy thing I've ever had."

Ridge gave Sardelle a curious look, but her face had gone expressionless. She didn't even offer a these-people-are-obviously-crazy eyebrow raise.

"It's odd enough that a woman would have made it down into the mines," Heriton said, "when the trams are operated by soldiers, and they're the only way in and out."

Possibly. Someone could slip down into the mines without using one of the cages. The diagonal shafts were steep, but not *that* steep. Sardelle was obviously gifted at sneaking in and out of places. Ridge reminded himself to question the gate guards later. For now, he remained silent and nodded for the captain to continue.

"It's even odder that she would be all the way down at the end of a new tunnel, in the rock itself, if this man can be believed."

"This self-confessed murderer?" Ridge couldn't keep from asking. How reliable a witness should they consider him?

"I got no reason to lie about this," the shifty man said. "I know what I seen."

"It's hardly the only unusual thing that's happened revolving around this woman," Heriton said. "I've been wondering if it's a coincidence that the Cofah showed up on the same day she did."

"They showed up on the same day *I* did as well," Ridge said.

"*You're* a national hero. She's... " Heriton groped in the air, as if he couldn't get a grasp on Sardelle. At least Ridge wasn't the only one. "I'll be blunt, sir," the captain went on. "It makes me uneasy having her walk around here at your side, like she's your trusted aide. I... I'd like to discuss this further with you in private."

"Yup, I figured you would." Ridge sighed. Inviting Sardelle up for coffee was going to be every bit as unlikely as he had feared. "I have a funeral service to arrange and five thousand other things to do, but I'll talk to you this afternoon."

"Very good, sir."

"Now, go find work. All of you." He shooed the captain and the rest of the soldiers away, until only Sardelle remained, her hands clasped behind her back as she gazed up at the mountains. Ridge would have paid a lot to know her thoughts. "You'd better go back to work and stay out of trouble for a few days, at least until something else distracts Heriton." He smiled at her, though he felt guilty for sending her back to the laundry and those crowded barracks rather than finding her a nice room. His room, perhaps? The problem was, he shared all of the captain's concerns. Whatever she had been looking for down in the mines when she had been discovered, Ridge doubted very much that his superiors would want him to give it to her.

"Work?" Sardelle asked. "I thought I had the day off. Eight days off, wasn't it?"

The book reports. Right. He almost told her that the days off wouldn't start right away, but curiosity changed the lay of his tongue. "What would you do if those days off started today?"

"Research in the prison library. I thought I'd try to find your flier for you."

"My what?"

"The flier you were talking about yesterday, the one that crashed ten years ago." Sardelle spread a hand. "Maybe you could drag it back here and fix it up so you would have a way to defend against further incursions from the airship."

He frowned. He had caught her hesitation and suspected she'd had something else in mind for research until this inspiration struck. Yet, this was exactly the right thing to say to win him over. If he could find that flier and fix it somehow, he wouldn't have to stalk uselessly back and forth on the ramparts when enemy airships flew circles around the fort.

"Three days," he grumbled. Ridge hadn't even known her for three days, and she already had intimate knowledge of the controls on his dashboard.

"Pardon?" Sardelle asked.

"Nothing. Go. Research." Ridge waved. "The library is on the second floor over there. I'm skeptical you'll find it particularly extensive or useful though. I doubt records of crashes are kept in there."

"I won't know until I look." Sardelle bowed her head toward him. "Thank you."

Such a formal parting of ways. It seemed a crime after their intimacies in the cave. Yet this was how it had to be. He shambled off in the other direction, heading for his office, his heart feeling like a crashed flier.

***

Colonel Zirkander hadn't been exaggerating about the library. Ridge, Sardelle reminded herself with a smile. He had invited her to use his first name. It wouldn't be appropriate in public, with half of his men giving her hard, suspicious looks, but she would think about him that way. Nobody here had access to her thoughts, fortunately.

She ran a finger along the backs of the dusty tomes lining the library's single bookcase. She recognized many of the titles from his list. A few gaps on the shelves suggested that at least some of the prisoners had taken him up on his offer and were going to try to read the classics. Sardelle had been lucky so many of them were old enough that they had been classics even when she had gone to school. Albeit that book on flight hadn't been anything she had read. Jaxi had coached her through summarizing it.

You're welcome.

Sardelle smiled. *Do you have any idea where the crashed flying machine might be?*

No good morning first? You simply want to send me straight into researching for you?

I apologize. Good morning, Jaxi. I'd like to thank you for your discretion last night.

Discretion? You mean the fact that I kept my mental lips shut so you could make the rocks shake with your colonel?

Sardelle blushed, though it wasn't as if she had any secrets from her soul-linked sword of nearly twenty years.

Three hundred and twenty years. And don't I always stay out of your head when you're being intimate with someone?

Yes, though it's been so long that I thought you might have forgotten my preferences.

As I recall, scrawny sorcerers with ink smudges on their fingertips are your usual preferences. I must say the colonel was a welcome change.

Sardelle's heart quickened at the memory of how *much* of a change Ridge had been, how enticing it had been to run her hands over his lean, muscular body... *That's why I want to find his flying machine for him.*

She made herself focus on the task at hand, pulling a journal from the shelf, one hand-written by a general from two decades past. It was too old to have anything to do with the crash, but maybe it would contain information on common flight routes or something of that nature.

So he'll feel so grateful that he will send his minions digging in my direction?

Something like that.

Just don't forget your mission here. I doubt you're going to have much time left to act freely.

As long as Ridge is commanding, I don't think I'm likely to end up in shackles.

If swords could shrug, Jaxi did. *If I were you, I wouldn't presume too much. He's loyal to his military, and you're a problem as far as that military is concerned. Don't get cocky because he slept with you. It's not like there are many options here.*

Thank you for your bluntness. When you're not busy sounding like a teenager, you sound like my grandmother.

Just so long as you know I know what's best.

You're just grumpy because you don't think I'm working to free you, but that was my original intent in coming to the library. Sardelle sat at the room's only table and opened the journal she had selected. *If I can figure out what they're looking for in these mines, and there's a way I can help them find it, I'm sure I could get a tunnel dug in your direction.*

You haven't figured that out yet? Jaxi sounded genuinely surprised.

No...

Laughter echoed in Sardelle's head. A lot of laughter. She imagined Jaxi wiping tears before asking her next question. *Why didn't you ask?*

Sardelle scratched her head. *I thought I had.*

Hm. I don't remember that. Anyway, the magical mystical energy sources these soldiers would die defending are... lamps.

Lamps?

Yeah, those illumination prisms that hung on the ceilings in rooms and tunnels throughout our complex.

Sardelle leaned back in the chair, picturing the glowing white light sources. *And they call those crystals?*

The rock does take on sort of a crystalline texture when it's melted and fused, then imbued with power.

Well, I was right to be befuddled that they were mining in the backside of the mountain then. That must be where they first chanced across them. I guess we had tunnels—and lamps illuminating them—back there, though there would be a lot more in the main living areas.

Yes, and I'm quite sure there are a couple in the room you left me in too.

Sardelle nodded slowly. *Yes, I can lead them right to you. Or close anyway. I'll have to sneak back down there and pull you out myself. If they find you first, and I take you, they'll call it theft and chase me halfway across the world.*

Nah, I can make sure they have no interest in me. Rashes are the least of the things I can do to any grubby miner who puts his hands on me.

Sardelle choked at the imagery that flashed through her mind, courtesy of Jaxi. *I think your three-hundred-year imprisonment has made you punchy.*

If by punchy you mean filled with bitterness, loneliness, and barely contained vitriol, you are correct. I'm aching to return to work. And I'm quite curious to see how the world has changed. A ride in an airship would be fabulous.

I'll see what I can arrange once we're the masters of our own fate again. Now, if I can just find that wreck, I'll have a reason to report to Ridge's office.

Get a map. I'll show you where it is. I don't know how serviceable that flier will be after ten years in the sun, wind, and snow, but if it'll make your man happy...

You already found it?

Yes, did you think our conversation was consuming all of my vast mental resources? I am a soulblade, you know. Powerful and gifted.

And cocky.

Naturally.

Sardelle was poking through a rack of maps, searching for a topographical one of the mountains, when the door creaked open. She looked up, hoping for Ridge, though she couldn't imagine what would have brought him by so soon. It had only been a half hour. He couldn't be missing her yet, though maybe he had been thinking of her and how delightful it would be to share that coffee with her.

Now who's cocky?

Hush.

It wasn't Ridge but a young soldier who entered, a soldier carrying a steaming mug of coffee and a couple of books under his arm. He was watching the black liquid carefully as he walked; it was filled to the brim and threatened to slosh over. Her first thought was that he had the morning off and had come to use the library as well. She started to push her book to one side so he would have room to join her if he wished, but he stopped at the head of the table and set the mug and the books down in front of her. He also dug a slightly smashed muffin out of his pocket and laid it next to the coffee.

"Ma'am, Colonel Zirkander sends these items with his well wishes for the success of your research."

"Oh, thank you. Thank him for me, please."

"Yes, ma'am."

He remembered, Sardelle thought as the soldier strode out, closing the door behind him. *I think I'm in love.*

I may gag. Do you have my map yet?

Just a moment. Let me see what he sent. Sardelle opened the first book. It was a journal like the other one, but more recent, written by a general's assistant from… yes, dates ranging from twelve to nine years ago. The crash should have happened during that time. The second book was an atlas.

There you go. Don't you love him now too?

He does *have a sexy chest.*

Sardelle snorted and flipped through the pages, finding the correct mountain.

That's the spot. Jaxi used her finger, guiding it across the contour lands. Sardelle always felt it a little strange when the soulblade took control, but, as an early instructor had pointed out, it was only fair given that humans got to swing swords around whenever they wished. Once Jaxi had even ambulated her unconscious body after a battle, moving Sardelle to a safe spot where she wouldn't be captured by the enemy.

An image flashed through her mind of a narrow, snow-covered plateau overlooking a ravine with a river and a lot of jagged rocks far below.

You're saying it will be difficult to retrieve, eh?

There's a reason the only thing the soldiers recovered after the crash was the power source.

Maybe Ridge can disassemble it somehow. Or bring out a team and repair it up on that plateau. If I had a schematic, I'm sure I could help.

Better leave it to him, Jaxi thought. *I doubt he's going to believe you're an engineer* and *an archaeologist.*

Possibly right. Sardelle pushed back her chair.

Where are you going?

To tell him, of course.

You've only been in here for thirty-seven minutes, and you've only had his books for seven. Don't you think he might find that efficiency a little unlikely?

You may be right. Sardelle settled back in the chair and picked up the coffee mug. She took a sip. It wasn't as sludgy as Ridge had threatened. Maybe he had put someone else on coffee-making duty this morning. *An hour? That would be long enough, wouldn't it?*

You just want to see him again, don't you? I am definitely going to gag.

Careful. You wouldn't want to inhale a rock.

* * *

Ridge stifled a yawn as he followed Captain Bosmont, the engineer responsible for keeping the mine machinery in working order, to the bottom of yet another tram line. The officer hopped out of the cage and pointed at the pulley system at the bottom. "This is the last one, sir. Let me get the part number for you."

The captain rolled up his sleeves, dug a wrench and pliers out of the coveralls he wore over his uniform, and clanked and tugged at bolts the size of apples. The burly officer had shoulders and forearms that would have impressed a smith, along with tattoos that covered most of the skin Ridge could see, including one of the schematic of a dragon flier. That had been what had convinced Ridge to work past his office hours, following the man around and writing down his parts requests. A private could have handled the job, but on the off chance Sardelle found the location of the downed flier, it wouldn't hurt to make friends with the fort engineer.

"Need a hand?" Ridge asked.

"Nah, I got it. You make yourself comfortable, sir. This'll just take a minute."

Ridge eyed the open chamber, with its six mineshafts shooting off at irregular intervals, and wondered where one might find comfort. Perhaps he could sit on one of the rusty ore carts lined up on the rail. He yawned again, not bothering to hide it this time. Though he and Sardelle must have been stuck in that cave for twelve hours, he didn't remember getting all that much sleep. How odd.

The captain glanced over, and Ridge wiped the smug expression off his face. "I appreciate you coming down here, sir. And ordering the parts. The general always said there wasn't any money in the budget, and he expected me to make do. Well, you can only make do for so long before things start busting, and when stuff breaks down here, people get hurt or killed."

"There wasn't money in the budget because he had no idea how many people were actually working here, so he had to overestimate on his supply orders. That's been fixed now, so we'll only be ordering what's needed and nothing extra."

Bosmont nodded and pulled out a torso-sized part that must have weighed a hundred pounds. His voice wasn't at all strained when he said, "Number's on the back, sir, if you want to write it down. 'Preciate it, thanks."

Ridge hurried to do so, so the captain could return the clunky piece before he threw his back out. After he refastened his bolts, they headed for a cage up to the top.

"You ever work on fliers?" Ridge waved toward the man's tattoo.

"My first duty station, sir. Love them babies. Got to fly a couple times, too, but nothing like what you do of course." Bosmont threw the lever to start them up the tramline.

"*Did.*" Ridge sighed.

"Yeah, was wondering about that. Seems a waste, them sending you here when you could be blowing up enemy airships. How, ah, did that come to be, if you don't mind my asking?"

"I threatened to rip off the wrong diplomat's cock."

It was hard to tell in the dark cage, but Ridge thought the man looked at him in shocked silence. It was silent for a moment, anyway, with nothing except the clank and grind of the cage rolling up the rails. Then Bosmont laughed.

"Something similar happened to me, sir."

"With a diplomat?"

"Nah, with a commanding officer."

"Well, I trust now that we've bonded like this, I won't have to worry about such threats from you."

"No, sir. Glad to have you here."

They stepped out of the cage up top, and Bosmont shook his hand before walking off, whistling a tune. Ridge wished all men were so easily pleased.

He turned, intending to make sure nothing important had been left on his desk before finding his rack, and almost tripped over someone in the dark.

"Sorry, Colonel," came Sardelle's voice from beneath the hood of a parka. Did she have it pulled up because of the cold, or because she was skulking about and didn't want anyone to see her? Or maybe she wanted to secret him off to some dark corner for a repeat of the previous night's activities? That would be scandalous, completely inappropriate and... appealing. "I've been trying to meet with you all day," she said, "but your captain wouldn't let me in the admin building to see you."

"He wouldn't?" Ridge squashed irritation at the captain. Heriton was just doing his job, however annoying certain aspects of that job were at the moment. "I apologize for that. What did you want to see me about?"

"I believe I've found the location of your flier, and I think I can help you find something else too." She glanced toward a pair of miners heading out of a tram cage and toward the mess hall. "You might wish to discuss it in private. And I need some light to show you on the map." She held up the atlas he had sent her.

"The furnace should still be warm in my office."

"I'll follow you. I'm fairly certain the captain won't deny *you* entrance."

"I should hope not."

Heriton had left for the day, so nobody charged out to deny anything. Ridge was relieved. He knew he would get more concerned looks if the captain saw him taking Sardelle up to his office. Ridge had been too busy working and watching the skies for returning Cofar ships to worry about rumors and gossip during the day, but he didn't doubt that word of his night spent alone in the cave with Sardelle would have gotten around and that Heriton would have heard. The captain had made it clear that while he respected Ridge very much, yes, sir, he suspected Sardelle was a witch who had put a hex on him, something to make him sympathetic to her cause. Whatever that was. Maybe he was about to find out. He doubted she had spent the whole day researching flier crashes.

Ridge stepped inside the office and turned up a couple of lamps. He thought about inviting her to sit with him on the couch—perhaps doing *more* than sitting—but she went straight to business, laying the atlas out on his desk and opening it to a page she had dog-eared. She had circled and X-ed a spot on the southern side of the mountain. "It's been exposed to the elements on the top of a cliff for ten years, so I don't know if there's hope for making it flight-worthy again, but you can check at least."

"Yes, I'll send out a team." And hope there were no owls haunting that side of the mountain. "Thank you. And there was something else?"

"Yes." Sardelle had pushed back the hood of her parka, and her black hair tumbled around the silvery fox fur rim, making for an eye-catching contrast. She looked around the office. "May I see the mine map again?"

Ridge pulled it out from behind the bookcase. While he

spread it out, Sardelle grabbed a pen out of a drawer.

"You're going to mark up the official copy?" he asked.

"With likely locations of crystals, if that's all right?"

His breath caught. She couldn't possibly know, could she? With the mine producing so few of them, getting them back from crashed fliers was always paramount, and every time one went missing meant a reprimand on someone's record, even if the pilot had been facing overwhelming odds. Ridge had heard rumors that there weren't any left in the king's vaults. He couldn't let that information out, though, not to Sardelle, not to anyone who might repeat it.

"So long as it's not graffiti," Ridge said, making his voice casual.

"I'll try to restrain my doodling tendencies."

Sardelle bent, one hand on the map and one holding the pen. Ridge held his breath. She marked an X, then another, and a few more. "These are approximate, of course, based on my studies of the Referatu. The maps I've seen were from before the mountain was bombed."

Ridge, noticing his mouth was dangling open, snapped it shut. "Where and when did you study these people so closely?" And how could she know so much about the history of an area owned and operated by the government when he had known so little? Though he supposed the military had only been mining here for fifty years or so. Before that, perhaps someone else had been doing research? He had no idea, in truth. Maybe he needed to spend some time in the library. "I can't imagine it was during your days as a pirate."

"No."

"I only mention this because Heriton found your record." Ridge pulled the folder out of a drawer. "It actually confirms the story you were telling the other day, if you can imagine that."

Sardelle didn't appear surprised or uncertain in the least. She gave him that serene smile and said, "I must be more honest than I sound."

"I think not." Ridge suspected she had planted the record. If she could sneak in and out of the guarded fort and the guarded mines, the archives room wouldn't present that much of a challenge.

She spread her hands. "There are a lot more crystals off the edge here. I can point more out to you if you have another map of the other half of the mountain, but maybe you want to see if you can verify these first."

Ridge tossed the folder back into the drawer and studied all the Xs she had made. Eight. If he found crystals in half of those locations, he would probably get an award when he got back home.

"I would have told you sooner, if I had known what you were looking for," Sardelle said. "It was only when I was digging around in the library that I came across the information."

"And what are *you* looking for?" Ridge gazed into her eyes. "While I appreciate all this assistance, especially if something comes of it, I'm quite certain you didn't come here for me."

"What brought me here was largely an accident."

"But you're searching for something. Nobody stays here without a purpose."

"No," she murmured, gazing at the dark night beyond the window.

Ridge thought about taking her hand, but clasped his hands behind his back instead. This was a professional discussion, not anything else. Though maybe she could be teased into sharing more if he confessed the times he had considered finding creative ways to extract information from her. "I knew I should have tried my seduction plan."

That pulled her attention back to him. She raised an elegant eyebrow and murmured, "Hm?"

"At one point, it crossed my mind that you might be here to seduce me. Then I decided you weren't and thought perhaps I should attempt to seduce you, so I could learn your innermost secrets. But I was afraid I lacked the sexual allure and charisma for the task."

Her lips curved upward. "The deceit required for the task, more likely."

"So my allure is fine?" Ridge wiggled his eyebrows.

"It's quite nice."

"Good to know." He tapped a finger on the freshly marked map. "I am going to keep trying to wheedle the information out of you until you relent. I hope that fact won't damage my allure overmuch."

"So long as you keep delivering me coffee in the mornings."

"Any particular care over which of these Xs we mine toward first?"

Sardelle pointed at two in close proximity. Interesting. They were down deep and not particularly close to the shaft where she had supposedly been discovered wandering.

"If you tell me what you're looking for… " Ridge started, though he wasn't quite sure where he was going with the offer.

"You'll help me find it?" she asked, her tone dry. She must understand that the military considered all of this their property and anything found within the mountain theirs.

Ridge licked his lips. He had to be careful. To promise anything that hinted of treason… he couldn't do that. But if she could truly help him find crystals, and what she wanted lacked in military significance, then what would it matter if he never mentioned it in his reports? He closed his eyes. The thought of withholding information from his superiors made him uncomfortable. But maybe he didn't have to withhold it. The crystals were of paramount importance. He would be justified in trading something valuable for them.

"Though I fully acknowledge that what's in that mountain isn't mine to trade, I think I could make it work for my reports if I received crystals in exchange for something else. So long as it's not some huge ancient weapon that will be used to destroy the continent."

"This is my homeland too. I wouldn't do anything to harm it."

He believed her. And it sent a wave of relief through him. "Good."

Sardelle studied the map, or maybe the floor at her feet, or maybe nothing. Ridge felt her debating with herself and didn't say anything. He had already pushed enough. If she didn't— couldn't—trust him, he understood. He had suspected from the beginning that they were on conflicting sides.

Finally, she looked up, meeting his eyes. "It's a sword."

"A sword?"

"A six-hundred-year-old Referatu soulblade."

Part II

Chapter 9

Sardelle had known it would get colder, but she wasn't ready for how much colder. Now she understood why her people had put their homes *inside* the mountain instead of on it. If they had been less feared, maybe they wouldn't have had to use such a remote part of the world, but relationships with mundanes had always seemed to work better with separation. Until that didn't work anymore either.

Sardelle sipped from a coffee mug—she had another mug in her hand, a cover over it in a vain attempt to keep it from chilling—and watched as Ridge and his engineer friend worked on the rusted flying machine now residing in the center of the courtyard, its dragon "feet" perched near the frozen stream. There wasn't a building large enough to house it, and there wasn't room to work on it anywhere else. Just getting it here had been a gargantuan chore, she understood. It had come in pieces, pulled around and across the mountain in stages by strange machines the engineer had said were usually used in the logging industry. Whatever route it had taken, it was here now, and the miners, soldiers, and even the women working the laundry room were taking bets as to whether it would ever fly again. Given the amount of snow that had fallen overnight—there were at least nine new inches blanketing its metallic carapace and wings—Sardelle wasn't even sure it would be able to remain standing upright through the day.

Like everyone else working up top, she checked the sky

often. It had been nearly three weeks since the encounter with the airship and the owl. She wanted to believe the Cofah had forgotten about the fort and had gone home, but she suspected they were still out there. Ridge thought so, too, and there was an urgency about the way he worked on the flier, as if the small one-man craft could stave off an attack from an airship that claimed a sorcerer among its passengers. He said they had the cold and the snow to thank for the peaceful days, citing airships' sensitivity to changing weather conditions and thin air, but Sardelle wondered if the other sorcerer had sensed her somehow, and if they were acting more warily because of her presence. She would have preferred to be a surprise, someone to lie in wait if needed, especially since she couldn't reveal to her allies that she had powers. She wasn't all that certain she was a match for this jungle shaman anyway. Maybe once she had Jaxi…

Ridge had ordered new tunnels opened in the directions she had indicated, and they had already found three crystals. It was the reason she was allowed to stand around, drinking coffee and watching the men work, even though she had run out of days off some time ago. It was also the reason Ridge had a bounce to his step, she assumed. Or maybe that was because he was working on a flier, however rusted and dilapidated. She knew it didn't have anything to do with bedroom exploits, since she hadn't been invited up to his room for any of those. Not that she had expected it here in the fort, where she was under scrutiny from Captain Heriton and several others—she hadn't had to use her mental faculties to catch whispered gossip going around about her. Ridge himself must be under scrutiny from associating with her too. No, she hadn't been expecting exploits, but she did miss them. At the least, it would be enjoyable to try bedroom activities with an actual bed. The lumpy, rocky cave had made things a little awkward, though she had found the experience quite enjoyable. The memory could still cause her to smile into her coffee.

"Morning," Ridge said, ambling over in his full parka, fur cap, and mittens, all three smeared with grease. For a pilot, he definitely had a hands-on approach to flier repairs.

Sardelle tamped down the urge to wipe off a smear on his nose. Even though it was snowing again—or maybe it was still snowing, as she couldn't remember the last time it had stopped for more than five minutes—there were people in the courtyard, miners tramping off to work and soldiers in the middle of shift changes. "Good morning, Colonel." She handed him the second mug. "How is the progress?"

This had become a ritual, her showing up with coffee, asking after his progress, and him spending a few minutes chatting with her about it. Just because he wasn't sending her invitations for midnight trysts didn't mean he didn't care, or wouldn't *like* to send those invitations. In the meantime, he smiled and chatted amiably with her, and despite the frozen courtyard setting and the walls of cannons surrounding them, she had come to find a comfortable familiarity in the daily sharing of their morning coffee. She looked forward to it.

"With the flier, about the same. We're building an engine from scratch from scrap parts pillaged from around the fort. I swear Captain Bosmont was eyeing the cook's metal pans this morning in the mess." Ridge removed the cover on his coffee and took a big gulp. "The miners also found another crystal last night." He beamed at her, and Sardelle melted a little inside at his obvious pleasure. "That makes four. I won't need to worry so much about testing the flier now."

"Because you'll need to borrow one of the crystals for it?" It still floored her that these people were using three-hundred-year-old lamps to power their flying machines.

"Because this pile of wings and rust might fall out of the sky and plunge to the bottom of a canyon on its test run. It would be difficult for anyone to retrieve the crystal then."

Sardelle blinked at him. She knew it was questionable whether they would actually be able to get the flier in the air, but had assumed they would know if it was feasible before risking their lives. "And its pilot as well?"

"Well, I'm not sure they would bother going down to scrape his pulverized bones off the rocks. But the crystal, that's valuable." Amazingly, he smirked as he described this scenario. He had to be joking.

"You're a unique individual, Ridge Zirkander," Sardelle murmured. She didn't use his first name when anyone was close enough to hear, but believed the snow would insulate their voices from those crossing to the trams behind them.

"I've heard that a lot in my life, though usually with cursing rather than fond smiles. You must be unique yourself."

Sardelle smiled into her cup again. "I think you've already figured that out."

He grunted. "I still haven't figured out much about you. No signs of swords down there yet. Do you think we're close?"

Sardelle shook her head. Though she had relented and told Ridge what she sought, she hadn't plotted a direct shaft to it on his map. So long as the miners, with their powerful explosives and constant shoring up and supporting of the tunnels they built, got close, she should be able to drill the rest of the way in.

"If the men do find it, will it look like anything other than a sword?" Ridge hadn't asked much about it when she had revealed it as the item she sought; if anything, he had surprised her with his lack of surprise, but she supposed it fit with this relic-hunting archaeologist persona he had constructed for her. "Will it... it won't be a danger to them, will it? Burn them if they touch it or something like that?"

"Of course not." Sardelle lost her smile. "The Referatu weren't evil."

"Uh huh, that's not what the history books say." Ridge frowned as well, giving her that concerned look he did every time she spoke of magic, like he was worried for her soul.

What was she going to do if he found out the truth about her? For that matter, what was she going to do when she got the sword? At that point, she could leave, unless she somehow wanted to try and dig out more artifacts. She wasn't sure how she would do that, but it did irk her a bit, imagining the descendants of those who had buried her people alive coming back later to paw through their belongings.

"What will you do when you find it?" Ridge asked.

Indeed, just the question on her mind. "Study it," she said, though she already knew Jaxi's every inner and outer contour intimately. Sardelle had a vague notion of traveling the world and trying to find more of her people, descendants of them anyway. Not *everyone* had been at that birthday celebration. Almost everyone had been—which was no doubt why their enemies had chosen that day to attack—but more people than her had to have survived. Had they fled the continent? Were they hiding in some distant corner of the world? Would they welcome her into whatever community they had managed to create? Or could she somehow live amongst the mundanes and be happy?

"Back at some university, I suppose," Ridge said, studying the liquid in his cup.

"Aside from one handsome and generous fort commander, I have not found many people to welcome me here."

"And he's not enough of a reason to stay?"

Sardelle swallowed. This was the first time he had suggested he wanted her to. "I…"

"It wouldn't be forever. Just a year. Eleven months and five days now. Not that I have a calendar I'm marking on my desk or anything." Ridge gave her that quirky smile of his, the one that made his eyes glint as if he were planning some mischief. "I have a much nicer place down near the coast. A little cabin in the woods, next to a lake with some great fishing. It's very private and peaceful. Did I mention private? Nothing except the raccoons and owls—normal-sized non-freaky owls—to pay attention to what's going on out there at night."

"I see, and if I were to stay here for a year—" or go off and check on the world and on her people and then come back for him in a year… "—would I be working in the laundry and sleeping in a tiny bunk surrounded by dozens of snoring women the whole time?"

"I'm quite certain you've only worked in the laundry one day so far," Ridge said dryly.

"True enough, but there's only been one night when I haven't slept in the snore chamber." Sardelle wriggled her brows at him.

"Yes, I've regretted that, but I've felt somewhat inhibited with Captain Heriton next door. The man has actually had the gall to knock on my door before dawn a couple of times and glance behind me to see if anyone else is in the room. I'm going to have to make sure he's not slipping any reports onto the supply ship. I don't need a spy in my own camp. Assuming that supply ship ever comes." He looked to the cloudy sky. "They should have been here four days ago."

Sardelle didn't want to talk about supply ships. She wanted to find a way to circumvent his spies. Of course she couldn't tell him that she could insulate his walls and keep the nosy captain from hearing anything. "Perhaps a less closely monitored location?" she suggested.

Ridge pulled his gaze from the clouds. "Oh?"

"Would anyone think it odd if you visited the library in the evening for some quiet reading time?"

"Reading time, eh? You don't think the library will be packed with miners eager to check out the classics?"

Sardelle grinned. "Have you had anyone take you up on that yet?"

"Actually, yes. I listened to four book summaries just yesterday afternoon, delivered in between pickaxe blows on the sixth level, since their supervisors wouldn't let them leave to come up to see me."

"Good. Now as to the library hours… perhaps later, we would be less likely to run into earnest readers. There is, after all, only the one table. Which we might like to use." Sardelle wasn't used to propositioning men—those with the nerve to do so usually asked her—so she wasn't sure if she came off as smooth or awkward.

Ridge grinned and bumped his shoulder against hers. "Goodness woman, you're either as libidinous as I am, or you're willing to do anything to get out of sleeping in that barracks room."

"It *is* a less than restful environment."

Ridge winked and opened his mouth, doubtlessly to suggest the library table wouldn't be restful, either, but a shout of "Colonel Zirkander" came from the ramparts, and he turned away, the humor in his eyes disappearing.

More than one soldier was pointing toward the western sky.

At first, Sardelle couldn't see anything other than snow, but then she picked out a dark balloon hugging the heavy gray clouds as it flew over the peaks toward them. The markings were different than that of the Cofah aircraft, all grays and blacks instead of gold and wood tones, and it had an enclosed cabin rather than an open ship design where one could see people standing on the deck.

"That's our supply ship," Ridge said, fishing in his pocket for something.

"That's good."

Now Ridge would have an opportunity to send word back to his headquarters about the enemy ship. It shouldn't be long until reinforcements arrived.

"Except that it shouldn't be coming in on that route, and I think that's..." Ridge extended the spyglass he had dug out of his pocket and watched the sky.

Alerted by the tension in his voice, Sardelle reached out with her senses. The ship was still far away, but she immediately felt the emotions of the people aboard because they were so intense. There wasn't much of a crew—two, no three—but they were all scared. Terrified.

"Smoke," Ridge said. "They've been struck." He raised his voice to yell at the soldiers on the ramparts. "Ready the weapons. We might have company." He gave Sardelle a quick, grim look, handed her his coffee mug, then ran for the stairs.

The clanks coming from the flier paused, and the big engineer stuck his head out. "Sir, you going to want me at the—"

"Keep working on the flier, Captain," Ridge answered as he raced up the stairs. "We may need it sooner than we thought."

Sardelle, remembering the image he had painted of a possible failed launch, grimaced. She returned her attention to the incoming airship. There weren't any other vessels in the sky, at least not that she could see or sense, but—no, wait. At the very edge of her reach, behind the mountain peak, there was a familiar presence. The Cofah airship. It didn't seem to be coming closer. Indeed, she had the sense that the captain was struggling with the wind and the snow, but it didn't matter. It had already damaged its target.

By now, a spyglass wasn't needed to see the smoke streaming out of the gray airship's engines. Sardelle wondered if she could do anything to fix the problem, or at least slow the craft's descent. It was streaking across the sky more quickly than she thought might be normal for an airship, dropping altitude at an alarming speed. Its balloon wobbled and the sides rippled—it had been damaged, too, she realized, and was losing gas. They must have originally intended to land it in the fort, but the steering didn't seem to be working; it was veering toward the right. If it continued on that path, it would go full circle and crash into the mountain it had just crested.

Sardelle found the problem. The smashed rudder was stuck in one position, not responding to the pilot's frantic pulls at the controls. A cannonball was wedged into the steering mechanism. Sardelle pried it out, dumping the iron weight into the snow far below. She turned the rudder in the opposite direction and imagined she could hear its pained squeal from two miles away. It wasn't going to be enough to correct the problem. The vessel would still crash. Maybe that was inevitable, but better to crash close to the fort rather than into a mountain cliff.

She attempted to maneuver the craft against the wind without making it appear unnatural. Dozens of soldiers atop the rampart were watching. Fighting the wind was as much of a challenge for her as it was for the ship, and heat pricked at her skin, making her feel as if she were running laps around the fort instead of standing still. When the craft crashed, she had done what she could. She had brought it down on snow rather than letting it smash into a cliff. She didn't know if it would be enough.

"Watch that ship," Ridge called to someone before sprinting down the stairs. "Sergeant Komfry, grab some men. We're going to look for survivors."

At first, Sardelle thought his command was meant for the supply ship and couldn't imagine why it would need to be watched—it certainly wasn't going anywhere now—but the Cofah vessel had sailed into view above that mountain peak.

It hovered there, watching. Preparing an attack? More snow had gathered on the high mountainsides. Would they try the avalanche maneuver again? If so, she was ready. This time, she would stop them before they dropped any explosives. One way or another.

No sooner had she experienced the thought when a whisper sounded in her mind. *Who are you?*

The warmth of Sardelle's body vanished, replaced by a chill. The words came from the Cofah ship. From the other sorcerer. There was no doubt.

Come any closer and you'll find out, she responded.

The laughter in her mind rang dark and disquieting. *You could do nothing against my pet. You'll be even less trouble for me.*

Sardelle didn't point out that she had been limited as to what she could do because she couldn't let the soldiers *know* she was doing something. For one thing, she still had that problem. For another, it would be better for this foe to believe her weaker than she was.

She sensed the man—and she could tell it was a man now, someone older and experienced—trying to dig deeper and read her mind. She bricked off her thoughts. She could have prevented him from contacting her further as well, at least at that moment, but she didn't. Any intelligence she might gather from him could prove useful. And maybe there was a part of her that wanted to hear from another telepath, another sorcerer. Even if he was the enemy and from an unfamiliar country and mage line. By default, she had more in common with him than with anyone here in the fort she was so determined to defend.

Why are you protecting these people?

Sardelle licked her lips, wondering if he had somehow slipped past her barriers to read her thoughts after all. No, it was a coincidence. Nothing more. She would have sensed him rummaging inside her mind. Besides, logic dictated that if he had to ask, he didn't know.

They are my people. Sardelle made sure not to think of Ridge as she sent the words across the wind. As the commander here, he would already be a target. No need to make him more of one.

Impossible. All of the Iskandian sorcerers were killed long ago.

Sardelle was glad nobody was watching her, or paying attention to her at all—Ridge had led a team through the gates on snowshoes, and everyone else was keeping the miners in the shafts or watching from the walls—for pain must have flashed across her face. She had been certain there would be *some* survivors. She was tempted to reach out to Jaxi, to ask how the soulblade read the situation, but not while this other sorcerer was monitoring. The last thing she wanted to do was make some enemy aware of the artifacts buried within the mountain.

Even if some ancestors of yours survived, the enemy sorcerer went on, *I don't understand why you would defend these people. They were the ones responsible for the purge. You* must *know that.*

You cannot blame a man for the faults of his ancestors.

Please. Do you think these people would be any different? They shoot, drown, and burn anyone with a hint of dragon blood. Nothing has changed. I'm surprised they haven't... ah, they don't know, do they? They don't know who you are.

Sardelle didn't respond to the smugness in the voice. How proud he was to have figured it out. Twit.

I will not share your secret. He chuckled. *Though I will be shocked if you succeed in keeping it. To always hide your true nature, it must be painful.*

What do you care?

Now? Nothing. But I... could care. You could leave these people. Come with me.

To what end?

I'll take you to where the others of our kind live. You would be more comfortable there.

Sardelle swallowed hard at an ache in her throat. She *did* want to find out where other sorcerers might be, but if they were the types to join in with conquering armies, did she want anything to do with that? Of course, just because one man had made that choice did not mean they all did.

Or... The sorcerer's words grew softer, almost husky in her mind. *You could come with me.*

What are you offering?

A union. There are few left with dragon's blood, even fewer whose lines haven't been diluted to near worthlessness through the centuries. Those who remain rarely produce offspring when they breed with each other. The blood is too close, too intertwined.

Sardelle found herself gaping at the distant ship, which was still hovering over the snowy peak. Had she just received an offer to *breed*? And from an utter stranger? How romantic.

He would probably say anything to get her away from the fort. Maybe he considered her more of a problem than he had let on.

For a brief, immature moment, she thought of sending him an image of herself entwined with Ridge, but that would be idiotic. All she said was, *I'll keep your offer in mind.*

Do so. It will be a shame to kill you when we attack.

Uh huh. *And when will that be?*

Soon. Make your decision soon.

The enemy ship turned and drifted out of view, heading back to whatever docking space it had carved out in these inhospitable mountains.

Sardelle climbed the stairs to see if the crash site was in view and if Ridge had found any survivors. What she witnessed made her suspect he wouldn't be meeting her in the library that night.

* * *

It took Ridge and two other men to pull open the dented metal door of the gondola. The shouts they had heard when they first approached had stopped. He hoped that wasn't a sign of injured people falling unconscious—or worse. Unfortunately, he and the six-man team he'd brought out had needed to dig away a lot of snow to reach the door. The windows at the front of the enclosed cabin were still buried, so nobody could see in. The frame inside the balloon had been smashed as well, the gas bag ripped and torn, with shreds smothering the rest of the craft. In short, the crash site was a mess.

He was relieved when a cranky, "It's about time," snapped out of the darkness as soon as the door opened. His relief faded somewhat when the follow-up was, "Get us out of here, you buffoons."

Ridge was about to state his name and rank, in the event that might result in friendly relations, but the speaker added, "I'm not sure the pilot is going to make it," in a softer tone.

"Oster, Rav." Ridge waved for them to follow, then crawled inside first. The only light came from the doorway, and it took a moment for his eyes to adjust. "I'm Colonel Zirkander. Who's barking at me and where's the injured man?"

"He's up front," came a woman's voice—and Ridge gaped into the darkness in surprise. Who would bring a woman up here unless she was one of the prisoners? Or maybe this supply ship had been carrying prisoners as well as goods? "He was trying to keep us from landing hard. He wouldn't pull away from the controls, even when—" Her voice tightened in something close to a sob. She sounded young.

"As to who's barking, Colonel, you're speaking with General Melium Nax. You can call me sir."

Great. Ridge had heard the man's name spoken before. Usually in a fearful tone.

"Yes, sir." He could make out the general's form now—he seemed to be comforting the other passenger, the woman—though Ridge was focused on crawling into the smashed cockpit. "Rav, is that you behind me? Do you see the pilot? We're going to have to pry that busted panel off his legs to pull him out."

"Yes, sir." The burly infantryman brushed past him. "Hurrying."

Ridge patted about, trying to locate the pilot's throat to take his pulse. He encountered a lot of blood. Hells. The man had some ripped metal beam thrusting into his chest. And no pulse.

"Never mind, Rav," Ridge said softly. "There's no hurry."

Behind him, the general sighed. The woman sniffed and wiped her face.

"Let's get you two out of here," Ridge said. "I'm sure you've sustained injuries as well. I'll show you to the medic."

"You'll show me everything, young man. I'm here to check up on you."

"Yes, I gathered that. I'm honestly more concerned about the Cofah right now. Rav, have the rest of the men unload this ship. We need the supplies, whatever survived the crash. And cut this poor pilot out as well, please."

"Yes, sir."

Ridge climbed out ahead of the others, offering the general a hand. The white-haired, stern-faced man looked like the no-nonsense sort—also known as the utterly humorless sort—and Ridge doubted that they would get along. Oh, well. He had to admit he wouldn't mind handing over fort operations to someone else, at least while the Cofah threat remained, so he could focus on defense and getting that flier off the ground. The general had a few scars on his hands and face. He must have seen some battles, so he should have useful advice. So long as his scars hadn't come from street toughs he hadn't been able to bribe with pies.

The thought brought Sardelle to mind. Seven gods, how was he going to explain *her* to a new commanding officer? Captain Heriton wouldn't have to send a secret report anywhere to find someone to inform.

"Careful, Vespa," the general said to the woman, who was climbing out now.

Without thinking about it, Ridge offered her a hand. The general scowled—if he was the husband, he was at least thirty years older than the woman, maybe forty—but she beamed as she accepted the offering. She was attractive with a delicate nose and pointed chin, and lush blonde hair mostly tamed by a braid, though several wisps had come free in the crash. She didn't appear injured, though when she stepped into the snow, she floundered and ended up leaning against Ridge, grabbing his parka to stay upright.

"Oh, it's deep here."

It wasn't that deep, but Ridge said, "Yes, ma'am."

"Vespa Nax is my daughter, Colonel." The general scowled at Ridge, as if *he* were the one who had grabbed *her*.

"Yes, sir." Ridge extricated himself from the embrace. "Why, ah, I wouldn't have expected you—or anyone—to bring a woman here." Ridge wasn't usually so circumspect with his superior officers, but he had never met Nax before and didn't feel as comfortable mouthing off to him as with those in his chain of command. Maybe because he had something to lose here. Back home, he knew they weren't going to take him out of the air for long. Here? He was going to have to tread lightly if he didn't want Sardelle locked up.

The general scowled—it seemed to be his normative state. "Vespa, Professor Vespa Nax, I should have said, is a geologist. The king suggested I bring her along to study the rock formations in the mountain and determine where more crystals might be found. We lost two fliers in ocean fights not two weeks ago. That's two crystals lost. Production must be increased."

Ridge had been about to lead the way back to the fort, but he froze. "Which squadron?" Not his people... He didn't want to hear about *any* downed pilots, but especially not those who flew under him.

"Which squadron, *sir*."

Was the bastard kidding? Even being circumspect, Ridge was going to have trouble with the general, he could tell already.

Nax pointed a finger at his nose. "I know your reputation, Zirkander. I've seen you strutting around HQ like everyone there should bow down to your brilliance, but you're an insubordinate nobody. Your family is full of drunks and delinquents. How you got into the academy, I can't even imagine. Must have been some female recruiting officer falling for a handsome face."

At that statement, Ridge was all too aware of the man's daughter looking on, her expression somewhere between surprise and exasperation. Ridge didn't mind getting his butt scrubbed with the porcupine brush, but he always hated those officers who did it in front of others. Vespa didn't matter that much, but the men unloading the dirigible—men working very hard to pretend they weren't hearing this—were soldiers Ridge might have to lead into battle later. They needed to respect him, not think he was some joke around HQ.

"I don't know how you got promoted this far," Nax went on, "but if you give me any shit, I'm going to knock your ass back to lieutenant."

"Wonderful," Ridge said. "Now, if you're done with that speech, which I get the feeling you were rehearsing all the way here, I'd appreciate it if you told me which squadron—which men—went down. Sir." And so his plans to be circumspect lasted all of three minutes. As they said in the academy, no battle plan survived past first contact.

"Hells if I know," the general growled. "All you dragon kissers are alike. Now, if you'll show me to my office, I'd like to know what's been going on here since you took command." He scoffed and walked away—the black stone walls of the fort were visible through the snow, so he couldn't get lost. Ridge didn't hurry after him.

"I didn't realize my father had met you before," Professor Vespa said.

"He hasn't. At least not so far as I know."

"Oh, odd. Usually he reserves that level of vitriol for lobbyists, liberals, and his most loathed enemies."

"He must know I don't vote conservative at the holiday costume contests."

Vespa chuckled. Ridge hadn't been trying to be funny. Oh, well. "This way, ma'am. I'll show you to the, uh, guest quarters." Those being some dusty, unused rooms in the officers' billets.

"Thank you. And, Colonel? Can I call you Ridge?"

"Yes," he said though he didn't want to. He didn't want to breed any sort of familiarity with the general's daughter. Grumpy old Nax was going to be trouble enough without that. What had the king been thinking sending her out here among the hordes of horny men? An image of him in the cave with Sardelle flashed into his mind, and he flushed. Horny men indeed.

"Good. Ridge, then. It was Wolf Squadron. It was in the newspapers."

"Wolf." All of his indignation from the general's treatment drained out of Ridge. That was his team. What did self-righteous superior officers matter if his people were back there dying? "Do you remember the names?"

"It was a man and a woman. Dash and... Ann? Orhn?"

Ridge stopped in the middle of the trail, his boots suddenly feeling like lead weights on his feet. He closed his eyes. "Ahn."

"They flew with you?"

"Yes."

"I'm sorry." The professor put a hand on his shoulder. "If you want to talk about it or to share a drink tonight, I would be happy to do so."

The woman's familiarity surprised him. Up ahead, the general had stopped and was scowling back. Ridge resisted the urge to push her hand away. He forced himself to say, "Thank you," and started walking again, knowing the hand would fall away on its own.

The snow had lightened, and numerous men were watching from the ramparts. He hoped they were paying as much attention to the sky as they were to him and the newcomers—the Cofah ship had disappeared, but that didn't mean it wouldn't be back. He spotted Sardelle up there, the breeze tugging at her long black hair, and hoped she hadn't seen the overly familiar professor putting her hands on him. Something about the way she turned away as soon as he looked in her direction made him suspect she had.

Chapter 10

The snores reverberated from the ceiling, walls, and floors of the women's barracks. Whoever had designed the building should have considered carpets, curtains, tapestries, or at least something with sound-dampening properties. The decorator probably hadn't known many women who were so nasally challenged. Sardelle hadn't until she arrived here. Thus she lay awake in the darkness, listening to the audible slumber of tired women. She was tired herself, since she had spent the day in the laundry room. Though the other women had treated her like a leper since she hadn't been in there in so long and had been, as they called it, kissing balls and freeloading, it had seemed a good place to hide from this General Nax, who had been dragging Ridge all over the fort, making angry gestures and yelling.

Sardelle had instantly disliked the man, even though she hadn't been in the same room with him yet. Captain Heriton had shown up at some point, trailing along on what appeared to be an inspection. She had stayed out of his sight, not wanting him to be reminded of her. She found it highly unlikely this general would be someone who would make a deal with her when her sword was discovered.

She hadn't figured out who that woman was yet either, except that she was young and pretty and seemed just as out of place here as Sardelle. She was obviously Someone Special though, for the soldiers had all been bowing and smiling at her whenever she came around. She didn't think all of that could be the result of good looks.

After lying awake for an hour, Sardelle crawled out of bed and put on her boots and clothing warm enough for a trek across the courtyard. She didn't expect Ridge to be in the library, or even thinking about her, but she couldn't sleep anyway, so on the off chance he was there...

He's there.

Sardelle, in the process of sticking her feet into her boots, nearly tipped over. Jaxi had been silent all day, probably sharing her concern about being discovered by that sorcerer.

Yes, I'll lie low whenever their ship is around. I didn't like that smarmy know-it-all. Jaxi sniffed.

By lying low, you mean listening in on our telepathic conversation? Sardelle dressed more quickly, affected far more by the first thing Jaxi had said than by anything else.

I have to keep abreast of what's happening. I assure you, he didn't sense me.

That's good. Sardelle tugged on her parka. *When you said 'he's there,' did you mean—*

I'd hate to be wielded by some smarmy mage stinking of the jungle and joining in with conquerors.

I'm glad you also didn't like him, but what I really want to know is—

Yes, yes, your boyfriend is waiting for you. Though I'm not sure sex is what he has in mind.

Sardelle strode outside, still buttoning her parka. The snow had stopped and the sky had cleared, though the air was cold enough to freeze the hair out of her nostrils.

An attractive image. I recommend you don't share it with your lover.

Thank you for the advice, Jaxi.

There were fires in the watchtowers and braziers burning on the ramparts. Though it was late, the soldiers strode about, their eyes toward the sky. Yes, with the clearing weather, the Cofah might think it time to try a new attack. She swept the skies with her senses, though she didn't slow down from her brisk walk toward the library building. She didn't feel anyone out there. Good.

The library was only one room, upstairs in a building dedicated to equipment storage and welding. For a moment, Sardelle worried the front door would be locked, but it wasn't. There weren't any lamps lit in the open bay downstairs, and she had to use her senses to pick her way past everything from ore carts being repaired to giant flywheels from the machines that operated the tram. There was usually a clearer path to the second-floor stairs, but maybe things had been moved about for the general's inspection.

As she climbed to the upper hall and still didn't find any lamps lit, she began to doubt Jaxi's promise. But she sensed someone in the library room. Maybe Ridge had brought his own lantern and not bothered lighting any on the way. Perhaps a good idea if they didn't want to be discovered. Although with this general here now, Sardelle was reluctant to do anything with him that might get him in trouble. For all anyone here knew, she was a prisoner. Ridge was the only one who had thought of her as anything else.

She paused with her hand on the doorknob. Maybe she shouldn't risk contacting him. But she couldn't stomach the idea of leaving him in there alone. He was…

Drunk, she guessed as soon as she opened the door and smelled the alcohol. And sitting in the dark, staring toward the library's lone window, which had a lovely view of the drab stone ramparts.

"Ridge?" Sardelle whispered. "Are you… do you want to be alone?"

He took a deep, audible breath, letting it out slowly before answering. Considering his answer, perhaps. Whatever had brought him here, Sardelle doubted it was she or an urge for sex.

"No," he finally decided.

"Can I light a candle?"

"Yeah." His voice wasn't slurred, but he definitely sounded off. No, he sounded *down*. Defeated.

"Well, I don't like this new general already if he drove you to drink," Sardelle said lightly.

Ridge grunted.

"Is he in command now?"

"Yeah. HQ gave him the authority to take over if I wasn't doing an adequate job." He flipped his hand, as if he didn't care.

After fumbling in a couple of drawers, Sardelle cheated, using her senses to locate candles and a box of matches. She brought them over to the table where Ridge was seated. He looked away when the match flared to life. The brown glass bottle next to him didn't have a label; maybe it had been concocted in some tub in the back of the barracks. Whatever it was smelled strong. A little wooden dragon figurine rested next to the bottle, the paint on its bulbous belly worn off. She had only had glimpses of the charm, but she recognized it. There was a little metal eyehook on the top with a braided golden loop attached. Maybe he hung it in the cockpit when he flew.

Sardelle sat in the chair next to him. "Perhaps you could give me some context. I'm not certain whether I should be trying to cheer you up or commiserating with you. Or simply sitting in silence."

Ridge used the back of his hand to push the bottle toward her.

"Or joining you for a drink," she added.

"Two of my pilots were killed."

"Oh." It wasn't the general that had distressed him so, or not only the general. "Men you flew with? That you knew well?"

"A man and a woman. A girl, really. Ahn was only twenty-three, barely out of the academy, but she had a real feel for the flier and the archer god's gift for accuracy. She—" Ridge swallowed audibly, then cleared his throat and picked up the bottle. He took a long swig.

Sardelle wondered if this Ahn had been more than a fellow pilot for him, but kept herself from asking. This was not the time, and she refused to feel petty jealousy toward a dead woman.

Ridge set down the bottle. "She was a good kid. Would have had a great career. Made a difference, you know?"

Sardelle didn't have any words, none that wouldn't sound pointless and inane, so she simply laid a hand on his forearm.

"Dash, too," Ridge said. "Even if he was reckless. They both were. Probably got that from me. And then I wasn't there when—" He broke off again, gazing into the dark nothingness.

"I'm sorry," Sardelle whispered. It seemed so inadequate. For him, and for her too. Her thoughts drifted to those she had lost, friends and relatives who also would have had great careers if the fates had allowed it. Some had been younger than Ridge's lieutenant when the mountain had come crashing down.

They sat there in silence, letting the candles burn lower, their lights dancing with shadows on the bookcase. After a time, Ridge pushed the bottle toward her again.

"You should drink. I'm more interesting when you do. Better company."

Because he wished it, Sardelle took a sample of the strong-smelling brew. As she had suspected, it burned like fire going down her throat. She managed not to cough and sputter—barely. "As I told you this morning, you don't have to do much to be better company than a brigade of snoring women."

"Yeah? Guess I'm lucky standards here are low."

Sardelle too. She thought of the pretty blonde girl and the way she had fallen over Ridge from the moment she stepped out of the plane. It occurred to her that the hero worship she had seen from many of the soldiers must extend to women when he was back home. He must have his choice of female companions. If she were to knock on the door of his cabin by the lake someday, would she find him alone? Or, with so many other interested parties around, would he forget about her?

You never used to be insecure.

I never used to date much.

You're an attractive woman, Sardelle. He's in the library with you, not drinking with that blonde girl. She offered.

I'm sorry, were you trying to make me feel better?

No, just making observations.

Time for a different topic. "It sounded like that general was giving you a hard time. Will you get in trouble over the changes you've implemented?" Or over me, she added silently.

"Already did. He thinks I'm running the place like the officer's club back home. He figures I'll bring in masseurs to rub down the prisoners next."

"Wasn't he at least pleased by the crystals you've found?" Sardelle asked.

"He was so happy he almost didn't scowl for a second. Wouldn't credit me for them though—not that I've had anything to do with finding them—" Ridge nodded toward her. "Even though Heriton told him differently, he's convinced they came out of the ground on General Bockenhaimer's shift."

"Well, your men are close to another one. He'll be able to see that one for himself when they dig it out."

"Yeah."

"If I were down there, I might be able to find even more. Pretty soon, you're going to get into some of the old rooms, and there'll be a higher density of..." Sardelle stopped because Ridge had twisted in his seat to face her.

He clasped the top of the hand she had been resting on his arm. "Listen, Sardelle. You need to make yourself scarce. Don't let him see you, and don't show up when Heriton is around either. If he starts blabbing about what that prisoner said or about any of the admittedly unusual things that have happened since you came around, you'll be in danger. I won't be able to protect you. As much as I'd like to, I can't throw a superior officer off a cliff."

"I'd never ask you to."

"I know you wouldn't." Ridge lifted his hand and stroked the side of her face. "You're more mature than I am." His eyes moved, following her face as his fingers traced her cheek down to her jaw. A pleased shiver ran through her. "Sexier too," he murmured.

"I would refute that statement. You're quite sexy. Especially when you smile."

He managed a small one. "No argument on mature, eh?"

"No."

Ridge chuckled softly and leaned closer. He kissed her gently on the lips, then lowered his face to the side of her neck. Sardelle wasn't sure if he had commiseration in mind or something more, but her body was certainly responding to his touch. It would be a shame to go back to the barracks now. He pushed his hand through her hair and massaged the back of her neck.

"I suppose being pawed over by a drunk wouldn't be much of a reward for you coming all the way out here to keep me company," he murmured against her throat, his lips grazing her skin.

She wondered if he could feel the rapidness of her heartbeat there. "Depends on the drunk," she whispered, slipping her hand behind his head and wondering why their chairs were so far apart.

"Oh?"

"You still seem to have... " That massage felt so good, her brain slipped a cog and she momentarily forgot the rest of her sentence. Good and stimulating. Not to mention what his lips were doing on her throat. "Retained your faculties," she breathed.

"I was hoping you'd come." His other hand found her thigh. Even through her clothing, it charged her with heat.

Sardelle left her chair to sit in his lap and wrapped her arms more firmly around him. "Me too." That didn't make sense, but she didn't care.

"You're the only thing keeping me sane tonight," Ridge whispered, and it was the last thing either of them said for a time.

* * *

After spending the night with Sardelle, something Ridge resolved to do more often, whatever he had to do to manage it, he found himself struggling to pay attention to the lecture from the general's daughter. Oh, Professor Vespa surely didn't mean it to be a lecture, but by the time she had explained the significance of the tenth type of rock from her sample case, Ridge was hoping General Nax would show up to send her away. Odd, when Sardelle had recited summaries of all those books, he hadn't found it pompous or boring, but Vespa had an air of self-importance that made him want to pull out something else to work on while she spoke. He also got the impression she thought he wasn't that bright.

"It's important that we start getting the miners to categorize the non-valuable debris they clear out in each level," Vespa stated. "I'm here to determine the most likely types of rock that we can find crystals in."

"Someone has already determined that," Ridge said. "That's why we've found four in the last couple of weeks."

"Someone." Vespa crinkled her tiny nose. "A geologist? An expert?"

"I'm not sure what field she studied. She's a prisoner."

"You're taking excavating advice from a prisoner? Oh, Ridge."

"She's educated." Ridge probably shouldn't be talking about Sardelle at all, but he didn't want to have to institute some idiotic rock cataloguing system—he could just imagine how well that would go over with the miners, having to separate and label every chunk of dirt they removed—when they had a better way.

"From where?"

"She didn't say." It occurred to Ridge that he might have an unexpected resource to unearth a little more about Sardelle's mysterious past. "Although, maybe you've heard of her. I think she was an archaeologist or in a similar field before ending up here." Did geologists and archaeologists work together from time to time, read each other's papers?

"What's her name?"

"Sardelle Sordenta."

Vespa shook her head. "I've never heard of her."

"Hm. She has some interesting ideas about where the crystals come from. Have you ever heard about there being a Referatu outpost here at some point in the past? Here, inside the mountain itself?"

Vespa took a step back. "The sorcerers? Of course not."

She was genuinely surprised. Huh. Ridge had thought he simply didn't spend enough time in the halls of academia to have stumbled across the information himself. Well, a geologist wasn't an archaeologist. "You might find it interesting to actually go down into the tunnels," he said. "See the mine shafts. You can tell that some areas appear to have been mined before, and then collapsed."

"Truly? That's fascinating." She smiled, flashing a pair of dimples at him. "And did I just hear you offer to take me on a tour down there?"

"Er. I'm actually already late to meet Captain Bosmont to work on the flier."

Vespa held up a hand. "I wouldn't go near that thing if I were you. My father was furious when he saw that rusted junk pile—his words, not mine—in the middle of the courtyard."

"Yes, I was there to receive his opinions on the project yesterday." His opinions on *everything*.

"I heard him say he wants it scrapped."

"He'll think differently if we're able to use it to defend against the Cofah, who could be back at any time." Another reason Ridge didn't want to dither around giving tours. The skies were clear. The snow and wind that had been keeping the airship away wouldn't be a hurdle now.

"I'm sure he will. I would love to see you fly."

Ridge would love for *Sardelle* to see him fly. Her background might still be a mystery to him, but he had gotten the impression that she had never seen a dragon flier before, despite her academic familiarity with the Denhoft book.

A door banged open out in the hallway. "Colonel? General?" came Captain Heriton's excited voice. "News from the mines!"

Ridge pushed to his feet. "Shall we see what it is?" He held the door open for Vespa.

"Thank you, Ridge."

She walked out first and as Ridge stepped out, General Nax strode out of the office next door. Not surprisingly, he scowled at the back of Vespa's head, then at Ridge, having caught them both coming out of the same room.

"Hurry," the captain called from the base of the stairs. "Out by Tram Three. This is unbelievable."

"A crystal?" Vespa asked.

"Must be," the general said.

Ridge wasn't so sure. Heriton had been as excited as anybody at the finding of the first crystal—the first one in over a year—but now that it had become more common, he didn't shout for everyone to come look when a miner walked out with one.

Ridge jogged across the courtyard. Quite a few people, soldiers and miners, had gathered around the tram exit. An ore cart full of something that wasn't ore rested in front of the shaft. The dusty contents looked to be...

"Books?" Vespa asked, jogging too. "Dug out of the *mountain*?"

Her face screwed up in disbelief.

Ridge was less surprised, having been warned of the Referatu by Sardelle. This must be the first true proof, other than the crystals themselves, as to a prior civilization living down there. One that had apparently had a mountain collapsed upon their heads.

Men moved aside for Ridge and the general to approach.

"We found 'em just this morning," a miner was saying, "and some old dusty carpets too."

Another miner standing beside him elbowed him and pointed to Ridge. "Tell them about the bones."

"I know, I know, I'm getting to it."

"Be quiet," General Nax snapped. "Everyone. Except you." He pointed to the first miner. "Explain everything. No one interrupt him."

Several men muttered yes-sirs. A couple of them glanced at Ridge, as if they felt betrayed he had allowed this more authoritative—or despotic, depending on how one looked at it—figure to take charge. He kept himself from rolling his eyes or doing anything else that would let the men know how he felt about Nax. Channeling some of Sardelle's maturity, perhaps. He took a deep breath and listened.

"It looked like an old room that had caved in. Part of some kind of underground fortress or castle or something. There were two crystals. Two! Within ten feet of each other. The engineer took those right away, but we brung up these books too. But, like Two-five-three said, there were bones too. All smashed from the rocks, but human skeletons for sure. Two of 'em that we got to right away. Could be more. Bunch of us are still digging down there."

The general was staring at the books and didn't seem to be paying attention.

"Good find," Ridge said. "Thank you for the hard work."

The miners knuckled their foreheads in something approximating a military salute. "Sure, boss. Sure."

"What *is* this?" General Nax asked, touching the spine of one of the books with a single finger. The title was written in

Iskandian, albeit an archaic-looking version of the text, with more flowery touches than one usually saw on a book.

"What is it, Da?" Vespa squeezed past two men for a better look.

"Rituals of the Harvest Moon," Nax read, then jerked his finger back. "Rituals. These are sorcerous filth." He looked at a few more titles. "All of them."

"If this was a Referatu stronghold," Vespa said, "those titles make sense."

Ridge winced. He hadn't told her that believing she would speak openly of it. A mistake. He shouldn't have said anything at all, a notion reinforced when the general's head whipped around. "Who told you that?"

Vespa looked at Ridge, a question in her eyes.

He snorted to himself. She might as well have thrust a finger at him.

"I heard it from a prisoner," Ridge said when Nax's scowl turned in his direction again. "I thought it might be an accepted fact in the academic world, so I brought it up to the professor."

The miners were looking back and forth, sharing confused expressions. Ridge couldn't blame them. They ought to be proud of finding such an old and unique find, but the general certainly wasn't giving them that impression.

"Burn them," Nax said. "Burn everything that comes out of there."

"What?" came a familiar cry from the back of the crowd.

Ridge winced again. He couldn't blame Sardelle for protesting this, especially if these artifacts were what had brought her all the way out here, but he wished she hadn't let that cry slip out. In truth, it sounded like one of surprise as much as one of protest, and when he spotted her, wearing the usual prisoner's garb and with a laundry basket in her arms, he also spotted the regret in her eyes, the cringe on her face. She, too, knew she had made a mistake.

Chapter 11

Sardelle kept her hands clasped behind her back and stared steadily at the snow in front of her. Ridge had warned her, and she had warned herself, yet when she had chanced upon that crowd, seen the books, and heard that vile proclamation from the general...

To destroy what little remained of her people, it was unthinkable. And yet, she had brought this about herself. If she hadn't been so eager to help Ridge find some crystals, the miners might never have delved into that half of the mountain. Now they might destroy every remaining piece of her culture.

That's not fair. You sent them that way to recover me. If anything, this is my fault.

That doesn't make the situation any better, Jaxi. I—we—miscalculated. We couldn't have foreseen Slug Breath taking command.

"Her record says Sardelle Sordenta," Captain Heriton was informing the general. Ridge stood a few feet back, his arms folded over his chest, his face flinty. Not at her, she knew, but at the situation. Heriton, of course, was smiling cheerfully. "A record that didn't appear until she had been in the fort for two or three days. When it appeared, it was in a spot I had already checked. It hadn't been there the day before. And then there's the fact that she was originally found wandering in the mines by a..."

Sardelle had heard the accusations before and listened in silence, watching as the books were unloaded from the cart and carried to an empty area in the center of the courtyard. Someone set a can of kerosene next to them.

If you don't do something, I will. Jaxi sounded as irritated by the situation as Sardelle.

I'm already on the verge of being accused of witchcraft here. What can I do? After I get you, it doesn't matter— Sardelle glanced at Ridge and admitted it would still matter, *—but until then, I can't let them...*

Kill you?

Yes.

That would be inconvenient. I've grown attached to you and missed you when you were sleeping for three centuries.

I'm glad to know you care. If you do something, don't hurt anyone, please.

The grumbles that sounded in Sardelle's head weren't encouraging, but she knew Jaxi wouldn't physically harm anyone unless it was to defend her. They had both taken oaths long ago to protect, not to hurt.

"You have anything to say, woman?" General Nax asked.

Sardelle shook her head.

"You knew about this spy, Colonel Zirkander?" Nax's voice grew soft, dangerous.

For a moment, Ridge looked like he might go with a mute answer as well, but his lips thinned, and he chose to say, "I don't know what she is, but if she's a spy, she's a considerate one. She's the one who pointed out the locations of the new crystals."

Sardelle didn't want him to get in trouble for defending her, but with so many eyes upon her, she didn't know how to signal him.

You don't think he's ready for telepathy?

Remembering the way he had lost his composure when she had teased him about being a telepath, she didn't think so, no. He had run afoul of sorcerers before, he had admitted as much. The moment she allowed him to find out she was one was the moment she lost the only thing she had here. In the world.

The last of the books had been piled up, and a soldier uncapped the kerosene can.

"And how did *she* know the location of the crystals?" General Nax regarded her through slitted eyes.

"Is she the one who knew this was a Referatu stronghold?" the general's daughter asked, stepping forward and speaking for the first time.

Sardelle kept herself from frowning at Ridge, but it hurt

a little to realize he must have been talking about her to this woman. Trying to defend her, she sensed, but she still wished he had said nothing. She could get herself into enough trouble without anyone else's help.

The soldier lit his match. Sardelle made a point of not looking in his direction as she snuffed it out. Nobody except the soldier noticed. Good. He had a whole box full of matches. Not good. Oops, it seemed the heads had grown damp in the snow at some point. The soldier tried to light several more before grumbling to himself and heading for one of the buildings.

"I *will* have answers to these questions," General Nax said. "If not nicely here, then in an interrogation room."

Ridge dropped his arms. "That's not called for, sir. She's been helping us."

"No doubt so she can steal the crystals once we've pulled them all out. And take them back to wherever she's from. Did the Cofah plant you, girl?"

"I am Iskandian, through and through," Sardelle said. "I grew up in these mountains. I would not betray them to invaders."

The soldier returned, a fresh box of matches in his hand. She dampened them before he reached the pile of books.

"We'll see if you have the same answer when a little pressure is applied," the general said.

"Sir." Ridge stepped forward. "Are we really going to start torturing women, here?"

"You wouldn't object if she were a man. Spies can come in either sex, Colonel. Don't be naive."

"I haven't yet seen a reason to torture anyone. She's helping us. Don't you want to see how many crystals she can direct us to? If we can't keep a hold of them after that, that's our problem, isn't it?"

Nax scowled at him. "Isn't it, *sir*."

A muscle ticked in Ridge's cheek. Sardelle realized she hadn't seen him angry yet, not truly. He wouldn't do something to ruin his career on her behalf, would he? She couldn't let that happen.

"*Sir*," Ridge amended.

"I also think we should wait, sir," Captain Heriton said. "If she's truly the one who has been locating the crystals, we should use her as long as she's willing to help."

At first, Sardelle thought Heriton had changed his allegiance, deciding he liked Ridge more than the general, or at least that he liked the crystals more than he disliked her, but there was nothing friendly in his eyes as he regarded her. Even without brushing his mind, she could sense the suspicion there. More than that, she sensed he was perhaps the only one to have a true idea of what she was. Oh, he wouldn't think her a three-hundred-year-old sorcerer, but someone with a few mental tricks? Yes, that was exactly what he thought. Maybe he was waiting to say something until he had some evidence.

The soldier by the books cursed loudly enough to draw the general's attention. "What's your malfunction, private?"

"Sorry, sir. Can't find any matches that will light. Everything's damp."

"Odd," Heriton said, staring at Sardelle.

I think I'm going to have to come down to find you tonight, Jaxi. Whether the tunnels have been bored close enough or not.

I am more than ready to assist you in my un-burial.

"Damp," General Nax said. "Private, I don't want excuses. I want burned books. Throw them in a furnace if you have to."

"Yes, sir."

"Airship spotted," came a cry from atop the wall.

Sardelle had never been so pleased to see the enemy on the horizon.

The general cursed and jogged for the ramparts. His daughter, the captain, and most of the men gathered to watch the book burning did the same.

Ridge must have been itching to run up there, too, but he stepped up to her side. His gaze was on the sky, on the gold and wooden ship that had appeared over the western peak again. "I won't let him torture you, though it will mean my career, if not my life. I understand this sword is worth a lot to you..." He didn't say, *but is it worth my life?* He must have been thinking it, but instead he sighed and looked at her out of the corner of his eye. "So you might want to disappear until you have the opportunity to retrieve it."

Sardelle looked toward Tram Three, the shaft that led down to the room where the books had been found, the shaft that would get her as close to Jaxi as was possible. Ridge glanced over, following her gaze. He didn't say anything else, merely walked toward the stairs, very deliberately not turning to look back at her.

Watch the books, Jaxi. I'm going down.
It's about time.

* * *

A soft boom sounded to the north. A cannonball arced away from the Cofah airship and landed in a drift a hundred meters from the fort wall, sending up a shower of snow that was visible even down in the courtyard.

"We going to be ready for a test run today, Bosmont?" Ridge asked.

"Let's see if we can start the engine first, eh, boss?" It couldn't have been more than ten degrees, but the burly captain had his sleeves rolled up. Maybe all the tools he had squirreled away in his pockets kept him warm.

"If the engine starts, I'll be tempted to hop right in and take off. Who's to say it'll start more than once, or stay started?"

"Have more faith, Colonel. This girl will purr like a kitten after all we've done to her." Bosmont gave the engine a loving pat.

Ridge winced as his wrench slipped off a nut, his fist banging into the side of the compartment. That was what he got for tightening bolts at the same time as he was watching those bastards taking the range-finding shots.

The crystal glowing in its slot on top of the engine winked out. Bosmont frowned at it and slapped the casing, and it flared back to life.

"Auspicious," Ridge said.

"Just a faulty connector. I'll open it up and see if there's more rust I can scrape off."

A louder boom came from one of their own cannons. Ridge

eyed the snow-covered peaks around them. Even though he had been the one to tell Sardelle that avalanches would be unlikely at this range, he had still deemed it wise to take all precautions, especially with the enemy out there, doubtlessly hoping to goad the fort into causing trouble for itself. Apparently General Nax wasn't worried about avalanches.

"Because his hairy gray ass wasn't caught in the last one," Ridge muttered.

"What's that?" Bosmont asked.

"Said I'm going to go up and check the weapons system. Just getting in the air won't be enough to scare off the Cofah."

"Ah, is *that* what you said? I thought I heard something about asses. Figured you were talking about the general."

"I'd never be that disrespectful." Ridge crawled under the control panel in the cockpit to check on the connectors leading to the repeating guns in the nose of the plane. Flying was important, but doing damage was even more crucial.

"Were you talking about his daughter? Because that's an ass I wouldn't mind respecting."

"You've been stationed here too long, Bosmont."

"Got that right." Something thunked shut. "I'm going to fire this dragon whelp up."

"Good, I—"

"Colonel," a voice said from outside the flier.

"Yes?" Ridge wriggled out from beneath the console.

Captain Heriton stood there, an open book in his hands. The ever-scowling General Nax stood behind him, along with his daughter. Ridge hoped neither of them had heard his engineer's comments.

"As it turns out, it's fortunate we didn't burn those books," Heriton said.

Fortunate? Hadn't they tried? "Oh?"

"Where's the witch?" Nax demanded.

"Who?"

"Your helpful witch girl."

"Sardelle?" Ridge rubbed his head. Why would they think... his gaze fell to the book, and his stomach sank into the bottom of the cockpit. It was open to a bunch of text he couldn't see well from there and a picture he could. The face looking up at him, a slight knowing smiling turning up the corners of the mouth, was very familiar. But how? "That's one of the books that was pulled out of the mine, isn't it?"

"Yes." Heriton pointed at the page. "According to this, Sardelle Terushan was born three hundred and thirty-four years ago."

"How is that possible?"

"She's a witch is how," General Nax snarled. "And you've been aiding her since she showed up here. *More* than aiding her if the gossip can be believed." He squinted at Ridge. "Your career is over, boy. Now where is she?"

Ridge turned his back on them so he could climb down from the flier—and recover his equanimity. Or at least figure out how to mask his features and control the roiling unease in his belly.

"Even if she were a witch, I've never heard anything about tainted people being immortal," he reasoned, facing them again and holding out a hand for the book. "It must be a mistake. Maybe she was named after this person because of a resemblance."

Heriton didn't release the book, but he did hold it up so Ridge could see the pages better—and read the text. He puzzled through the entry. Apparently it was one of several in some sort of roster. The picture... damn, that was undeniably her. The words had been laid down with a printing press, but the portrait was hand-painted, its colors faded somewhat with time, though the book itself had been well preserved in its rocky tomb.

"Position... *sherastu?*" he wondered aloud, picking words from the description. "And healer." The latter made his stomach start writhing all over again. His hand drifted to his chest, where the scratches from the giant owl had healed extremely well, leaving only the faintest of scars. "Seven gods," he whispered.

"I repeat," Nax said, "*where* is she?"

Ridge met his hard eyes. "What are you going to do to her?"

"Answer the question, Colonel!" Nax lunged forward, as if to grab Ridge by the collar—or neck.

Reacting on instinct, Ridge stepped back. He thumped against the front of the flier, but he blocked the attack. The general barely seemed to notice. His finger came back in, this time pointing at Ridge's nose. "Boy, you've been helping her from the start. I've gotten the whole story."

When Ridge glanced at the captain, Heriton swallowed and looked away.

"Your career is dead. If you don't want to get pounded by a firing squad, you'll tell me where she is right now, and you'll damned well help us figure out a way to imprison her."

"You won't find anyone to shoot him here, Father," Vespa said. She had been watching this whole exchange with wide eyes, and lifted her hand a few times as if she wanted to intervene, but she ultimately let her arms fall to her sides.

"I'll shoot him myself," Nax roared.

"I've read that iron boxes are supposed to nullify their artifacts," Captain Heriton said. "Perhaps we could line one of the solitary confinement cells with iron, and she wouldn't be able to escape until we've thoroughly questioned her."

"Gotten the location of the rest of the crystals, you mean?" Ridge asked.

"I don't care for your tone, Colonel," Nax said.

"What? Not sarcastic enough for you? I'll work on that."

"*Sir*," Heriton whispered. Nax was too busy fuming to respond.

"Look, General. I don't know where she went. I've—" Another boom drifted across the mountainside. Judging by where the snow flew up, that shot had landed much closer. Thanks to its elevated position, the airship had a greater range than the artillery weapons on the wall. "I don't have time to talk about this now. We're straw bales on the rifle range right now. We've got to get this flier off the ground to have a chance at defending ourselves against an air attack."

Heriton eyed the battered and dented craft. "If that's our only chance..." He must have decided morale wouldn't be served by voicing the rest, for he merely shut his book and walked away, shaking his head.

Nax still had smoke coming out of his ears, but his face had grown a shade less red. "Fix it up, Zirkander. But know that after we deal with the Cofah, you're joining the witch in a lead cell. I've got enough on you at this point to have you hanged tonight." He stalked off, shoulders bunched into knots.

"With that ability to inspire courage and devotion, it's shocking he doesn't command legions of troops." Ridge was talking to his engineer—who had never stopped tinkering with the engine, gods love the man for his single-mindedness—but Professor Vespa was still standing there. She stared back and forth between Ridge and her father's departing figure. He thought about apologizing to her for maligning the general but couldn't bring himself to do it. He merely touched the rim of his fur cap, offered a polite, "Ma'am," and pulled himself back into the flier.

"You know where the girl is?" Bosmont asked after they had finished ratcheting down that engine the best they could.

"Not really. You care?"

"Not really." The captain flashed a grin. "But if you had a way of warning her not to come back, you might want to do that. I figure Nax will have a squad of armed men waiting for her if she shows up again."

"I don't know how to contact her. I don't even know if I should if I could." Ridge removed his cap and rubbed his hands through his hair. No, he would warn her if he could, but he wouldn't... he couldn't have anything to do with her after that. A sorceress. He had slept with... By all the gods, living and dead, how had he ended up with a sorceress in his fort? And had she ever cared a whit about him? Or had she been using him to get to what she wanted? Pretending she was helping him find those crystals, but secretly wanting the tunnels dug in a certain direction so she could get that sword? *Her* sword, he realized belatedly. Or one she wanted to use for some reason, doubtlessly a magical blade to increase her power. Wasn't that what the stories said? What would she do once she had it?

"Do me a favor, will you, Bosmont?"

"What?"

"Sneak me in a beer every once in a while once I've been court martialed, and I'm a prisoner here."

"Will do, boss."

Chapter 12

Sardelle knelt near the bottom of the tram shaft, crouching behind a cage. A few feet away, two soldiers stood to either side of the tunnel, their backs to the wall. The clanks, scrapes, and curses drifting out of a couple of the passages announced more people nearby. There were a lot of men she would have to sneak past to reach the freshly excavated tunnels.

A few ore carts had been left on a rail part way down one of the shafts, each full of dirt to be dumped. She waved her hand, and they rolled into the chamber.

"What the—"

"Who pushed those out here?" one of the soldiers demanded, striding toward the tunnel they had come out of.

As soon as he was even with them, Sardelle shoved the cart over. Dirt spilled out onto his boots. The man stumbled back, cursing, and his comrade ran toward the tunnel entrance.

Sardelle made a hard right, obfuscating her form so they wouldn't see anything more than rock, albeit a moving rock, if they glanced over. They were more focused on the tunnel and the ore carts. She slipped into a different passage, the one that should lead to the newly opened area where the miners had found the crystals—and the books.

Jaxi did the telepathic equivalent of clearing her throat. *Speaking of those books...*

Yes?

Did you know some of the annual rosters were in that pile? The ones showing where everyone who does field work is currently stationed?

No.

You should have let that soldier burn the books.

Sardelle forced herself to keep padding down the tunnel,

passing through the shadows between each lantern hanging on the wood supports, though she wanted to stop and spend a few minutes cursing and kicking things. *They found something with me in it?*

Yes.

Did Ridge see it?

Yes.

So he knows who—what—I am now?

He does. Everyone does.

Oh.

Sardelle kept walking though her legs felt numb. What else could she do? All that was left to her was to get Jaxi and go... where? She had no idea.

Somewhere you won't be hanged, drowned, or shot.

Yeah? And where's that? Sardelle remembered the shaman's offer, but the thought of going off with him made her stomach twist in knots.

I'm not sure yet. We'll find it.

Damn. Sardelle didn't want to leave, not by herself anyway. She wanted Ridge to come with her. Or she would have stayed here with him if that abominable general left... and he still wanted her to stay. She could help defend the mountain from enemies. It wasn't that different from the work she had done before.

*Are you sure you **want** to defend these people? People who would kill you if they got a chance?*

Ridge wouldn't.

When an answer didn't come, the silence unnerved Sardelle. What did Jaxi know that she didn't? Sardelle was tempted to reach up through the layers of rock and try to find Ridge up in that courtyard. He would doubtlessly be back at that aircraft. Or up on the wall if the Cofah were attacking.

She jerked at the reminder that the enemy airship was up there. This wasn't the time to worry about loves lost. She shifted from a walk to a jog, running between the iron tracks in the center of the tunnel. Only when the sounds of voices reached her ears did she slow down again. The bangs and clanks had grown much louder too. She sensed no less than ten people working at the end of the shaft. Extra men must have been funneled into the area after the book discovery.

Any ideas on how to get those men to take a lunch break, Jaxi?

The owl is back.

Er, the shaman's pet?

He seems to have sent it ahead. It's harassing the men up top.

While the airship sneaks in unnoticed?

Jaxi didn't answer for a moment. Sardelle crept farther down the tunnel, until a half-full ore cart came into view, along with the back of the man loading it.

It's still staying out of range, but that may change. It's possible the shaman realized you're not up in the courtyard anymore.

Me?

You're probably the only reason they didn't come in and try a more committed attack earlier. The fort's defenses are paltry. It's clear that when this place was built, attacks from the air weren't common yet.

Yes, they need someone to make it out of here to inform the rest of the military of this problem. Sardelle thought there was room enough in that partially filled ore cart for her to hide in, but she needed to convince all of the men to leave for a while.

Methane, Jaxi suggested.

That's poisonous.

Thus why it would scare them away, at least until their ventilation system could be extended down into these new tunnels.

That might actually work. Is there some down here we could siphon into the tunnel? Of course, I'd have to think about how to shield myself. The real gas would be rather poisonous to me too.

Why not just make them think *they smell methane?*

Sardelle grimaced at the thought of tinkering in people's minds. *That's a little ethically ambiguous.*

Less painful than rashes.

Sardelle sighed and leaned her head against the earthen wall.

I'll handle it. You can keep your ethics pure.

Sardelle should have objected, but she didn't. She didn't know how much time she had and how long it would take to dig out Jaxi.

She waited for the miner near the cart to move forward around the bend, then trotted up and hopped in. There was a box of dynamite next to the wall. If she couldn't pry Jaxi out with magic, she supposed explosives were an alternative. Though she might end up burying both of them if she tried that.

She curled into a ball and camouflaged herself to blend in with the rubble beneath her. *I'm ready.*

Already working on them.

"You smell that?" someone asked.

The scrapes of pickaxes died away. "What?" A few noisy sniffs sounded. "Is that gas?"

"It's leaking out of somewhere. Back up, get back."

The thuds of boots approached the cart, then shadows fell across Sardelle as the men raced past. She held her breath. She knew she was camouflaged, but it was hard ignoring the feeling that she was in plain sight as they trotted past. One frowned down at her, opened his mouth as if he might say something, but the man behind him gave him a shove, and he continued on. That one might have a few drops of dragon blood running through his veins if he had sensed something off about her illusion. She hoped that wouldn't come back to trouble her later.

Just get me, and we'll worry about it then.

Feeling antsy, are you?

It has *been three hundred years.*

Everyone cleared out without further trouble, and Sardelle climbed out of the cart. She grabbed a couple of the sticks of dynamite before jogging toward the end of the tunnel. She hoped she could reach Jaxi without using dangerous explosives, but there were limits to what she could do against a mountain.

I'm about two hundred meters from the end of their tunnel.

Sardelle grabbed the last lantern hanging on the wall before the passage grew dark and narrow, fresh earth upturned along the sides, waiting to be shoveled into carts.

You're almost there.

I'll need you to lend me some of your power, Jaxi.

That works best when you're holding me, but you know I'll try. I don't want to be burned along with the rest of the artifacts those people

pull out of here.
   I'm sure you could withstand the heat of their incinerator.
   Maybe so, but I don't relish the sunburn.

   A low passage to Sardelle's right made her pause, one that opened into a room. Ah, this was where they had pulled out the books. She ducked into the space and walked a few paces, holding the lantern aloft. She gave it extra energy, so the flame flared, and she could make out the smashed remains of what had once been bookshelves and carpets. The air smelled stale, and the ceiling had been caved in completely in places, but part of the room had withstood the quaking, thanks to a couple of sturdy marble supports still standing. Sardelle touched one, the stone cool and smooth. The miners had already removed most of the artifacts—odd to think of books and trappings she had passed by mere weeks ago, as far as her brain knew, as artifacts now—but there would be others in the mountain. She wished there were a way to recover them, to preserve them, instead of letting them be taken out to be destroyed, or perhaps carted off as quirky treasures.

   She climbed back into the main tunnel before Jaxi could remind her that one particular "artifact" was the priority.

   The ceiling lowered further, the walls raw from fresh pickaxe gouges, and Sardelle was crouching by the time she reached the end of the passage. She set down the lantern and touched the wall. She felt Jaxi's aura through the rock, calling her hand like a beacon. Fifteen degrees to the left and about twenty degrees downward. The miners would have gotten closer, but they never would have chanced across the sword. That was, she reminded herself, what she had wanted.

   Here goes, she warned Jaxi.

   She burned into the rock with her mind, winnowing a small hole, as if she were a termite gnawing through wood. She would widen it later, but for now, she emulated water, finding the route of least resistance. At first, the way was easy. Some of this was, after all, rock that had already been excavated once, rather than the solid core of the mountain, so much of it was packed rubble rather than solid slab. But she reached a spot where nothing except several meters of granite lay ahead.

The dynamite?

I'd hate to cause a cave-in. Especially when I'm standing here. Give me time—I can burn through. Sardelle's thighs ached, so she dropped to her knees. How long had she already been at it?

You may not have time.

The miners are coming back?

Not yet, but something is going on up top. People gathering.

All right. Sardelle inserted one of the cylindrical sticks into the hole she had created, then pushed it through with her mind. She had to widen the hole in places to maneuver it around bends, but she would have had to widen the tunnel anyway to get Jaxi out.

Soon the stick nestled against the granite. She lit the fuse with a thought, then retreated to the wooden supports farther back in the tunnel. As the flame burned closer to the stick, a fit of panic washed over her. She imagined the mountain falling all about her, as it had that horrible day weeks—centuries—before. She almost sprinted all the way back to the tram, but there wasn't time.

With all that intervening rock, the explosion was muffled. A faint tremor ran beneath Sardelle's feet, but the massive cave-in she had worried about didn't come.

Did that even do any good?

Big hole, Jaxi replied. *Come back. Keep going.*

Sardelle checked her termite-passage. "Hole" wasn't the precise word, as it was still filled with rock, but now the granite was crumbled, and she could continue burrowing down. She wiped sweat out of her eyes. A dull ache had started in her head—though all she was doing was standing there, the mental work was wearying. She was thinking of telling Jaxi she needed to rest when a fresh wave of energy surged into her. Even separated, a soulblade had power to share if it wanted.

You're close.

Sardelle came across something metallic sooner than expected, but it wasn't Jaxi. Right, she had been buried in a training room among a lot of practice blades. Sardelle wagered the soldiers up above wouldn't be so quick to destroy *those* types of relics. She weaved past what must have been a rack of swords and shields, and kept going, drawn closer until—

Yes!

Sardelle smiled. *You see the light?*

No, but I got a draft of fresh air. Make that stale air.

I didn't know swords were connoisseurs of air.

We're not. I'll take anything.

Sardelle wrapped a mental hand around Jaxi's hilt and began the task of pulling her back through the small tunnel. She was distracted midway by water dribbling out of the hole she had made in the main passage.

Uh, are you wet, Jaxi?

Yes, it's ruining my stale air, but I'll survive.

The water turned from a dribble to a faster flow. Sardelle shifted away from the opening and returned to navigating the soulblade through the tight passage, though she let her awareness seep into the rocks around, searching for the source of the water. It seemed to be coming from behind that huge slab of granite she had broken up. Her first silly thought was that one of the pipes her people had installed to supply indoor plumbing had erupted, but surely that had happened long ago. This was probably some hidden spring she had stumbled across. A spring that—

Hurry, Jaxi urged. *Something's groaning in here. It sounds like a dam about to burst.*

Great.

At least they were close. Sardelle stretched out her hand, certain Jaxi's sleek steel form would float out of the hole at any moment.

But an alarming crack emanated from the rock first. The mountain groaned, not just from the direction of the granite, but all around her. A tremor ran beneath her feet, this one fiercer than the one the dynamite had caused. And it was followed by a second and a third, until Sardelle had to brace herself against the tunnel wall to keep from tumbling to her knees. Behind her, dirt shifted and trickled down from the ceiling.

With single-minded determination, Sardelle kept her focus on Jaxi, on pulling the blade out, on—

There. The soulblade flew out point first on a gush of water that spattered Sardelle in the chest. The sword might have struck her, too, but it flared with a silvery glow and pivoted in the air. The hilt came to rest in her hand, even though Sardelle had been focused more on flailing and staggering back from the gushing water than on catching it.

Go, Jaxi urged, the word echoing in Sardelle's head with twice the power now that they were touching.

She would have sprinted away regardless. More than dirt was falling around her now. With the shaking of the earth, rocks flew free and smashed down from the ceiling with the intensity of meteors slamming into the earth. Thanks to Jaxi enhancing her mental energy, forming a shield around herself was a simple matter, but neither of them had the power to unbury themselves if the mountain fell on them.

Sardelle leaped ore carts and abandoned tools as rocks and dirt bounced off her barrier, inches from her shoulders and head. A boulder as big as she was crashed down not three feet in front of her. She almost smacked into it—Jaxi did gouge a chunk of it away before Sardelle stopped. There was no way around it, so she climbed up the side. There was only a foot of space at the top, and she had to suck everything in to squeeze between the boulder and the dirt ceiling. Rocks clawed at her shield.

The lighting grew dimmer—the lanterns behind her being shaken out or smothered by dust. She glanced back, and her heart nearly jumped out of her chest. It wasn't dust. A torrent of water was racing toward her, knocking off the lanterns and dousing them as it rushed closer.

She scrambled the rest of the way across the boulder, tearing her fingernails in her effort to pull herself over faster. She tumbled down the other side, managing to land on her feet, then sprinted again. The open chamber at the base of the tram came into view.

Almost there. Ten more steps. Five.

At three steps, the river smashed into her back. Her shield kept it from hurting and dulled some of the iciness, but it didn't keep the flow from sweeping her up into its grasp. The force knocked her into a wall and then tumbled her feet over head, mocking the power she thought she had.

If not for the big chamber, Sardelle would have drowned in a tunnel flooded with water, but the flow spread out, its height diminishing. She scrambled to her feet as it gushed out around her. Thinking she would have to deal with guards, she lifted the sword, ready to deflect bullets if she had to. But nobody was there. A good thing, since Jaxi was glowing like a comet.

Calm that down some, will you?

Sorry. I'm excited to be out.

It'll be hard to sneak out of the fort with you outshining the sun.

Is that the next goal? Out of the fort?

Sardelle thought of Ridge. It pained her to say it, but she whispered, "I think it has to be."

Water continued to gush out of the tunnel they had exited. Some of it was being funneled into other tunnels, but the level was rising in the chamber too. Sardelle sloshed toward a cage resting at the base of the tram shaft. It would be easier to sneak out if she climbed up the long passage, but going up would be much harder than sliding down it had been. Even on the way in, it had been a tedious slog.

Speaking of slogging... More water coursed toward the shaft, making the cage wobble on its track.

Yes, I'm hurrying. Sardelle pulled open the cage door.

She waved at the lever outside. It flipped upward, but the machine that powered the tram groaned. Its big flywheels were half underwater.

Uh oh.

We might be climbing after all, Jaxi thought.

We? You have some legs tucked under your hilt that you're going to use to help?

Hush. I'll see if I can get that machinery moving.

Sardelle had the engineering knowledge of an ox, so she was happy to leave that task to Jaxi. The ever-rising water level made her nervous though. "We can always get out and climb if we have to," she muttered.

She imagined the water rising up the tram shaft, threatening to drown her if she couldn't climb quickly enough.

No, numerous other levels existed above them with countless miles of tunnels. It would take an ocean to flood them all, and even if she had chanced across a spring that big, it would take a long time for all that water to fill in.

A thunderous crack sounded, so loud Sardelle brought her hands to her ears for protection, clanging the sword on the roof of the cage. More cracks followed, each one like an explosion of dynamite.

Jaxi, if you can't get that contraption moving...

The cage lurched. Sardelle couldn't hear it over the snapping rock and groaning earth all around her, but she felt it. After a few awkward trembles that nearly hurled her into the walls, the cage started upward. It bumped and twitched, as if it were going over rocks on the tracks—and maybe it was—but it continued upward.

You were doubting me?

Who, me?

All the lights disappeared below, swallowed by water and collapsing rocks. Jaxi didn't know if the entire level had gone down, but she prayed that all of the miners had fled because of the ruse with the gas.

Guess they won't be finding and burning any more artifacts for a while. Jaxi sounded smug.

Sardelle couldn't summon a similar emotion. She hadn't meant to create all that chaos. She was lucky to be alive.

She lifted her gaze toward the top of the shaft. Darkness must have fallen while she was digging around, for she couldn't pick out anything. Had the soldiers and miners above heard all the noise? Did they know she was down there? She stretched out with her senses... and cringed.

No less than fifty people were gathered around the mouth of the shaft. She doubted they had come together to play card games. She also doubted that their presence had anything to do with enemy attacks—everyone would have been on the walls then.

Maybe we should stop the cage and climb out, Sardelle suggested.

But what would that do? She would have to crawl up the steep, slick shaft, and she had a feeling those people would still be waiting there when she arrived.

Yes.

Yes, we should stop it, or yes, they'll be waiting?

They've been there a while.

Sardelle remembered Jaxi's earlier warning.

Because of me. She didn't make it a question.

Yes.

Sardelle made sure Jaxi wasn't glowing as the cage traveled the final meters. If she had to, she could fight her way out, shielding herself from bullets and blades the same way she had against falling rocks, but she didn't want to warn anyone of her powers by emerging with a glowing sword. Although thanks to that book, they probably already knew what to expect. And even if she fought her way past everyone, what then? Magical talents or not, she wouldn't be able to navigate that pass in the winter, not without a ship. She wasn't about to call down that shaman for a ride.

It's a possibility.

She shuddered—or maybe shivered, thanks to being wet and feeling the icy drafts coming down from above. *No. It's not.*

Maybe she could figure out how to fly Ridge's dragon contraption. Powering it wouldn't be a problem, but the rest? She had been daunted by the simple tram machine.

"Let's just see what's waiting for us," she muttered.

She might have sensed fifty people, but when they came into sight, it seemed like a thousand torches out there surrounding the tram cage. After the ride up in the darkness, Sardelle squinted at the light. It didn't keep her from seeing all the rifles aimed at her. Even miners were armed, albeit with pickaxes. Fear hung in the air. Fear of her? Gods, she had been helping them all month. How could they forget about that? How could they think she was an enemy now?

Through the cage bars, she spotted General Nax at the back of the crowd—he also had a rifle aimed in her direction. Ridge stood next to him. He had a rifle, but the butt rested on the ground. Only his frown was aimed at her. Somehow that was worse than all of the weapons.

Sardelle blinked back tears. A sorceress striding out to fight shouldn't be weeping.

I can send the cage back down if you want.

It's flooded by now, I'm sure.

Not all the levels.

Sardelle shook her head. With all of those men, Nax could guard this exit indefinitely, and she couldn't stay down there forever.

She was tired after her ordeal below, but she threw her remaining strength into a shield around her body, then pushed open the gate door. The men tensed, their fingers tight on their triggers, but nobody fired.

Of course not. The general wants to know where the rest of the crystals are first.

Hopelessly mired under the new lake, I hope. Sardelle held her arms out and let the soulblade dangle in her grip. Unthreateningly.

She met Ridge's eyes. He didn't look away, but he did mask his expression. She could have probed a little and figured out what he was thinking, but she had a feeling she didn't want to know.

"Take her sword," General Nax said.

Her hand tightened on the hilt. Fight now or fight later? If she fought now, she risked hurting a lot of people. She ought to be able to escape whatever cell they locked her in and find Jaxi later. At night, when most people would be sleeping.

Sighing, she turned the soulblade, extending it hilt first toward one of the twitchy privates who crept forward. Once she was unarmed, two other soldiers walked up, grabbed her by the backs of her arms, and steered her toward a building she knew held cells. She looked up at the sky, at stars so big and bright they seemed touchable, and hoped she hadn't made the wrong choice.

She almost tripped at a sight below the stairs—while she had been down in the tunnels, one of the wall towers had been obliterated. Now that she was out of the crowd, she could see rubble in the courtyard, too, dark rocks against the stark snow drifts. So, she had missed the first real battle. How had it gone? Had Ridge and the others driven off the Cofah? Brought down their ship?

You found a soulblade, came a hungry and unwelcome thought in her head.

Sardelle's shoulders slumped. The shaman. He, at least, was still alive.

Now I see why you've been here, what you wanted. Brilliant.

Thank you, Sardelle responded though she knew it was more Jaxi's existence he found brilliant than anything she had done.

A soft laugh sounded in her thoughts as the soldiers led her into a cell-filled basement hallway. *Better sleep with it under your pillow. As rare as they are anymore, I'll be looking for it when we return.*

Ugh. Not three minutes had passed, and she was already certain she had made the wrong decision. Jaxi was getting locked in some office or supply closet—where a powerful shaman would have no trouble finding the blade—and Sardelle was getting locked in a cell.

A heavy iron door thumped shut behind her, and a latch was thrown. Utter darkness filled the tiny room.

I think we need to break out tonight, Jaxi.

Sardelle expected an answer along the lines of, "That's obvious," but she didn't get an answer at all.

Jaxi?

Silence.

She realized with an alarming start that she couldn't *feel* Jaxi anymore, either. Not on the fort, not anywhere. Even when the soulblade had been buried in the mountain, she had sensed it. What had they done? Thrown Jaxi off a cliff?

Sardelle dropped her hands to her knees and told herself hyperventilating wouldn't do her any good. The advice didn't help.

Chapter 13

Sardelle needed to escape and find Jaxi—wherever the soulblade was—but she had to wait until some of those milling soldiers and miners went to their beds. Maybe the guard outside her door would grow less alert too. She paced in circles around the tiny cell. The carnage she had left down below had people buzzing around the courtyard, going up and down on the tram. And she sensed Ridge and the engineer working on the flier again. Er, wait. No, he wasn't up there anymore. She swept across the fort with her senses—others she might not have been able to identify so readily, but she knew his aura well by now. She halted in the middle of her circle and faced the door.

He was on his way down here.

To see her? Her heart swelled with relief, but the emotion soon faltered. She didn't know what he felt, what he wanted. Maybe the general knew they'd had a relationship and had decided to send Ridge to question her. And if, instead of strong-arming her, he gave her that quirky smile, she would tell him whatever he wanted. No, she would do that anyway. What did the crystals matter to her? What mattered was finding Jaxi. She would trade him whatever information he wanted if he gave her the soulblade's location.

It took Ridge longer than she expected to come down the stairs and into her hallway of cells. There was an uncharacteristic anxiousness about him. Those pauses… was he stopping to listen? To glance back over his shoulder? The general hadn't sent him at all, she realized. He was sneaking down. Did he know about the guard? What was he going to say to the man?

Soft murmurs started up outside the door. Sardelle leaned her ear against the cold iron, but she still couldn't make out words.

A soft thunk sounded below her ear—a key turning in the lock. She stepped back.

"Sardelle?" Ridge whispered, pushing open the door a couple of inches.

"Yes." Ridiculous that her heart was beating so loudly that he could probably hear it. His opinion of her shouldn't matter so much. But it did. She could fight against everyone else in the fort, but she didn't want to fight him.

"I thought you might have sneaked away already." Ridge stepped inside, a lantern in hand.

The hallway outside was dark, and Sardelle didn't see the guard. Ridge leaned his back against the wall, not coming close.

She tried not to let that distance sting. He was here at least.

"Not without Ja—my sword."

"Ah." Did he sound hurt by her answer? Did her feelings toward him still matter?

"And," Sardelle added, "I would not wish to leave you without… " Knowing if he still cared? Knowing if he could possibly see past that which he feared in her?

Ridge sighed. "Saying goodbye?"

"No. I mean, I don't want to say goodbye."

Sardelle shifted from foot to foot in the silence that followed. She didn't regret saying the words, but maybe she should have waited and let him talk first.

"You're not saying anything," she observed oh-so-helpfully.

"You can't read my thoughts?"

"I don't. We aren't like that. Very few ever were, except for those who went rogue and quite literally ruined the world for the rest of us. There are rules that we swear by and hold dearly. Or did."

After another long pause, Ridge asked, "How old are you?"

"Thirty-four."

"How… "

"This is hard to believe—trust me, I had a hard time believing it myself when I woke up, but I basically missed three hundred years."

The single lantern didn't provide a lot of light, and Ridge's face—which had been carefully neutral through most of their conversation—didn't change much, though his bottom lip did lower a few millimeters.

"I was here when the original attack came that collapsed this mountain," Sardelle said. "It was actually your ancestors, I suppose. They figured out a way to sap in beneath our community when nearly everyone was home for a big celebration, and I'm not sure how it happened exactly or where they found such powerful explosives—your dynamite hadn't been invented yet, so far as I know—but it was devastating."

"My ancestors." He sounded like he didn't want to believe her.

Sardelle shrugged. "Well, maybe not *yours* specifically. Yours might have been off inventing flying machines somewhere."

She watched him, hoping for a smile, but he was either too stunned or wasn't believing anything she said.

"Ridge," she said, then paused, half-expecting him to tell her not to call him by first name anymore. He didn't. "The sword. It's mine. I don't mean in the I-found-it-so-I-have-the-strongest-claim-on-it way, but in the... we were bonded when I was sixteen and passed my exams. There's a spirit inside, that of someone who was once a sorceress but who died young and placed her soul in the blade so she could continue to live on, in a manner of speaking. This happened over three—er, six hundred years ago, and Jaxi has been bonded with several handlers since then, but most recently with me."

Somewhere during her speech, Ridge had leaned back against the wall, one hand propped on his hip. If he weren't holding the lantern with the other, he probably would have propped that one up too. The stance said... I'm not buying this.

"I don't need you to believe all that," Sardelle said, "and it's perfectly understandable if you don't, but I just wanted you to know what Jaxi—the sword means to me. She's all I have left of my family, my friends, my *life*." Her voice broke, and she took a few breaths, struggling for equilibrium. The last few weeks had been busy enough to distract her from all she had lost—aside from a few nights in those awful barracks when she had allowed herself to weep silently—but that didn't mean the emotions weren't there, hovering beneath the surface.

Ridge stirred, lifting a hand toward her, but he let it drop again. Uncertain.

"I sense that something's been done," Sardelle said when she could find a more normal tone again. "You don't owe me anything, but if you could tell me where she—the sword—is, I would appreciate it."

"Actually, I owe you... much. More than what I thought, I'm beginning to realize."

Was that why he was here? Because he felt he *owed* her something?

Sardelle swallowed. It was better than not having him talking to her at all, and yet she wished he had come simply because he cared.

"What's a *sherastu*?" he asked.

"It's a title. Mage advisor. We worked alongside the military and the clan leaders to defend Iskandia from the Cofah and other invaders."

Ridge nodded to himself. "This afternoon, when that owl showed up again, distracting us so the airship could sneak in for attacks, no odd little blasts of wind hit it."

So, she hadn't been as circumspect as she had hoped with her attacks. "Sorry. I was busy down there. I didn't know the fort was under attack."

"Yes, when the general got the report on the devastation down there, his face turned so red, I thought he would pass out."

"What happened down there wasn't intentional," Sardelle said. "I was just trying to get the sword. If I'd had more time, I could have been more careful. I wasn't expecting a water source."

"Nax is certain you sabotaged the tunnels on purpose so we couldn't pull out any more crystals."

"I almost crushed and drowned myself in the process. I assure you it wasn't intentional. Also, these crystals you value so much, they're meaningless to me. They were our light fixtures."

"I believe you. I—did you say *light* fixtures?" For the first time, a hint of Ridge's humor shown through. Tickled by the concept, was he? Good.

"They hung on the ceilings. Honestly, if you gave me a few days to study, I could probably make them for you."

Ridge's response was somewhere between a snort, a cough, and maybe that was a laugh. "Well, that would be one more argument I could make for keeping you alive." His comment sobered him though. He stepped forward, his face grim. "The Cofah are on the horizon again, or the general might already be down here with his chosen interrogator. He thinks you're too dangerous to keep alive. You need to... " He glanced toward the hallway, perhaps making sure the guard hadn't returned. "You need to not be here when he comes."

"Did you come to leave the door open for me?"

"Do I... need to do that? That young man out there—" Ridge waved toward the hallway, "—he'll be back soon, and he respects me. I would rather not have him think I'm a traitor. I just wanted to make sure you knew and that you could find a way out on your own." He gazed into her eyes. "Can you?"

"Yes. I was waiting for things to quiet down out there, and I was hyperventilating a little because I couldn't communicate—er, feel—my sword." Sardelle studied his face. She wanted to ask him if telling her Jaxi's location would make him a traitor in his people's eyes—or in his own, which probably mattered more to him, no matter what he had said about the guard. But at the same time, she didn't want to press him to go against his morals. She could find it on her own. Someone else would have the information and she could, despite what she had told Ridge, access it.

"It's in an iron box in what used to be my office and is now Nax's," Ridge said.

Iron. Of course. It blocked the sensing of magic in a way miles of stone didn't. Sardelle slumped against the wall. Jaxi was in an office fifty meters away, not at the bottom of some distant chasm. "I see your people haven't forgotten *all* Referatu lore in the last three centuries."

"Heriton studied up after he found that book." Ridge wanted to say more—his thoughts burned at the front of his mind with such intensity that she got the gist without trying to read him. He wanted to elicit a promise from her that she wouldn't hurt anyone on the way to retrieving her sword, but he didn't want to have to ask. He wanted to trust her. He just wasn't sure anymore.

Though that uncertainty stung, Sardelle chose to see it as a good sign. In time, maybe he would get used to the idea of her as a sorceress. Maybe...

She shook her head. She would worry about that later. For now, she had to escape and retrieve Jaxi before the mob dragged her out for a shooting.

"Thank you for the information," Sardelle said. "I'll be careful. Nobody will see me."

Ridge exhaled slowly, surreptitiously. "Good."

Sardelle sensed someone walking into the building upstairs. "My guard is returning."

Ridge glanced toward the hallway. "I'll try not to find it disturbing that you knew that before I did." He sighed and looked back at her, holding her eyes for a moment.

Hoping for a kiss would be too much at this point, and yet...

"Want to rub my dragon?" Ridge asked.

Sardelle blinked. "What?"

He fished the wooden figurine out of his pocket.

"Oh." She offered a sheepish shrug—that was *not* where her mind had gone—and stuck her hand out. Enh, why not?

Feeling silly, she rubbed the belly of the wooden dragon and handed it back to Ridge.

"Sir?" the guard asked from the hallway.

"Yes, I'm done." Ridge pocketed his lucky charm. "Thank you, Private."

The young man squinted into the cell, assessing Sardelle but not quite meeting her eyes. "You're brave, sir."

"Uh huh." Ridge stepped into the hall.

"Is it going to be all right for me to be out here, sir?" the private whispered. "General Nax said the iron door was supposed to keep her from getting out, but I... I also heard—*overheard*—him tell someone I was expendable."

Ridge snorted. "*Nax* is expendable. You'll be fine, soldier.

Now, shut the door, eh? We wouldn't want her to escape."

"Yes, sir. Of course."

The door thumped shut, and if the men spoke further, Sardelle didn't hear it. An iron door? They thought that would keep her in here? If they had lined the whole cell in iron, it would have kept her from sensing or communicating with the outside world, but it wouldn't have done anything to nullify her actual power. Still, Sardelle couldn't help but feel very alone again when the key thunked in the lock. Ridge had helped her, but she also had a feeling that had been a goodbye as well.

***

Ridge hadn't taken more than three steps out of the confinement building when shouts started up on the wall.

"They're coming again."

"To the weapons!"

Ridge couldn't spot the airship in the night sky yet, but he trusted the lookouts. He jogged not to the wall but to the flier perched on its landing legs near the frozen stream, its hull as clean and rust-free as it was going to get. He wasn't surprised to find Captain Bosmont standing next to a wing, the engine already humming in the back of the craft.

"Ready for that test run, sir?" he asked.

Ridge glanced toward the horizon. "Yes."

"I figured you might be. Got her as ready as I could while everyone was worrying about our witch."

Ridge's jaw tightened at the word witch, but he didn't correct Bosmont. That didn't matter now. Getting in the sky and helping the fort did. "Thank you, Captain."

"If anyone can take that airship down, you can."

Ridge climbed into the cockpit. "I appreciate your faith."

"Good. But you should also know, if you wreck this baby I spent so many hours on, I'm going to hunt you down in whatever level of hell they stick you in."

"I'll keep that in mind, Captain."

"Oh, and one more thing, sir," Bosmont said, a grin splitting his broad face. "I made a little something extra for you, to keep you warm up there."

"Chicken soup?"

"Not exactly." The engineer winked. "They're down by your feet."

No sooner had Ridge slid into the stitched up leather cockpit seat and pulled his harness across his chest when an irritated call came up from below. "Where in all the cursed realms do you think you're going, Colonel?"

"To stop that airship, General."

"Were you going to ask for permission first or just do whatever you felt like, as usual?"

Ridge smirked down at the man. "The latter, naturally."

He fired up the lift thrusters, drowning out Nax's reply. He was going to be in so much trouble after this was all sorted out that it hardly mattered what he did at this point. Maybe if he took down the Cofah airship, his disrespect—and his dalliance with Sardelle—might be forgotten or at least treated with lenience. And if he failed utterly against the Cofah, the only threat he had to worry about was Bosmont's.

When the thrusters pushed into the earth, the engineer and general scurrying back, and the flier inched off the ground, Ridge let out a relieved breath. If he hadn't gotten off the ground, he would have felt idiotic about his insubordination. But the craft responded to his touch, if more sluggishly than he would have preferred. The crystal in the back glowed, illuminating his control panel. At least that was at full power. A ceiling light. The ridiculousness of it all almost made him throw his head back and laugh.

Later. The Cofah ship was visible now, not hovering above the distant peaks, but sailing straight toward the fort.

Ridge hit the switch that lowered a cover over the crystal, and the light disappeared. No need to make it obvious to the enemy that he was coming. His hands knew the controls well; he didn't need to see to fly this craft.

As it rose above the fort walls, wind whipped through his short hair, and the chill air burned his ears. Usually he would have a leather cap and goggles, but he hadn't been expecting to fly out here. All of his piloting gear was back in his locker on base. Tonight, he would have to make do without. One way or another, he doubted he would be in the sky long.

Once he had enough altitude, Ridge nudged the controls, taking the flier toward a rocky ridge the airship was paralleling. Maybe he could sneak behind her that way—the dark metal hull blending in with the bare slope—and attack from behind while the Cofah were focused on the cannons and rocket launchers in the fort. The soft clink-thunks of the engine shouldn't be audible over the wind and the airship's own machinery. He hoped.

Ridge took the flier to a higher altitude than the airship, though he was careful to keep the rocks behind him, and not the snow. He would stand out like a beacon against a white backdrop. Higher was often better, though, especially with airship captains who rarely took their slow-moving craft into battles. When they did, they were often used to looking down to drop bombs, not up to fend off attacks.

The men on the deck were visible as Ridge passed by, bundled so heavily against the icy wind that they seemed to waddle from place to place. The number of people manning the cannons disturbed him. Not only that, but the sheer number of cannons. He supposed he should have expected that, based on the damage the craft had done to the fort during its last attack. Clearly this particular airship had been created for war, maybe even specifically for this mission: to destroy the only source of the Iskandian dragon flier power supplies.

Ridge was tempted to bank and veer in, tilting his wings as he flew by so he could strafe the deck with his bullets. They were preparing something to one side, a smaller balloon and a big basket. An escape craft? Something for launching bombs? Or maybe for delivering troops. He almost attacked it, but he wanted to go for a more important target on his first run. He could only surprise them once.

The flier passed the airship, and, staying above them, keeping the stars at his back, he glided through a turn. He grimaced at the pull in the controls, the jerky way the craft responded.

Tonight's run might be all she had in her. He could only hope it was enough.

He leveled the craft and headed toward the back of the airship. If this one was true to other Cofah designs, the engines would be in the rear, hidden below decks and behind those wooden planks, planks that might be reinforced with metal. The airships might *look* a lot like the Cofah sailing ships that plundered the seas, but they were more advanced, usually with superior defenses. His guns could still do damage though. And he could always target the balloon, though it would take a lot of holes to let out enough gas to bring it down.

With the lights of the fort visible between the deck and the balloon, Ridge struck. He squeezed a trigger, and guns blasted, punching holes into the rear of the ship. Shouts arose on deck, just audible over the wind. Men raced for cannons at the back of the deck.

Tears burned his eyes, streaking back into his hair, and Ridge again lamented his missing goggles, but he didn't falter in his mission. He kept firing until those men were close to targeting him, then he pulled the nose up, hurling a few rounds into the balloon before rising above it. He slowed his speed as much as he could, putting that balloon between him and the deck so he would seem to disappear to those below. The flier would drop out of the sky if it tried to pace the airship, so he made tight circles above it. He couldn't see the Cofah any more than they could see him, but he hoped he had them consternated—and distracted.

A boom came from the fort, the first cannon firing from the walls. The ball sailed by a few meters to the side of the airship, but another cannon blasted on the heels of the first. Those on the airship deck should be busy now. Time for Ridge to do some more damage.

He guided the flier away from the balloon, rising again so it would be difficult for them to see, then swooping around to target the airship from the rear once more. That was the intent anyway. Something streaked out of the darkness, arrowing right at him.

A cannonball, that was his first thought, but that would have moved too quickly to see, and this was bigger anyway. Much bigger.

Ridge banked hard, his left wing tipping toward the sky. The object—no, the *creature*—blurred past him, missing by inches. Far more agile than he, it turned back toward the flier before he realized what he was dealing with. If he hadn't seen it before, he would have been mystified, but this wasn't the owl's first appearance.

Ridge swooped left and right, trying to make a difficult target for the creature, even as he distanced himself from the airship. He didn't want to be visible to their cannons while the owl distracted them. It screeched, raising all the hair on his body. Not only was the unearthly cry eerie... it was close. He glanced back, searching for it against the snowy peaks and the stars, but it was playing the same game he had with the airship. Only better. How could a mechanical contraption rival the grace of nature? Granted, some sorcerer had perverted the creature, but it still had all the agility of a bird of prey.

Something slammed into the top of the flier. Metal screeched in Ridge's ear. He shrank low in his seat, though he kept his hands on the controls. He twisted his neck and glimpsed spread wings and beady yellow eyes—the cursed thing had its talons locked around a bar on the frame. It wasn't more than three feet from Ridge. The cockpit was partially enclosed, but not fully. A giant owl could slip its talons in and slash his neck.

"So attack it first, eh?"

Easier said than done. Ridge banked hard, shaking the creature free. Then he accelerated, flying over the fort. He wasn't sure it was the best direction—with that idiot Nax in charge, Ridge might very well get shot down by his own people—but it was the only way that offered room to accelerate without having to climb over a mountain.

He pushed the engines to maximum power, hoping the owl couldn't match the speed. In a dive, a bird could drop as quickly as his flier, but surely wings couldn't flap as quickly as propellers rotated. He twisted his neck again, looking behind him. His own personal flier back home had mirrors, but he hadn't thought to install them here. Silly of him not to anticipate attacks by giant birds.

The owl was trailing him, its massive wings flapping, but falling behind. Ridge thought about trying to pull up right before he hit the side of the mountain ahead—hoping it would be so intent on chasing him that it smashed into the rocks—but he reminded himself that this wasn't another pilot-flown machine, this was a bird, something far more agile than his flier. Especially *this* flier.

Instead, when he had pulled ahead as much as he could without running into a mountain, he banked hard, turning back toward the owl. He lined up that dark silhouette, which was easier to see with the lights of the fort as a backdrop, and pounded ammunition into it. He remembered that their bullets hadn't done much in that canyon, but the flier's big guns had more power. He hoped it was enough.

Ridge hit it. Many times. But the owl kept coming. It flew straight at him.

With visions of it tangling in his propeller, he swerved at the last moment. The creature clipped his wing, and the flier shimmied like a top spinning on an old cobblestone drive. The nose of the craft dipped, and the rocks and snow of the hillside below filled Ridge's vision. He forced himself to keep a loose grip on the controls, though his instincts cried for him to yank on them, to pull the flier up before he crashed. Instead he waited for the wings to find equilibrium again, then eased the nose up. He swooped so low to the ground that snow sprayed in his wake, but he started climbing once more. An intermittent kerchunk-clink joined the engine's regular noise.

"A little longer," he murmured to it. "Hold out a little longer."

He searched all around for the owl, hoping he had injured it enough that it couldn't continue to fly, but not daring to believe that was the case. Nothing streaked out of the sky at him. Maybe, just maybe, luck had favored him.

Before he could think to celebrate, he spotted the Cofah hovering directly over the fort. Cannonballs blasted upward at the wooden hull, but impossibly they bounced off. The sky burned beneath the airship, lit up like an inferno as it spat a hailstorm of flames down onto the courtyard and walls.

"What the—" Ridge shook his head. Whatever weapon that was, he couldn't identify it. All he knew was that his people were in trouble.

Chapter 14

Sardelle crept down the hallway toward the front door of the prison building. She had left the young guard slumped on the floor outside her cell, snoozing in a deep slumber. It would take a cannon going off in his ear to wake him. Making him drowsy had taken time, but it had been a better alternative than giving him a rash.

Missing Jaxi's usual commentary on the subject, Sardelle cracked open the door to peer into the courtyard. It was surprisingly empty.

A cannon boomed from atop the wall, and she had her answer as to why. The fort was under attack.

Usually, she wouldn't root for that, but it gave her the opportunity she needed. She didn't have to throw illusions around or camouflage herself to trot unnoticed to the headquarters building. She did falter for a moment when she realized the dragon flier wasn't perched near the creek as it had been for days. A hasty sweep of the fort revealed that Ridge wasn't around either. The buzz of a flier's propellers drifted on the breeze, and she spotted the craft near the mountains south of the fort, a dark shadow against the snowy peaks. At first, she couldn't guess why he was there when the airship was floating in from the north. Then she spotted a second shadow. That shaman's overgrown owl.

Sardelle chomped on her lip, torn between going for her sword and trying to help Ridge from there. Seeing a soldier jogging down the stairs from the wall and turning in her direction made up her mind. He was heading toward the armory, but he would see her if she didn't duck inside. She pushed through the door, vowing to return shortly. With Jaxi's help, she would be able to do more damage, maybe even stop that shaman, not just his pet. She prayed Ridge could survive against the owl for a few minutes on his own.

Sardelle jogged straight up to Ridge's—now the general's—office without seeing anyone. It was so easy that she paused with her hand on the knob, half suspecting a trap. No, she didn't believe Ridge would do that to her. It was more that she worried she would open the door and find Jaxi had been moved. What if the general, knowing the soulblade's value, had taken it with him when he ran out to command the fort defense?

"Look first *before* worrying," Sardelle grumbled, and tried to turn the knob. It was locked. Well, someone must have had her in mind.

An explosion sounded. It hadn't come from the cannons on the wall but from somewhere above, and she sensed the approach of dozens of people—and one shaman. He wasn't talking to her this time. Maybe he was up to something more important. Like planning how to raze the fortress, destroy her, and take Jaxi.

"Not happening."

Another boom rang out. The floor quaked beneath her feet, and for a moment, she clutched her chest, remembering the disaster in the tunnels below. Something clanked to the floor on the other side of the door. The sword case? That brought her back to the moment, filled her with urgency.

Sardelle's first thought had been to carefully disable the lock, but with the Cofah floating ever closer, she simply blasted the hinges off the door. Let the general scratch his head over that later.

The office hadn't changed much, and she spotted the out-of-place iron box on top of a bookcase right away. Several books and a filing cabinet drawer had been dumped to the floor from the quakes, but the long box remained in place. When she climbed on the desk to reach it, it reminded her of the day she had walked in on Ridge cleaning, and another twinge of worry for him ran through her. She tugged the box down, hardly caring that it was too heavy for her. She let it clank to the floor, jumped down, and tried to tug it open. Of course it was locked. She hissed in frustration at all the delays and tore off another set of hinges. The general wouldn't know if a sorceress or a tornado had swept into his office.

Sardelle yanked open the lid on the box.

It's about time.

She sank to her knees on the floor in relief. *After three hundred years of being trapped, that half hour shouldn't have fazed you.*

It was well over an hour, thank you.

There was a piece of paper tied around the blade. Sardelle yanked it free, opened it, and found an address. She snorted. Nax had the blade all ready to ship off to some military research facility, did he?

Cannons boomed outside the window. Reminded that Ridge and the rest of the fort were in trouble, Sardelle stuffed the paper in her pocket, grabbed the soulblade, and raced back into the hallway. At the bottom of the stairs, she thrust open the front door and almost ran into a rain of fire.

The air sizzled with heat—and magic. Screams of pain erupted on the ramparts.

"Cover," someone cried, "find cover!"

"Stay where you are, soldier!" That was General Nax. Bastard.

Sardelle backed into the doorway to give herself a moment to think. A shield. That was what they needed. Yes.

Around the whole fort?

It has to be. Sardelle took a deep breath and concentrated. She created a translucent dome, so subtle that the fiery rain continued through it at first, slowed down but not extinguished. Gradually, she added more energy until the burning pellets bounced off instead of falling through.

Someone cheered from the wall. She doubted the soldier had any idea what was going on, other than the fact that fire wasn't falling onto his head, but Sardelle let herself feel bolstered—*appreciated*—nonetheless.

They're going to want to shoot through your shield. In fact, they're about to try now.

Sardelle grimaced. Ricocheting cannonballs would not be good. *Let me see if I can tinker with it and—*

I'll handle it. You look for a way to deal with the shaman. He'll know right where we are now.

Understood.

She would have preferred to search for Ridge and see how he was doing with that owl, but the shaman had to be the priority.

He found her first. With a mental attack. Something like a harpoon blasted into her mind. Pressure erupted from it, until her eyeballs felt like they would burst from her head. Sardelle dropped to a knee, pressing her fist into the cold earth for support. If not for Jaxi, the shield would have fallen. For a moment, all Sardelle could focus on was building her own shield, one around herself, one that could repel his attack. She gathered the strength to thrust him away, to return the assault, but paused before deploying it.

What if she played dead? Lured him down? She couldn't physically touch him as long as he was up on that ship, but if he came down, looking for Jaxi…

Yes, use me as bait. We invaluable swords love that.

Sardelle's head was still throbbing—if she fought him off completely, he would get a feel for how much power she had, and he wouldn't come down—but she managed a quick response. *Who told you that you were invaluable?*

All of the truly wise people who have known me. Go on. Crumple to the ground with theatrical flair. I won't give you away.

Sardelle opted for slumping against the doorjamb. She quieted her mind, as if she were unconscious. The attack continued to batter at her, but she gritted her teeth and endured it. If this didn't work in the next few seconds, though, she was going to get angry and start looking for ways to rip *his* hinges off, whether he was a hundred meters above her or not.

The flames have stopped, Jaxi reported. *Should I drop the shield?*

Yes, he'll be distracted with me for the moment. She hoped. Besides, to further the illusion, she had to stop doing anything that showed off her power. *Just be prepared to raise it again.*

Got it.

Then the shaman was probing her, the mental equivalent of checking her pulse at her throat. Neither she nor Jaxi thought a word lest he feel it. The sensation of letting him investigate without putting up defensive shields was like having ants crawling all over her skin, but she endured it, as she had the pain.

Eventually, he withdrew. The cannons were firing again—both from the fort and the ship—but Sardelle and the shaman had other concerns.

He's coming.

Flying? Sardelle had never heard of a sorcerer who could, at least not without the help of some sort of apparatus. *Or did someone drop a rope?* Was the airship close enough for that? Surely the soldiers would object.

He's bringing down a hot air balloon. Must be the airship equivalent of a lifeboat.

Are our soldiers attacking it?

Jaxi paused. *Yes, but the shaman is shielding it, just as you did, and he's protecting the airship, too, though it looks like your flying friend did some damage before the shaman was prepared.*

Ridge? Good. Sardelle felt a swell of pride for him. Though it quickly turned to worry. Would the shaman sense it if she stretched out, trying to locate him?

Stay still. He's landed. And he's walking this way.

Sardelle cracked an eyelid. She was surprised there weren't any soldiers racing down from the walls to attack the shaman.

Ah, but he wasn't alone. The bronze-skinned man who strode toward her in a cloak of black fur, his long white hair startling in contrast, was surrounded by no less than two dozen other men, shaven-headed Cofah warriors wielding short-swords and long double-barreled firearms that they shot one-handed from their hips. The soldiers inside the fort *were* shooting at them, but the shaman was shielding them.

Jaxi's hilt grew warm, ready for a fight. *You drew them in. Do you have a plan? I don't think he'll be bothered by a rash.*

Sardelle's plan had been to throw everything she had at the shaman and hope to take him by surprise, but if she could force his shield down, that might be enough. A sorcerer was as susceptible to bullets as the next person.

The Cofah warriors smiled as bullets bounced away from them and grew confident enough to launch their own attacks.

They started shooting at the men on the walls. The shaman raised a hand toward the mountainside, and the doors Ridge had ordered built over the tram shafts flew open amongst squeals of metal.

Sardelle cursed at herself. Inviting the bastard down hadn't been a good idea after all. If all those miners streamed out and started attacking their captors...

Time for her own attack. The shaman was less than ten meters away. Sardelle summoned her energy and blasted it at him, targeting his mind, just as he had done to her. She could only hope it was enough.

* * *

At first, Ridge had the airship in sight as he streaked across the sky, the wind tearing his eyes and scraping his cheeks raw. Then he saw the smaller balloon on the ground inside the fort, the bald Cofah troops striding across the courtyard in their crimson uniforms and cloaks. One distinctive white-haired figure at the center of their formation stood out. Ridge didn't know who he was—or why his own people weren't shooting those intruders—but had a feeling he was responsible for that fire that had been raining from the sky. Another sorcerer.

"Would have been nice if headquarters had had a clue about this ship," he muttered, tipping the flier's nose down to dive for that formation.

He fired, but realized the problem immediately. The bullets bounced off before striking the men. He adjusted his targeting, thinking he would blast a few holes in the ground next to the Cofah and see how well their invisible shielding protected them from heaving earth at their feet, but his finger froze on the trigger. Someone was crumpled on the ground in the doorway of the admin building. Sardelle.

Ridge swallowed—had she been shot retrieving that sword? Or had the shaman done something to her?

Necessity made him pull up, and she disappeared from his sight. Rage and fear formed a lump in his throat, and he almost missed the significance of a blast from overhead, a cannon firing. At him. It blazed past the cockpit, missing his wing by inches.

Ridge turned away from the fort, knowing he was all-too-well-lit by the fire and lanterns below. He aimed for high sky, though he kept the airship in the corner of his eye. If their sorcerer protector was on the ground, maybe they would be more vulnerable to attack now. He had already done *some* damage. If he could bring the ship down, the Cofah would be stranded, sorcerer or not. As much as he wanted to tear into the fort to protect Sardelle, he never should have fired into the courtyard to start with. He risked hitting his own men that way. This was the more logical attack.

"I hate logic sometimes," Ridge said, the wind stealing his words. Not that there was anyone there to hear them.

Once he was above the airship again, and they couldn't target him so easily, he veered in close. He strafed the oblong balloon, delivering dozens of small holes. With luck, the bullets might chew up the frame inside too. Unfortunately, those little holes wouldn't bring the craft down anytime soon.

Something streaked out of the dark sky and slammed into the front of the cockpit. He jerked back. The owl, he realized at the same moment as its unworldly shriek blasted his ears.

He banked hard, trying to hurl it off the flier. If not for his harness, he might have hurled *himself* out. The cursed magical bird hung on, its wings beating around the cockpit, keeping Ridge from seeing anything clearly. He glimpsed the balloon of the airship, approaching quickly. He tried to pull up, but that giant owl was either pushing down on the nose somehow or it weighed as much as another person.

Something rolled against Ridge's foot as he twisted and turned, trying to buck the owl free.

"What now?" he growled.

Then he remembered Bosmont's comment. Since he needed to duck a slashing talon anyway, he bent down and patted around his feet. He grasped something that felt like a cannonball. That didn't make any sense. He slapped at the switch that uncovered the crystal in the back, and light blazed forth.

The owl squawked and let go, flapping off to the side of the flier.

"Ten layers of hell, if I'd known it hated light, I would have tried that first." Ridge didn't give a whit that the glowing crystal would make him an easier target for the airship, not if it kept that demon bird away. He needed to see what his engineer had given him too. It was lighter than a cannonball, even if it had the same shape, and a wick stuck out of the top.

"Not a wick, idiot, a fuse." Ridge laughed. Bosmont had made him some bombs.

His first thought was that a bomb dropped onto the top of that balloon would definitely rip a big enough hole to bring the airship down. But the owl veered in again, its huge wings blotting out the stars. The light of the crystal might have startled it, but it had recovered.

"Let's see how he likes bombs."

Keeping one hand on the controls, Ridge unfastened the lid of the storage box next to his seat, and fished out the flashlamp used for lighting emergency flares. He thumbed the trigger on the side, and flint snapped against steel, producing a tiny flame. He jammed the bomb between his legs to hold it and hoped Bosmont knew what he was doing and that it wouldn't go off prematurely. He waited before lighting it, knowing it would take a lot of luck to catch that owl. From the length of the fuse, he judged he would have about four seconds before the bomb exploded.

The creature had disappeared for the moment. Maybe it knew what he intended. Ridge craned his neck in all directions and up, knowing death often came from above in aerial fights, and he was rewarded. He spotted the owl diving down at him from above, plummeting for a kill.

Ridge lit the fuse, grabbed the bomb, then waited, counting. The flier shimmied and jerked, needing two hands on the controls, especially now that it had taken damage.

"Just give me one more second, girl," he muttered.

He threw the bomb at the owl, as it extended its talons to grip the top of the cockpit again, or maybe to grip the top of Ridge's head. Whatever its intent, having a metal ball hurled at its face altered its plan. Ridge expected the bomb to strike it and bounce off—he was hoping he had timed it so it would explode before it bounced far—but the owl reacted by snapping its beak down. It caught the bomb in its mouth.

Ridge fought the urge to gape in surprise, instead taking the flier down, knowing he had to put distance between himself and that bomb before—

It erupted with a great flash of orange and yellow, and with a boom that rivaled that of the cannons firing below. The shock made the flier buck, but Ridge got away before any shrapnel hit him. For a moment, feathers filled the sky, as if a pillow had exploded.

Ridge blew out a relieved breath but went straight to his next target. The airship. He felt around with his foot. Hadn't Bosmont said he had packed a couple of those little gifts? To keep Ridge warm? Yes, there was another. He fished it out, setting it in his lap again. That would never cease to make him nervous, but nobody had thought to mount a bomb holder in the cockpit.

The flier fought him, and he didn't know how many more runs he would have, but he angled it skyward again. If he could take out the airship, surely the men below could do the rest. Sorcerer or not.

As he climbed, Ridge peered into the fort, wondering about Sardelle, wondering if...

This time, he did let his mouth fall open in a gape. Sardelle was on her feet in the middle of the courtyard, her sword blazing with an intense golden light that had to be hurting the eyes of anyone nearby. Except for that white-haired man in the furs... He was facing her, his hand outstretched, some sort of red mist pouring from his fingers. Ridge had no idea what was going on—or who was winning—and as much as he wanted to help her, he was glad to be far above. He would much rather deal with the airship than magic.

Around Sardelle and the enemy sorcerer, Cofah warriors were engaged with the fort defenders in close combat. Ridge's people had numbers and *ought* to have the advantage, but someone had opened the mine doors, and miners were streaming out, pickaxes in hand. There was no telling which side of the fray they would join. With that balloon on the ground, they would have to see an escape opportunity. They might simply brain anyone they crossed and sprint for freedom.

Ridge jerked his gaze from the courtyard and touched the bomb in his lap. He had to finish his part before worrying about the chaos below.

* * *

Sardelle advanced on the shaman, Jaxi glowing like a sun in her hand. She had surprised him with her initial attack, and his defenses had fallen, allowing the bullets to reach the Cofah warriors, but he had recovered enough to brick off his mind. That was fine. She had no problem stopping the man with her sword. So long as the Cofah didn't distract her overly much.

They were clearly acting as the shaman's bodyguards, whereas the soldiers on the wall would be as happy to shoot her as to shoot him.

A Cofah warrior aimed his firearm at her. When it blasted, Jaxi blazed, incinerating what turned out to be sprayed shot rather than a bullet. Fortunately, the rest of the Cofah were focused on shooting back at those shooting from the wall. With their shielding gone, they had the low ground. Some had already run to take cover behind buildings.

The shaman tried another mental attack, similar to the one he had originally launched. He wasn't the only one who had shored up his brain's defenses. The assault broke around Sardelle, like water passing a boulder in a stream.

She smiled at him and walked closer. Less than ten meters separated them. If he was armed, his weapons lay under that fur cloak. She eyed it. The wombat fur or whatever it was looked coarse and dry. She waved her hand, trying to ignite it. For a moment, smoke wafted up all around the shaman, but he squelched the attack.

He sneered at her, raising his hand, and tendrils of red mist floated toward her. Sardelle kept walking, not certain what that mist was—much of his magic was foreign to her, something from a distant continent—but trusted Jaxi's power to destroy it. For herself, she raised the soulblade over her shoulder, preparing for a physical attack.

Jaxi pulled the red mist toward her. It wrapped around the blade, then light flashed and it was gone, incinerated like the bullets.

The shaman's eyes grew round as he stared at her—at the sword. At that moment, he knew he was outmatched.

It's not too late, he spoke into her mind. *Forget these talentless apes. They're not worth wasting your power on. Come with me. I'll give you more than they ever could.*

Is this going to be another offer to breed? Sardelle didn't bother to hide her disgust this time. He should have offered again to take her to the other sorcerers in the world. That would have tempted her more. Not enough to lower her sword and stop advancing on him, but more.

Do you not want children? Children with power to rival your own?

If I choose to have children, I want them to have two parents that love them, and each other.

That could come in time. With his thoughts, he sent an image of them together, locked in a lovers' embrace.

Sardelle curled her lip. The shaman was backing away, even as she advanced. She increased her pace. Another five meters, and she would reach him. As she pressed forward, Jaxi cut down bullets that came close—one burst into flames a foot from her eyes. That had originated on the wall, not from a Cofah shotgun. It wasn't the first. No matter what the outcome of this battle, she needed to leave as soon as her confrontation was over.

You see them? The shaman flung a hand toward the soldiers on the wall. *They would strike you down as swiftly as they would me. To defend them is utter foolishness. You are not worthy of a soulblade.*

Your courting words could use some work. Three meters.

The shaman crouched like a tiger, as if he meant to launch a physical attack at her. Instead he threw up both hands, hurling a tidal wave of energy. Again she let it deflect off her mental shield, and it barely stirred her hair. Behind her, windows shattered and doors flew open. A soldier was knocked off the wall and cried out in pain.

Sardelle leapt forward, slashing at the shaman's neck with her blade. He scrambled backward, but his heel caught on slick ground. He flailed trying to catch himself. Sardelle lunged after him before he could recover, reminding herself that, weapon or not, he was *not* a helpless unarmed opponent. He had come to destroy this fort—and to steal Jaxi. She finished him with a stab to the heart.

Sardelle turned three hundred and sixty degrees, checking for fresh attackers, prepared to defend herself. Rifles fired and metal clanged in all directions. Red and gray uniforms mixed, as men fought hand-to-hand. The drab garb of prisoners was everywhere too. She had forgotten—the shaman had released the miners. A pickaxe slammed into a man's back. The victim wasn't, as she had feared, one of the fort's soldiers. It was a Cofah warrior. The prisoners were *helping* the soldiers, not hindering them.

Light flared in the night sky, and a cheer erupted. The rear of the airship had exploded, and shards of wood flew in every direction. Its balloon was already a misshapen, half-sunken mess. A single bronze dragon flier streaked out of the remains of the explosion, its frame gleaming with the reflection of the flames eating at the back of the airship. The wooden craft slumped in the sky, floating lower and lower, a crash inevitable.

Sardelle wished she could join in with the celebration and wait for Ridge, give him a kiss and a hug for his heroics, but she remembered those bullets all too well. As long as General Nax was in charge, she wouldn't receive fair treatment here.

With tears stinging her eyes, Sardelle checked the shaman one last time to ensure he was dead, then ran for the balloon craft that had delivered the Cofah. A single man waited in the large basket, the pilot doubtlessly. He was kneeling with only his eyes peeking over the rim. When he saw Sardelle coming, he leaned out and cut a line, then a second. They were attached to anchors holding the balloon down, and as soon as he severed them, the craft rose. Her run turned into a dead sprint. As dubious a craft as a hot air balloon might be for flying over the Ice Blades, it was all she had to escape these mountains.

She tossed her soulblade into the basket—that ought to alarm the pilot—then leaped, catching one of the dangling lines. Though she was weary from the battle, and no great athlete under any circumstances, she was motivated enough to find a way up. Half afraid the pilot would brain her, she rushed to claw her way over the edge and into the basket. Her sword was the only thing waiting inside.

I flared at him, and he jumped over the side.
You make an effective bully, Jaxi.
Thank you.

Sardelle pushed herself to her feet. In a minute, she would figure out how to work the controls. Sometime after that, she would contemplate her future and decide where she wanted the craft to take her. For now, she simply inhaled and exhaled the cold mountain air, feeling some of the tension ebb from her body as the fort grew farther and farther away.

The clank-thunk-kertwank of the dragon flier's engine drifted to her ear, and she found Ridge, the light of his power crystal illuminating him in the cockpit. He was flying toward the fort as she drifted in the other direction—by the sickly sound of that engine, it was doubtful his craft would make it much farther—and too much distance separated them for words. He gave her a nod though and lifted a hand.

Her throat tight, Sardelle returned the gesture. Even if nobody else in that fort understood, he did.

Is that enough?
Sardelle wiped her eyes. *It has to be.*

Epilogue

THERE WERE EITHER NO FISH, or his bait wasn't fooling them. Or he was too drunk to realize they had snickeringly made off with the bait an hour ago. He pondered whether fish snickered. And then he pondered whether he had the strength to get up from the chair, go inside the cabin, and make something to eat. It sounded like a lot of work. Much easier to lean back on the deck and enjoy the winter sun—if one could even call this weather "winter" in comparison to what the Ice Blades experienced. There wasn't any ice on the lake, and it felt more like autumn with the sun warming his skin.

On the other side of the water, a rooster crowed. There were only two other houses on the lake, part of the reason Ridge had bought it, but he wasn't sure he was enjoying the solitude at the moment. Given his mood, it might have been better to stay on base, to wait in the company of others for his squadron to return from their latest mission. But he hadn't given Sardelle his address there. He doubted she wanted anything to do with the military again.

Ridge picked at a sliver on the chair and wondered if he was being a fool. Did he truly expect her to show up? Was he even sure he *wanted* her to? After seeing… all that he had seen?

"You're sitting here, aren't you?" he mumbled.

What reason did she have to come though, now that she had her sword—her big glowing sorcerer-slaying sword? She didn't need any more favors from him.

"Drinking again?" came a soft voice from behind him.

Ridge nearly fell out of his chair. He *did* knock his fishing pole in the water as he jumped up and spun around, his mouth hanging open.

Sardelle stood at the head of the dock, wearing an elegant forest-green dress that hugged her slim waist and accented her curves far more nicely than the prison garb had. Her black hair hung lush and thick about her shoulders, and framed her face, including the spattering of freckles across her nose and cheeks. Somehow Ridge had never pictured sorceresses with freckles. He was glad for them though. They made her seem more... human. That and her archly raised eyebrow as she regarded his bottle.

"It's only the second time in a month," he said.

"Ah. I hope it's not because of bad news again?" Her eyebrow lowered, and her expression grew earnest. Concerned. Maybe she thought he had gotten in trouble because of her.

"Nope. I was allowed to return to my squadron, and I got an award for my—" Ridge rolled his eyes as he quoted the rest, "—cunning, bravery, and initiative." Some idiot had threatened to promote him as well, but Ridge had squashed that snowball before it could roll downhill and turn into an avalanche. Generals didn't fly; generals commanded brigades—sometimes forts. He had no interest in enduring that again for a long time, if ever.

"Oh, I see," Sardelle said. "And that's why you're sitting out here and drinking, as if you've lost your oldest friend."

"The king and general of the armies were so happy to get that pile of crystals that they just had to award someone. With General Nax gone, I guess I got it by default. I'm not a believer in awards that are given without being earned. I didn't do a single intelligent thing while I was out there, and in the end I didn't do much more than blow up an owl. Someone *else* was paramount in defeating the Cofah." Ridge gave her a pointed look. It had all been in her hands all along.

"All I did was defeat their shaman. You blew up their airship. And that owl was *big*." Sardelle tilted her head. "When you say General Nax is gone, do you mean...?"

"A little band of those Cofah sneaked up to the wall and got to him. I actually missed him when I got back down. There was no senior officer to foist all of the cleanup on."

"Regrettable," Sardelle murmured.

Ridge wondered if she would have kept flying away in that balloon if she had known the general had already been dead at that point. Probably. From what he had heard later, his own people had been shooting at her, right along with the other sorcerer.

"Sardelle, I... " Ridge stuffed his hands into his pockets and studied the dock boards at her feet. "I can't imagine it means much, but I want to apologize for the way you were treated there. I'd like to say things would have been different if you had told me the truth from the beginning, but... " He shrugged.

"I was afraid that if I did... Among other things, would you have spent the night with me in that cave if you had known?"

"Seven gods, no. I would have been afraid you would melt my dragon if I didn't please you adequately."

Sardelle snorted softly. "Just so we're clear, you're talking about... the little wooden figurine, right?"

Because a woman would find a man who called something else a dragon silly. Right, he knew that. "Of course."

"And the night in the library?" she asked.

"Oh, I was drunk enough then, that I might have risked your ire."

"I see."

Sardelle padded down the dock, soft green shoes that matched the dress whispering across the boards. He wondered when she had gone shopping—or how. Did she have money? Or had she simply snapped her fingers and willed the dress into existence? He swallowed as she drew nearer. He wasn't afraid of her, but at the same time... he couldn't pretend nothing had changed. She looked the same, but... it was hard not to see that aura that had enveloped her when she had held her sword aloft.

He glanced toward the yard and the cabin. "You didn't bring your shiny sword?"

Sardelle stopped a couple of paces away, her head tilting. "I didn't think I would need it here."

"No... it's generally safe, though the mosquitoes can be a powerful threat in the summer. Still, it doesn't seem like something you should leave lying around for anyone to find. Or for a mountain to fall on top of."

"I rode a horse here." She waved to the trees by the road. "Jaxi—my sword—and a pack are on it, but I wasn't sure if I should... presume to drop my things on your porch. I wasn't even sure this would be your porch. That address... at first, I thought it was some research facility the general had meant to ship my sword to."

"No," Ridge whispered, distracted by the thought that she wanted to drop her things on his porch.

"Then by the time I got that balloon over the mountains and down to civilization, and figured out what city that address was in, I was a little concerned I might find you here with... someone else."

"Who else would there be?"

"I don't know. Given how quickly the general's daughter—I presume she's still alive?—grew infatuated with you, I gather you don't have much trouble finding female company."

"Oh." Ridge decided not to mention that he had ridden home with Vespa, who had tried to convince him to console her physically over the loss of her father. "She was actually infatuated before she came, I gathered later, and more by my reputation than by actually knowing me. Once women get to know me, they often flee the other way." Not exactly true. The incompatibility issues didn't usually arise until they tried living together, and he was off for months at a time, trying to get himself killed—their words, not his—and leaving them alone at home to worry.

"Ridge, are you lying to me?"

"Maybe a little. I thought it was my turn." He smiled and crossed the last few feet between them, sensing that she wanted that from him, and took her hands. "If you can tolerate my mendacious ways, maybe you could stay a while, see if you find the knowing more appealing than others have."

She leaned against his chest, their hands still clasped. "I'd like that."

"Good," he whispered, locking eyes with her. His heart was beating as fast as a propeller. He felt like a teenager filled with that mix of exhilaration and terror as he mustered the courage to kiss her. But as soon as their lips touched, there was a sense of the familiar... and the right.

THE END

Afterword

Thank you for giving *Balanced on the Blade's Edge* a read. If you enjoyed it and have time to leave a review, I would appreciate it. If you would like to continue on with the series, the second novel, *Deathmaker,* is now available in paperback.

Printed in Great Britain
by Amazon.co.uk, Ltd.,
Marston Gate.